ACCIDENTS OF LOVE

Barbara Bleiman

Printed by CreateSpace, An Amazon.com Company
Available on Kindle and other book stores

Acknowledgements

I am indebted to Elly James, Jack Munnelly and Heather Holden-Brown at HHB Agency, for their wise advice, guidance and support in the writing and publishing of this book. I am very grateful to Sue Tyley for her excellent, clear-sighted and meticulous copy-editing and to Lucy Webster for her invaluable help with the publication process. Thank you to my husband, Adam Sharples, for his unceasing encouragement and for living with the characters of this book over many months and sharing their world with me.

Front cover image: Cultura Creative (RF)/Alamy

Typeset in Minion Pro 11/13.2

'If you could learn about life, books would teach you,' she said. 'But they don't. They just show you that you're not alone. Others have done exactly what you have done. And knowing that is some comfort. Hearing about someone else's life, the hows and the whys, that can provide some kind of relief.'

And when they asked her, afterwards, whether she regretted any of it, she always said no. She couldn't have done anything differently, she said. Even though now, she felt she knew so much more.

'You only have one chance at things,' she said, 'one bite of what sometimes turns out to be a rather sour cherry.'

But what if she'd made those other choices, and what if he had?

'Looking back, everything could have been different,' she said. 'That's the whole point.'

The Age of Experience, Rowena Mann

(Dodd & Co, 2015)

Chapter 1

Celia had been really looking forward to Bill and Judy Webb's party. It was Bill's sixtieth. 'Isn't it terrific?' Judy had said, when they'd arrived. 'Such a great place for a party, don't you think?' The venue was, indeed, wonderful – an old reservoir pumping station, tucked neatly behind Seven Sisters Road, down an unpromising potholed roadway that seemed, at first, to be leading nowhere, till a car park appeared and the sudden revelation of a massive expanse of water. The lake looked as if it had been put there as some kind of apology for the urban mess that surrounded it, an earnest attempt to make amends. The building itself, the pumping station, was freshly painted inside, in gleaming white gloss. It had clearly just been done up as a venue for weddings and parties, a great cavernous hall with all its inner workings visible, making a feature of the engineering. Industrial chic. It had huge windows opening out onto the water, and stripped wooden decking, not yet weathered, stretching expansively on either side.

It was a lovely early evening in October, warm enough for the guests to stand in coats and jackets out on the decking, looking across the surprising expanse of water towards the tower blocks and sprouting new developments of Manor House, sipping good-quality champagne from fine crystal flutes. She scanned the room, trying to remember the names of people whose faces had a troubling familiarity. Was that Carol thingy, who had lived in Bill's house in Bounds Green, in the early 80s? If so, she'd put on rather a lot of weight. Her face was distinctly jowly and her eyelids had sagged. She'd been a very pretty young woman then, much less so now. If it *was* her, of course. Increasingly, Celia struggled to know whether it was her own memory letting her down or whether the people she encountered had aged so much that they really had very little visual link to their former selves. She tried to catch the woman's eye, to see if there was any spark of recognition, but she turned away to engage in conversation with her companion, either not having noticed her, or failing to identify her either after all this time.

Celia let her eyes wander. That man and woman Judy worked with in her Social Services days were there, the ones she and Nick always referred to as 'The Goodies'. But what were their real names, should they wander over to say hello? It would be embarrassing to have forgotten, particularly if they remembered Nick's and hers. Nick had come up with 'The Goodies' after a particularly dull evening in their company at Judy and Bill's. 'Insufferably right-on and smug,' Nick had said. 'You'd think they were the only people who did anything worthwhile with their lives.' She'd scolded him half-heartedly for being intolerant, laughed despite herself, and the name had stuck.

In the corner of the room, she could see Annabel, talking animatedly to a man she didn't know. She'd have to catch up with her later. They'd met for a coffee at Sable d'Or in Crouch End only a few days previously, so there was no urgency about seeking her out now. And there was George Parker! He'd obviously come on his own as usual, poor George, but he'd found the Websters and seemed to be in reasonably cheerful conversation with them. She could understand the awkwardness he must feel, a man divorced and single for so many years now, surrounded by couples, and, worse still, at a party like this, where so many old friends were gathered together. It must be hard for him.

She turned to focus on the other side of the room. Would the Glassmans be there? She couldn't see them. Lois and Howard were good friends of Bill and Judy's and she had always enjoyed her conversations with Lois, though they never met socially on their own, only at parties or dinners organised by the Webbs. We should invite them over for a meal, she thought, or maybe I should ask Lois to meet up with me for a coffee sometime? Nick had never been that keen on Howard. Perhaps it would be better to try to strengthen the friendship between her and Lois instead?

She looked around for Nick. He was chatting to a chap from Bill's office, the rather dull man who'd done the conveyancing for them, years back, when they bought the house in Kentish Town. He'd been a decent enough lawyer, a little pedestrian perhaps, and Nick had had to ask Bill to keep a close eye on things at a few critical moments, but all in all he'd been helpful and polite and done a good job for them in the end. Celia wasn't in a rush to join them though. She could happily live without a conversation with Peter Warburton; she'd have nothing to say to him, other than to reopen dreary discussions about the planning permission for the dodgy extension that had been put on before they bought the place, still something of a sore point.

'Food's served. Help yourselves!'

And now there was a mad scramble for plates and cutlery, a queue that rapidly formed out of nowhere, people jostling to get to the mounds of spicy grilled chicken with za'atar and roasted lemon, the couscous and chickpea salad, the baba ganoush and flatbreads, the endive and grape salad, the whole salmon with salsa verde, the prosciutto and figs with basil and pomegranate molasses, the baskets of sourdough bread.

'Inspired by one of those celebrity chefs in Islington,' someone said. 'Similar style of food but a cheaper outfit just off Green Lanes. And jolly good it looks too!'

'Superb.' She turned to see Dena Lamont, Judy's psychoanalyst friend – the guru – piling her plate high; she'd got in fast. Others had made way for her, recognising her superior claim. Celia couldn't bring herself to say hello, though they'd been introduced several times before and Dena should surely know who she was by now. She always felt stupidly shy when they met, more like a gauche teenager than a fifty-seven-year-old woman with a career of her own. Or rather, like a small piece of inanimate debris floating in the vast orbit of Dena's planet.

Celia took what she hoped would be a first helping, of a reasonably modest size, then found herself a chair at a small square table tucked away in a corner. She pulled up another chair, hoping that Nick would come and find her when the food was served, as he usually did. He was always rather gallant in that way, making sure that she wasn't eating on her own, touching base to see how she was getting on. And five minutes later, as expected, he appeared, cheerfully carrying a plate that was full enough to need careful manoeuvring onto the table.

'Trust them to do a good job on the food,' he said. 'Just look at it!'

'Talked to anyone interesting so far?'

'No one special. Did you see me chatting to Peter Warburton? Nice enough guy but I got well and truly trapped. Not much conversation beyond extensions and leases.'

'Sorry I didn't come and rescue you. I couldn't quite face it.'

'There was a nice couple who knew Bill when he was at school. Nancy and . . . I've forgotten his name already. Something beginning with A – Alan, Adam, Andrew, Angus . . .' He tailed off. 'They were a friendly pair.' So much information that used to get neatly lodged in the brain for easy retrieval when needed seemed now to fail to spark the appropriate electrical reaction, trigger the right synaptic connection. More and more things were going in and getting lost forever. It had become a standing worry for them both, a standing joke.

'Alistair,' she said helpfully. 'Nancy and Alistair. You've met them before several times at occasions like this. He plays tennis with Bill.'

'Ah yes,' Nick said. 'I'd forgotten.'

She patted his hand. 'Crumble for tea, dear? Can't find your specs? Looking for your walking stick?' She put on her old-lady voice, as he so often put on his old-man one, when they joshed each other about the gradual onset of decrepitude and dementia. They laughed at the idea of growing old together.

'Not many people we know. No sign of Lois and Howard, for instance,' Celia observed.

'No. But Bill says there's a whole group coming a bit later – some Buntings people who've had to go to a colleague's drinks party first, and then the book-club people – they'd bought tickets for the National Theatre months ago and apparently couldn't change them. Maybe Lois and Howard will be part of that posse?'

'I thought the numbers were a bit low. Bill and Judy usually have a big crowd at their dos.'

There was a sudden burst of noise at the doors, a great bustle and flurry of people hurrying in, pulling off coats and hanging them on rails, smoothing down hair, straightening ties or silk scarves, organising their clothing to help them look their best, eyes searching the room to find their hosts, sizing up who else might be there. Some, seeing that the food had already been served, made a beeline for the big tables at the back; others went straight for the champagne.

'Here they all are, arriving at once,' Celia said, her spirits lifting again with the hope of fresh people to talk to. 'Oh good – look, there's Pete Daunt. You haven't seen him in ages, have you? He's gone so grey all of a sudden, though. And look, there's Lois, talking to Judy. I'll go over and say hello, shall I?'

'Of course. I'll see what Pete's been up to, get myself some dessert and come and find you later.'

Celia left her plate on the table and wandered over towards the group. She kissed their old friends Mary and Evelyn in turn and, after a few brief words, promised to come back to find them later. Pete Daunt had spotted Nick and hurried over to talk to him, so she took the opportunity to open up a conversation with Lois, who was warm and friendly as always. She seemed genuinely pleased to see Celia and they chatted happily before Celia suggested that she might like to get some food before it all went. They parted, agreeing to try to meet up for lunch one day soon.

Now what? Nick had disappeared and Celia was left searching for someone to talk to. Mary and Evelyn were now in full-flow talking to Judy, and she was reluctant to break in. No doubt they'd be engrossed in talk of gardens and allotments, Latin names for plants, fertilisers and pruning tips. She'd give that a miss. She'd already been through everyone she felt confident enough to engage in easy conversation and suddenly felt oddly awkward – unsure of how to thrust herself into a group, or approach a complete stranger with a clumsy overture. Instead, she helped herself to another glass of champagne. She wondered where Nick had gone, if he'd moved on from Pete Daunt, and whether it was too soon to admit defeat and go and find him again. When it came to it, despite her outward show of sociability, she'd really rather deal with events like this with him by her side.

A woman standing beside her, helping herself to a glass of champagne, came to her rescue.

'Hello. I'm Lavinia. Who are you?'

'Celia. How do you know Bill and Judy?' It was boring, she knew, to ask the usual, obvious, tedious question but it always seemed like the simplest way to proceed in social gatherings such as this.

'I work with Bill. On intellectual property rights. A junior partner.'

She was a striking-looking woman in her forties, with sleek black hair down to her shoulders, a stretchy black dress, low-cut and stylish, tanned, hairless skin and heels that Celia thought looked outrageously high and horribly uncomfortable. Clearly a city lawyer.

'He's a sweetie, Bill. A lovely man to work for. Just gorgeous! Not quite sure how he ended up where he is, given what a cut-throat place our little world is.'

'He *is* a sweetie, isn't he,' Celia said.

'How do you know him?'

'He's a very old friend of my husband's. They were at university together.'

'Ah, so you've known him a long time.'

'Years and years. More than thirty! He was there the night my husband and I met. He'd just started dating Judy.'

'Aaaah!' she said. 'How nice. Shared history and all that. So you must know loads of people here?'

'A few. Not as many as one might think, though. How about you?'

'One or two people from Buntings are here I expect, but otherwise probably not. We don't socialise much outside of work, given the long hours we spend together in the office.' She surveyed the room. 'There's that man from conveyancing, though – Pete Warburton. I'll steer clear of him. He's very dull! I'm pretty amazed he's stayed the course at Buntings to be truthful. And that's Wilfred Mainwaring – ex-senior partner – sitting over there at that table with his wife. Retired now. Set up the firm when Bill was just a junior. When I started at Buntings myself he was just doing the odd case, tying up loose ends for his long-standing, loyal clients. Frighteningly clever old geezer, he was. Could summon up case law quicker than anyone else in the building. If you wanted to learn how to be a serious lawyer, he was the one to try to emulate.'

'My father was in the law,' Celia said. 'I enjoyed hearing his stories about cases but the hideous workload put me off ever thinking of following in his footsteps. He was hardly ever at home. It was a treadmill. And my mother hated it. She saw law as the enemy.'

'No work-life balance. You don't have to tell me! Not many women stick it, I'm afraid. They get into their thirties, get broody and end up handing in their resignation. Luckily, I wasn't interested in having kids, so I've stuck at it. Career woman and all that.'

For people who'd never met each other before the conversation was getting surprisingly deep, Celia thought.

Lavinia shook back her hair and laughed. It reinforced the image Celia had of her, as the no-nonsense, tough, professional woman.

'Never interested in having children at all?'

'Not really. Usual story of not being able to find the right man at the right time. Like so many of us working girls! Half my friends are in the same boat, either hitched up with someone quite unsuitable, searching for Mr Right on the Internet, or shagging some married man.'

She was looking over Celia's shoulder. 'Talking of which . . . you see that man over there?' She was pointing towards the food table. 'The one with his back to us, helping himself to the puddings, the good-looking grey-haired guy wearing the striped shirt and cords.' She paused. 'I'm pretty sure he's the man who's been having an affair with one of the women I work with. It's been over a year now. He's married with grown-up kids and I swear he wouldn't leave his wife in a million years, but my colleague still hangs on in there in the hopes that one day it'll all come good, he'll ditch the wife, make it all legit, set up home with her, give her a few nice babies and the happy ever after she's been dreaming of. Fat chance! He's got his cake and he's eating it!'

'The man in the stripy shirt?' Celia said.

'Yeah, that's him. He takes her out to lunch sometimes.'

'You're sure about that?'

'I think so. His name's –'

'Nick?'

'Yeah, Nick.'

'That's my husband.'

Chapter 2

The woman had backtracked immediately. For someone so self-assured and sleekly presented, she had appeared flustered, gabbling her words as she sought to retract, her tanned face flushed, her poise shattered. The words poured out in a frantic torrent – terrible memory for faces ... probably not him at all ... older men all look the same to her ... just what she'd heard on the grapevine ... foolish workplace gossip ... just a silly story. They'd parted with Celia finding herself rather absurdly trying to make the woman feel better for her silly 'gaffe'. 'Look, don't worry,' she'd said, with an air of bright confidence. 'I'm sure it's just a mistake. I trust my husband absolutely. If it is Nick that you recognise, there'll be some simple explanation, I'm sure. Don't concern yourself about it in the least. I'd go and help yourself to some food if I were you, before it all disappears.' When the woman hesitated she reassured her again that she was fine; there really was no cause for concern. She'd even managed a brittle little laugh and a light pat on Lavinia's shoulder to lessen her anxiety.

Celia watched as she hurried off, teetering on her high heels, not towards the table of food but in the direction of a little cluster of young women who were standing near the stage, where the band was preparing to strike up. Celia looked away. Now that the woman was gone, she felt her legs begin to give way. She had to steady herself with one hand on the drinks table to stop herself from falling over. She felt clammy and nauseous and her head began to swim. She would have to find the toilet. She could not, would not, make a scene out here in front of everyone. It would be too public, too exposed.

As she started to move away, she looked over towards the stage and saw Lavinia in spirited conversation with the other women. She was gesticulating wildly. The other women's faces were turned towards Celia, looking right at her. Quickly she averted her gaze.

In the toilet, she threw up. When she was finished, she washed her face, wiped it with white paper towels from the dispenser, then sat on the upright wooden seat near the door and tried to calm herself, taking deep breaths and pressing her hands firmly against her thighs to try to stop them from shaking. She must, at all costs, prevent herself from fainting. After a few moments, the door swung open and Annabel came in.

'So, here you are, Celia! I've been looking –' She broke off suddenly. 'Oh my God you look awful. What's wrong?'

Celia burst into tears. 'I don't feel very well. I think I need to go home.'

'You just sit there. I'll go and get Nick.'

She sat and waited, trying to pull herself together enough to face him and the others. Soon the questions – what's wrong and why – would start. There was a noise of voices just outside the toilet, male and female mixed. She heard Judy's loud, 'Oh bugger! They'll miss the speeches and the cake!', Bill's practical, 'What coat was she wearing, Nick? I'll find it for you!', Annabel's concerned, 'She looks like death warmed up, poor thing! Her face is as white as chalk!' And then Nick's anxious voice, 'It's not like her to be taken ill so suddenly. She's usually strong as an ox. Barely ever had a day in bed.' 'Perhaps something she ate didn't agree with her?' someone said and Judy's emphatic reply: 'I think not!' and finally Nick, taking charge of things, 'I'd better get her home.'

And now Annabel swept in through the door, coming to fetch her, with her soft camel coat open and ready for her to slip her arms straight into and Nick was there just outside waiting, taking her gently by the arm, patting her hand, looking worried. He half ushered, half carried her towards the exit. The room was quiet, with just a faint murmur of whispered talk. From the decking outside came the sound of louder voices, where people hadn't yet realised that something was wrong. The members of the band were standing with their instruments in their hands, a little unsure about what to do, waiting for the signal to start playing.

'So sorry, Judy!' Celia said quietly as they reached the outer doors. 'Happy birthday, Bill! Hope I haven't spoiled the fun.'

Everyone offered their best wishes, hoped that she'd be better soon, assured her that no harm had been done and that the party would get going again in no time, though she'd be missed, of course.

'I'll call you tomorrow,' Annabel said. 'To see how you are.'

'Thanks, Bel.'

And now they were out in the cold air and Nick was helping her into the car and they were driving home in the darkness and Nick was asking her what she thought was wrong. Might she have a bug or food poisoning or something? Should they call a doctor or not? She reassured him that a doctor wasn't needed and that she just had to get herself home and to bed.

She wished he'd stop talking so that she could think, so that she could be left to her thoughts without having to listen or respond to him. She needed to get a grip, get a grip on things, get a grip. And decide what to do next. Ask him or not ask him? Know or not know? Ask other people first? Confront him? Shout at him? Cry? Scream? Tell him to fuck off, fuck off fuck off you bastard, how could you do this to me? Divorce him? Oh my God! Tell the children? Oh my God! Break it to the children? Ask Annabel if she knew, ask Bill – surely Bill must have known? – and Judy and Lois and Howard and Dena Lamont and all their acquaintances and all their friends who knew but never thought to tell her, or decided not to tell her. A conspiracy of silence? Listen to his explanations. Try to believe them. Too implausible, too plausible, impossible to believe. But that woman . . . Lavinia . . . knew what he looked like, knew his name, knew who he was. The man in the stripy shirt. The good-looking man getting the pudding. Nick. She'd said his name, the man her work colleague had been involved with for a year, a married man. She'd have to divorce him. She'd have to. And then what? Oh my God! Live on her own, at fifty-seven, just when they were coming up to the retirement years. So many plans, travel projects, what they'd been aiming for after a life of hard work. And the children. Oh my God! Daniel and Pippa. The children. Pippa and Dan and their partners. Oh my God the betrayal. And the hatred they'd feel for him, the pity for her. The worry and the anger they'd feel, the upset, the sadness, just when they were making their own lives. Christ. Christmas was not far off now and where would they go? To him or to her? And where would that be? At home, or somewhere else? And then he'd do what that woman Lavinia said he wouldn't do in a million years and divorce her and marry the woman from Buntings and set up home with her and give her babies, step-brothers, step-sisters for Dan and Pippa. Another family, without her. She couldn't forgive him if it were all true. She just couldn't.

But then – she tried to remind herself of this – other women, other men, did forgive. Eventually. She ran through the people she knew. Jenny was still with Trevor wasn't she? And what about Judy and her work colleague, a few years back? True or not true? Judy and Bill still together at sixty, retiring together. And of course, Annabel and Charlie. Forgiven? Forgotten? Could she do that? Forgive, not say anything, pretend nothing's happened, forget or pretend to forget? No. She couldn't even bear to look at him sitting next to her. All she could think of was what he'd done. The bastard, the bastard. The betrayal!

And then she thought about Lionel, her father. She'd have to tell him. He'd come straight out and say I told you so. He'd never liked Nick. Not the right man after what he did to Barbara. Going out with your ex-girlfriend's sister and marrying her instead when Barbara had been his girlfriend first and Barbara had been deeply upset and Lionel had always liked Barbara best, his number one girl, the apple of his eye, a First at Oxford, following him into the law. And they'd gone and got engaged, she and Nick, when Barbara wasn't properly over him yet. And – oh my God, she'd also have to tell Barbara. She'd have to ring her up in New York and tell her over the phone, that huge distance away, working out her reaction just by her voice and the gaps, the awful bulging silences that said it all. Well, what did you expect? It was inevitable, in the end, wasn't it? Though Lionel face to face would be worse, of course, much worse. Told you so, told you so. We never liked him, your mother and I.

She began to cry; she couldn't stop herself.

'Are you OK?' Nick asked, taking his eyes off the road to look at her.

'Just not feeling well,' she said. 'Get me home. I'll go straight to bed.'

'Yes, you do that. With a bit of luck you'll sleep it off, whatever it is, and be better by the morning. Otherwise I'll call for the out-of-hours doctor first thing.'

She didn't say anything.

'And if you're still not well tomorrow, I'll cancel my trip down to Alton to see Mum and Arthur. They'll understand. I won't leave you if you're still feeling like this.'

'I'll be fine by the morning,' she said. 'Your mum's expecting you and Arthur always looks forward to your visits. You should go.'

She'd forgotten all about his planned trip to see his mother and her partner, but the thought that he might be gone for the whole of the next day was something of a relief. She would be left alone. She would try to order her thoughts, pull herself together. By the time of his return, perhaps she would be calm enough to decide what to do, be clear what she should say to him and how she might act upon whatever he said in response.

She went to bed in the spare room, with the excuse of not wanting to disturb him, and had no sleep. All night her thoughts circled, around past episodes, past scenes. She retraced recent events, his absences – the regular ones, the expected ones and unexpected ones, the short and the lengthier ones – and the reasons for them, his behaviour towards her and the behaviour of their friends towards both of them. She could find nothing obvious to accuse him of, nothing to berate him with, nothing to suspect, other than the devastating testimony of a woman called Lavinia who seemingly recognised him as the man who had been shagging her work colleague for well over a year.

In the morning Nick came in bearing a mug of tea. She hoped that, in the semi-darkness of the curtained room, he would not be aware of the signs of grief – her eyes darkly ringed and puffy with tears.

'How are you feeling?'

'Better, thank you. But I think I'll stay in bed a bit longer. Whatever it was has left me exhausted. You're fine to go off down to Alton, though. I'll be much better off on my own here, just having a quiet day to recover.'

'If you're sure . . . I'll ring when I get there and I can always come back early if you're feeling lousy. Or call me on the mobile if you need to.'

'I'm sure I'll be absolutely fine. Give Celeste and Arthur my love.'

He was always admirably dutiful towards his mother, and remarkably patient with Arthur, who could be a dreadful bore. He listened to all Arthur's stories about the petty battles on the allotment committee, and his gripes about their neighbours, and he took in his stride Arthur's quite awful Little Englander attitudes about Europe and immigration and taxes, in a way that she always found far more difficult to tolerate. He was admirably forgiving of their flaws. She wished she could say the same of her own behaviour towards Lionel. But then Celeste was easy to be fond of, and undemanding, while Lionel was so very difficult. He didn't make it easy for her to be the dutiful daughter.

Thinking of Nick's kindness to others wasn't a comfort now, though. It made her feel sick to the stomach. Something else on the way to being lost.

He kissed her on the forehead, then left, quietly closing the door behind him. She heard him downstairs, packing up a few things to take with him, probably the usual little box of groceries for his mother, a couple of box sets of DVDs to lend them, his drill and some tools so that he could do a few odd jobs around the house while he was there, along with his walking gear, in case Arthur felt up to a stroll through the fields at the back after lunch.

Celia crept out of bed and drew back the curtain a fraction so that she could watch him loading up the car. He was doing everything so simply and normally. She felt a sudden rush of feeling for him; he was entirely unaware that anything was wrong. She watched him go, then stumbled back towards the bed, climbed in and pulled the bedcovers up high so that she was buried beneath them. Whatever he had done, or not done, already everything had changed.

Chapter 3

Celia finally dragged herself out of bed at 10 a.m. and had a shower. There was some relief in letting the water flow over her body, between her breasts, down her back and legs, hot and soothing. The smell of the lavender was a comfort too, so familiar and safe – she always treated herself to high-quality products, Neal's Yard or Molton Brown, simple luxuries she felt they could easily afford at this stage in their lives. Looking at her body these days, though, she was painfully aware of the flaws – the sagging of her breasts, the rough, discoloured patches on her skin, the old stretch marks from the babies, the way her hips had expanded and her stomach had lost its taut control. The body of an older woman. Fresh tears. He'd always loved her breasts and look at them now! The woman from Buntings would be young and firm, of course, her flesh not yet damaged by age.

As she was drying herself she heard the phone ring. Quickly she grabbed a towel and, still dripping, hurried into the bedroom to reach it in time.

'Celia?'

It was Lionel.

'Oh, it's you. How are you, Daddy?'

'So-so. Same as usual. Getting by.'

She wished that just for once he might sound a bit more cheerful. She really didn't feel up to coping with him and his problems right now.

'I've lost my spare pair of reading glasses.'

'Oh dear, that's a shame.' She tried to keep a lightness in her voice, no hint of anything being wrong.

'I thought you might be able to take me round to Optical Solutions tomorrow – you know, the one on the High Road, with that nice young Chinese woman who listens to me. Not the one further up on the hill – Gunn or Bunn or whatever he's called – who just can't be bothered to make the effort. Will you take me? I need some new ones made.'

'Are they just your spares? You've still got a pair to read with?'

'My spares. That's what I said didn't I?'

Celia took a deep breath before continuing. 'If it's just your spares, Daddy, can it wait for a bit, maybe? I'm really busy this week and I simply can't afford to take the time off work. But –'

'OK. Don't bother, then. I'll ask Mr Booth across the road to take me. He'll do it. He's usually happy to step in when you can't do these things for me . . . when I make too many demands on you.'

She could tell by the tone of his voice that he was cross. The last thing she wanted was a row with him.

'It's not that. It's just –'

'OK, then. I'll ask Mr Booth!' And before she could say anything more he'd put the phone down.

Why was it always so difficult to get it right with him? And at this, of all times. Some people turned to their parents for support when things were going wrong, even well into their middle age. Annabel, for instance, seemed to be constantly phoning her mother for advice, despite the fact that Doris was well into her eighties and obviously in need of care and attention herself. She couldn't imagine doing that with Lionel. She would have no idea where to start. Nor would he. And talking about Nick was, in any event, completely off limits.

The phone rang again. Probably Lionel again, deciding that he'd been just a bit too sharp with her this time.

'Annabel. It's you. I thought it might be my father.'

'How are you this morning? Feeling any better?'

'I'm OK. Still not feeling great.' A moment's pause, then, 'Maybe something I ate. A tummy bug or something.'

'Is Nick there?'

'He's gone down to see Celeste and Arthur. I told him to go.'

'Shall I come round? I'm worried about you.'

Celia hesitated. Did she want to talk to Annabel? Was it a good idea? Maybe it would be sensible to be circumspect. If nothing came of any of this, if it were all a horrible mistake, no one need know and they could carry on as before. Her instincts were to keep it to herself for the moment, just until she'd had it out with Nick and knew where she stood, till the shock had subsided and she'd worked out what to do.

'I won't come if you'd rather not but I thought you might want me there. I thought you might want to talk to a friend.'

'Why, what have you heard?'

'Oh Celia!' There was a catch in Annabel's voice, like a little sob. 'There was some talk at the party.'

So they knew. The word had spread. Perhaps Lavinia had talked to Bill after they'd left, to let him know what had happened. She'd have apologised profusely for blundering into the revelation. She'd probably have wanted reassurance from him that she hadn't been at fault

– it had been an accident waiting to happen, hadn't it? Celia imagined Bill's reaction to the news. 'Christ! She's found out. The shit's hit the fan! Poor Nick. He's going to be devastated.' And what about Judy's response? If she'd known all about the affair, what would she be thinking? 'Damn and blast! Buggeration! Celia's going to work out sure as hell that we were completely aware of what Nick was up to. How could she not? She'll see it as a betrayal. I knew we should have talked to her, Bill. I always said it'd end in tears, with her the last person to know.'

'Celia? Are you still there?'

'Sorry. I'm not quite sure what I want right now. I'm not thinking straight.'

'Right. I'm coming over. I'll just need to sort out a few things with Charlie – he'll have to walk Buster for me – and cancel the arrangement with Alex and Daisy – they were going to come and have brunch with us – then I'll be there.'

'Don't cancel Alex and Daisy, Annabel! You really don't need to, honestly. You see so little of Alex these days. Sunday brunch, it'll be nice for all of you, a family get-together. I'll be OK, really I will.'

'Nonsense. He'll understand. So will Daisy. They can come another time.'

'You won't . . .'

'No of course not. I'm not that stupid. I'll tell him you're not well.'

'I wouldn't want Alex talking to Dan.'

'I understand. I'm not stupid. Honestly, I won't say a word.'

Celia slowly got dressed. She couldn't face breakfast but made herself a cup of camomile tea, the only thing she thought she could manage. She went to the front door to see if the Sunday newspaper had arrived but the mat was empty, the paperboy evidently having let them down once again. On the street it was quiet; a Sunday morning like any other. Across the road, her neighbour, Vincent, the retired film producer, was putting out the rubbish in his red dressing gown. Though he glanced over and clearly saw her, he quickly averted his gaze. It was an unfriendly road, she'd always thought, surprisingly so, given its rather homogeneous population of middle-class intellectuals – journalists, academics, people in the media or, like her, in publishing. Only the bigger houses, the multi-occupancy four-storey residences further up, had younger, more impecunious occupants, who came and went with great regularity, a shifting and anonymous population of short-stay tenants whom she hardly expected to get to know. But, with a few notable exceptions, the older owner-occupier residents of the road also kept their distance.

That woman from several houses down, Veronica somebody or other, was setting off on her morning walk to Parliament Hill in her waxed jacket and wellies, with her pair of lurchers almost pulling her off her feet in their urgency to get to the park and be let off their leads. If anyone on the road thought they'd be having a quiet Sunday lie-in, the lurchers certainly would have put paid to that, with their agitated yapping and barking.

In the other direction, a man she didn't recognise was running his engine and scraping a fine layer of ice off the windscreen. The temperature had suddenly dropped overnight; autumn was obviously finally setting in. A young woman in a big woolly hat and scarf, wearing a combination of improbably small shorts, thick knitted tights and Doc Martens boots, was unlocking her bike from the railings of the house next door. Other than that the road was empty. Celia looked out for the appearance of Annabel's car. Nothing yet; no sign of her.

She wandered back into the kitchen and paced the floor for a while, unable to sit down or settle to anything. She picked up an already well-thumbed magazine from the table and, still standing, flicked through it in a half-hearted way, then put it down again. Cradling her half-drunk cup of camomile tea, she went and stood in the utility room looking out at the garden. The trees were bare of leaves, most of the bushes stripped of any colour; only the grass looked thick and lush after a particularly wet summer and early autumn. Nick would need to be reminded to clear away the wet leaves that had drifted onto the patio, she mused, then instantly realised the absurdity of the thought, its hopeless banality. Sweeping the patio would be low down the conversational agenda when she next saw him.

The bird table was empty. They were so close to the Heath, to all that open space and woodland, yet sometimes it seemed that the wildlife had deserted them for good. She always greeted the occasional robin or blue tit with enthusiastic joy and relief but for now there was nothing, just the usual crop of slugs and snails creeping over the paths and flowerbeds, threatening to wreak havoc on their careful planting.

She went into the living room to look out of the front window, watching for Annabel's arrival. When she finally saw her silver car pulling up outside the house, she tried to compose herself a little, looking for a tissue in her pocket, to blow her nose and hide the signs of crying. Unable to find one, like a small child she wiped her eyes on her sleeve. Even now, even with Annabel, her closest friend, she would rather not reveal the extent of her shock.

As in an awful accident, when someone falls and hurts themselves seriously and instinctively tries to pretend that it's nothing, just a small graze, rather than the terrible, agonising trauma that it is, she wanted to keep to herself the horrifying intensity of what she felt. It was shameful to admit it to herself, let alone to anyone else. Embarrassment and self-reproof seemed like odd emotions in the circumstances – what, after all, had she done wrong? – but they were powerfully present nonetheless, humiliation at being thought not good enough, at being betrayed in such a conventional way, and uncomfortable shame for Nick, for the ugliness of what he had done. It reflected badly on both of them and she wasn't ready to expose either of them to outside scrutiny. Not yet.

Before Annabel had the chance to either knock or ring the bell, Celia opened the door.

'Oh my God, Celia. I'm so sorry.' Annabel dropped her bag on the doormat and reached for her, pulling her straight into her arms. Her voice was soaked in pity, thickly steeped in it.

'So it's true, then,' Celia said calmly, moving a step back to distance herself, before Annabel's kindness risked bringing on tears.

'I didn't know till last night, I swear to you. I promise, honest to God, I'd have told you if I'd known. Bill told me and Judy at the party. Judy was horrified. He'd kept it from her. It was only the Buntings people who had any idea about it at all. Even now, it's hardly got around – most people at the party thought you were genuinely sick and the evening went on as planned. But it was all a bit muted, to be honest. Bill tried to keep up appearances but

I can't say the speeches were all that they could have been. Judy disappeared into the kitchen while Howard did the toast. She was still cross with Bill, I expect. Showing her displeasure, in no uncertain terms.'

'That's something, at least. I was worried that everyone was in on it except me. I'm so glad you didn't know. And Judy. At least that's something. What did Bill tell you?'

'What do you already know?'

They were still standing in the hallway.

'Come in,' Celia said quietly. 'We should sit down.'

In the kitchen, she made Annabel a cup of tea and then when she tried to explain what had happened with Lavinia at the party the night before, the tears could no longer be brought under control. It was difficult enough to grasp what Nick had done, let alone say it out loud. Voicing it made it seem so much more real. Perhaps that was another reason why she felt so cautious about talking to Annabel.

Eventually she stopped crying enough to continue. 'She seems to be some kind of lawyer working in intellectual property with Bill. I don't know her name.'

'Bill told me last night. Do you want to know?'

'No, don't tell me . . . Yes, do. I ought to know.'

'Marina Jones.'

There was a silence while it sunk in. Marina. From the sea. A sea creature, a siren luring men onto the rocks, dragging them into dangerous waters away from the safety of the land.

'What else do you know?' she said finally.

'Do you really want me to say?'

'God knows. In some ways the less I know the better, but stupidly there's a part of me that wants to hear all the details, every last sordid thing, even though it makes me feel like throwing up to think about it.'

'I don't know that much, Cee. Just that she's a lot younger than Nick – in her late thirties or so. He met her when he was out with Bill for lunch one day and something happened. Bill says Nick's been agonising over it all. Full of remorse, keeps trying to end it, feeling he's behaved like a complete bastard to you. Bill says he'd never leave you, though. How you're everything to him.'

'Obviously not everything,' Celia said drily.

'Celia! He adores you!'

'Not enough to stop him shagging some cunt in Bill's office.'

'Celia! That's –'

'Don't complain about my language, for God's sake, Annabel. I know you don't like it. You don't ever speak like that. It offends you. And it offends me too. It's not like me. But that's how I feel right now! She may be a perfectly nice woman but she's been a fucking cunt. She's been sleeping with my husband.'

'He'll end it with her. He won't leave you, you know.'

'Maybe not. But what about me? What if I don't want him to stay?'

Annabel looked surprised, as if the thought had never occurred to her.

'Think about what that would mean. For all of you – you and the children as well as Nick. It's all very raw now and you feel terrible. But these things subside. People get over it. They forgive each other. They carry on. Maybe you'll end up feeling you want to do the same?'

People get over it. They forgive each other. They carry on. They both knew that Annabel had her own situation in mind. She had been through something like this herself, only it had been Charlie who had had to be relied upon to do the forgiving; it was Charlie who had made the decision to carry on. Carrying on – in that sense, rather than the 'philandering' one – had worked out all right for them in the end. In neither sense had it been allowed to derail their lives. Annabel had experience of these things, where Celia felt that she had absolutely none, but, fond of her as she was, Celia wasn't sure that Annabel's way of dealing with such matters was much help to her. And anyway, Annabel had been the wrongdoer, not the wronged. It was altogether different.

'The way I feel at the moment I never want to see him again. I'd change the locks on the door if I could. I'd throw all his clothes out onto the road. I'd . . .' She burst into a fresh flood of tears. 'I hate him for how he's ruined it all. Everything we've built up. Everything we've felt for each other. And for lying to me. For more than a year. Not just some horrible, stupid, one-off mistake, some drunken moment of lust. Not just sex. A whole year or more. A year of out-and-out lies. I don't think I can just shake that off. I don't think I can ever trust him again.'

Annabel frowned and Celia wondered whether she was thinking of her or of her own past actions, of Charlie's behaviour towards her.

'What are you going to do, then? Wait till he comes home and confront him? Is that what you'll do?'

Celia didn't reply but simply shook her head to indicate her uncertainty.

'And the children? What about them?'

She felt clearer about that. 'I won't say anything to them yet. Not till I have to. Not till I understand more about what's going on. They'll be utterly distraught when they find out.'

The phone rang. It was sitting on the table right beside her. She hesitated a moment, wondering whether to answer or not. Annabel looked at her expectantly. She picked it up.

'Celia? Listen, I need to talk to you.'

It was Nick. His voice sounded urgent and strained.

'I'm going to have lunch with Celeste and Arthur, then I'm coming straight home. I've told them you're not well. They understand that I need to get back to you.'

'OK,' she said.

There was silence at the other end of the line too. He was clearly searching for the right words.

'Celia, I've just had a call from Bill. I'm so sorry, so very sorry.'

She slammed the phone down before he could say anything more.

By the time Nick returned, Celia had packed an overnight bag, propped a carefully worded note against a jug on the kitchen table, locked up the house and gone. She didn't say where she was going but told him not to worry – she would phone him in a few days' time, when she could face talking to him and when she had worked out for herself what she wanted to do. She said that she was turning her mobile phone off, so he shouldn't try calling. She wanted some space to think, to be alone.

She took the Honda Jazz and headed off on the motorway towards Hertfordshire. She had already phoned her old school friend Anne, to ask if she could stay for a few days.

She told her that something had happened that meant she needed time away from home but left the explanations till later. Anne, sensitive as ever, did not press her. She said that a room would be ready for her when she arrived and reassured her that it was no trouble – she would look forward to her visit.

She drove on autopilot at first, barely aware of the roads she was taking, the changing traffic lights, the pedestrians, cyclists and other cars. The sun had come out, it was a crisp, sparkling morning and the roads were full, with people obviously having decided to make the most of the good autumnal weather, driving out into the countryside, going on an outing to one of the big shopping malls off the A1, or just visiting relatives for Sunday lunch. As the traffic slowed, she began to be more aware of the families in their cars, waiting at the lights, the women with their children, the husbands and wives sitting side by side, the elderly couple in the Rover, crawling along in the slow lane; people in relationships, people whose lives were connected, tied to each other by bonds that had endured. 'How could you do this to me?' she said out loud. 'After all we've been through together. To get so far and now this.'

They had met soon after university, when he had already started working as a lawyer for Hackney Council; she'd just finished her Master's and landed her first job in publishing. She'd come out of a rather unsatisfactory relationship with a bloke who'd messed her around, unable to make up his mind if he was really interested or not, constantly running hot and cold. In the end, she'd been the one to finish it, though not without some sadness and regret. When a girlfriend suggested that she accompany her to a party, she'd refused. She needed time to recover before risking fresh encounters. The friend had cajoled and wheedled, till finally she'd agreed to go along. The party was for someone's birthday – a girl called Judy, whom the friend had known from school. 'She's great fun!' she had said. 'She can be a bit crazy sometimes, over the top, irrepressibly upbeat but I'm sure you'll like her. Everyone does! And the party will be amazing – I can guarantee you that. Good music, great food, lots of drink, top-quality dope, groovy people. She's got an ace crowd of friends. And anyway, I want to meet her new man. He's very dishy, so I've been told.'

Celia hadn't had the heart to make much effort with her clothes. She'd slung on a little black T-shirt and some jeans, tied her blond hair back off her face and scarcely bothered with make-up, just a quick smudge of eye shadow and a few flicks of mascara. At the last minute she'd grabbed her red jacket, as a small concession to festivity. She'd only be staying a short time, so not much point in going to too much trouble over her appearance, but then, she did have her pride.

The party was already in full swing when they got there, heaving with people, pulsing with the beat of 70s disco, Wilson Pickett, Diana Ross, the Stones, Free. The girl who opened the door to them was very beautiful – petite, big-eyed, with masses of thick, dark hair. She was clearly tipsy, or mildly high on something else, swaying to the music as she spoke. She pulled them into the flat and hurried to find them food and drinks, solicitous for their well-being.

'That's Judy,' her friend had said. 'Lovely, isn't she?' Hovering near her was a tall, well-built young man, also rather good-looking but in an entirely different way – quite shy, she thought. In awe of Judy, he seemed, completely smitten. 'Must be the new man,' her friend whispered. 'William Webb. He's training to be a lawyer. Rather gorgeous, don't you think?'

She'd been attracted to both of them straightaway. Her friend had been right; Judy drew people in. While Judy was busy all evening, orchestrating things, encouraging her friends to dance, changing the records, topping up drinks, Bill hung around, cheerfully watching the goings-on. He clearly didn't know all that many people there. Celia's friend had managed to pick up a long-haired man with a droopy moustache and had gone off to 'have a bop' with him, so she'd spent some time chatting to Bill. She found that he was just as charming as Judy, but without any of her zany energy. He was a good listener – a rare quality in either men or women, in her experience, and that was very endearing. She discovered that he'd done his law degree at Oxford and knew her sister, Barbara, who'd been a year or so older and at a different college but was the ex-girlfriend of a very good friend of his at St John's. What a coincidence! Small world. Strangely enough, that friend actually happened to be there at the party. Did she know him? Did she want to be introduced? Nick Cabuzel.

Nick Cabuzel. She'd heard all about him from Barbara but had never met him. They'd gone out with each other in Barbara's third year and then broken up just before her finals. Barbara had been unusually thrown by it all. Their parents, Lionel and Marje, were desperately concerned that she'd flunk her finals and Lionel had travelled up and down to Oxford most days during that week to support her. Of course, being Barbara, she'd pulled herself together for just as long as it took to get her First, but after that she fell apart for a bit. It was her one and only setback in love and she took it hard.

Celia wasn't sure she wanted to meet Nick Cabuzel, the bolter, the cause of all that grief. But in the end she didn't have the chance to say no. A slim, curly-haired man with large brown eyes and an enormous smile came over and gave Bill a great big bear hug.

'Hey, Bill, how's things? Enjoying the party? I absolutely love Judy, you know! You're a lucky man. She's perfect for you. You will invite me to your wedding, won't you?'

They both laughed. Celia looked him up and down. He wasn't at all what she'd been expecting. Barbara's early descriptions of him had given her a very different impression and then, after the break-up, she could only think of this half-French, half-English law graduate as the devil incarnate.

'Nick, this is Celia. Barbara Brown's sister.'

'Oh my God.' He flushed red with embarrassment. 'I'm so sorry. I don't know what to say. I'm not often lost for words, you know, but really . . . this is a bit awkward.'

'Don't worry,' she'd said, trying to reassure him. 'It was a while back and Barbara's fine now. It was tough for all of us at the time but it's water under the bridge.' Celia had been doing her A levels when it all blew up and it wasn't only Barbara who had suffered. Lionel's absences and Marje's anxiety had meant that there hadn't been much attention to spare for her and she'd had to keep to herself all her own exam worries so as not to add to her parents' troubles. It hadn't been a happy time, not for her, not for any of them.

'I'm glad she's OK,' Nick said. 'I thought the best thing was a clean break. Terrible timing, I know, but then . . . it's a long story. I didn't feel I had much choice. I wasn't very grown-up then, I'm afraid. Didn't handle it as well as I could have.'

She'd watched him as he spoke. He really wasn't what she'd imagined at all. His open admission of regret was quite disarming. And he had a rather lovely, friendly face, a wide smile, an intent, warm gaze. But did she want to prolong the conversation? No. Under other circumstances, perhaps, but not these. She made her excuses and went off to find a glass of wine.

A few brief chats with other people, a glass or two of cheap wine and a few puffs of a spliff later and he had come looking for her and struck up conversation again, this time avoiding any mention of Barbara. She was confused by her own feelings. She liked him, more and more as the evening went on. She'd meant to go home early but by two in the morning she was still there, talking quite comfortably to Nick Cabuzel.

Finally, when the other guests had thinned out and they felt obliged to leave Judy and Bill and Judy's flatmates to themselves at last, he offered to walk her home. When he dropped her at her flat in Tufnell Park, he asked if he could call her the next day. To her astonishment, she agreed. She knew that it was crazy, that she'd have a lot of explaining to do if Barbara or her parents ever found out, but there was something about him . . .

It was almost morning. The night sky was turning pale, the first sign of the approaching dawn. He moved to go, but then, seeming to hesitate slightly, turned back, tipped her face forward and kissed her full on the lips. They clung to each other in a way that seemed to shut out everything else, the sirens on the Holloway Road, the wakeful yowling of the local cabal of cats, the noisy bread-delivery vans and milk floats starting out on their early-morning calls.

And that was that. The next day he called and the following day they went for a walk on the Heath together, a little stroll that turned into a long trail, up past the ponds, through the woods, up to Kenwood and over the top to Hampstead Village. On the spur of the moment, she invited him back to her place for something to eat. It felt like the right thing to do. He never left. Ostensibly he had his own place in Stoke Newington; ostensibly he was living there and paying rent. In practice, from that afternoon, he was always over at hers; from then on they were hardly ever apart.

Of course, eventually she had had to tell Barbara, and Lionel and Marje, who'd never met him but hated him with a vengeance. That had been tough. Barbara had been good about it; she'd cried a little when Celia told her, then put a good face on it, but their parents had been astonished, furious, perplexed, especially Lionel.

'Just think how he treated Barbara. He was a little shit, dropping her like that, just before her finals. He's not a good sort, Celia. Best steer clear of men like him. And anyway, it's really not fair on Barbara. Having it shoved in her face like this. Can't you just find yourself someone else, instead?'

But she couldn't and she didn't. Lionel had ended up having to live with the fact that Celia had chosen Nick as her partner. He'd had to lump it. Marje was nicer about it as time passed – or at least more tactful – specially after Barbara had met and married Nigel, but Lionel never managed anything more than frosty politeness towards Nick, not even after they'd finally got married, not even after Daniel was born, nor lovely little Pippa, Pipsqueak, his favourite grandchild. Even then, Lionel made it quite clear that Nick wasn't worthy of either of his daughters' affections.

'And now I'm going to have to tell you, Daddy,' Celia thought, driving out towards St Albans. 'I'm going to have to admit to you that Nick's cheated on me. And even if you don't say I told you so, that's what you'll be thinking, that it was only a matter of time. Thirty-odd years, maybe, but in the end the man ran true to form. He did the dirty on you, just like he did with Barbara.'

She pulled off the main road into the nearest lay-by, switched off the engine and sat there howling, full-blown, loud, uncontrolled sobs that no one else could hear but were shocking even to her. It was only when another car came along and a man and woman got out and started walking towards her, gesturing to ask if everything was all right, that she finally pulled herself together. She wound down the window and told them she'd just stopped to answer her mobile phone. Whether they believed her or not, looking at her red, swollen eyes, she was beyond caring. She thanked them for their concern, started the engine and drove quickly away, heading for St Albans, where Anne would be anxiously awaiting her arrival.

Chapter 4

Celia sat on the bed in the upstairs room that Anne had prepared for her. She took her mobile phone out of her bag. It had been two days now since she'd left home and she'd resisted the temptation to check it. She held the On button down, waited a moment and then tapped in her password. Unsurprisingly, there were several messages and missed calls. She flicked to the 'Recents' and 'Missed Messages' to see who had been trying to reach her. At least six or seven calls from her home number and an equal number from Nick's mobile. Her stomach churned. Poor Nick. On some level, she could feel sorry for what he was undoubtedly going through and a part of her even felt worried about him, but she wasn't ready to listen to his messages and hear his voice again. Not yet.

There was a text from Annabel, another from Judy, one from Dan and several from Pippa, along with a voicemail message. She looked at Annabel's first. 'Hope you're OK. Haven't told Nick where you are. Don't you think you should? He's in pieces. Call me soon.' Judy's was short and supportive: 'Thinking of you. Hope you get things straight soon. You & Nick mean so much to us. Judy & Bill.' Dan's message was just a keeping-in-touch text from his holiday in the Lakes: 'Hi Mum! Having a great time. Bikes in good shape. Tough at first but getting into our stride now. Lottie sends her love. Back next weekend. XXX Dan.'

But Pippa's series of messages was more of a problem.

Her first was a cheerful text message about planning a weekend in Barcelona with Daisy and another friend, wondering if she had any tips for nice boutique hotels, her second similar but a little more urgent, asking why she hadn't responded first time round. Her third, a voicemail message, was a rather more anxious plea to get in touch. 'I've spoken to Dad and asked him where you are and why you haven't replied to my calls. Can't get anything sensible out of him. What's going on and where are you?' The fourth, a text, was all in upper case: 'PLEASE PHONE ME!'

Celia sighed. She would need to do something. It wasn't fair to just disappear from view like that. She decided to take the call and almost instantly there was a click and Pippa's voice at the end of the line.

'Mum? Thank God! Where on earth are you? I've been really worried.'

'I've had the phone turned off, Pips. I didn't know that you'd been trying to get in touch.'

'I went round to the house last night to try to see you, since you weren't answering any of my messages. Dad was in. He's looking pretty grim – but he won't say anything other than that you've gone away for a few days and not to worry. What on earth is going on?'

'I can't tell you, Pips. It wouldn't be fair.'

'What do you mean, "it wouldn't be fair"? I don't understand.'

'I'll explain everything as soon as I can, sweetheart, but not now. When I'm back in London, we'll talk. I promise.'

'Are you sick or something?'

'No, no. Goodness, no. Not sick.'

'Really?'

'Absolutely not. I swear I'm not sick. Honestly.'

'Well that's good. I was starting to imagine all kinds of crazy things – getting a bit carried away – you know me.'

'I'm fine. You don't have to worry on that score.'

'So . . . what's up then?'

Celia hesitated for a moment. 'It's not something I want to talk about over the phone, Pips.'

'Something to do with Auntie Barbara? Or the dreadful Dora, working you too hard? Having a break for a few days?'

She let Pippa rattle on, working through a list of possible explanations, with sleuth-like but inept persistence. There was a doggedness about Pippa that she'd always noted with a mixture of pride and amusement, but now she wished her daughter would pick up the cues and slow down.

'Is it something to do with Grandpa Lionel?' Pippa continued. 'Has he upset you again? Is he being mean to you?'

Celia almost wanted to laugh. When would that be a big enough event to cause a stir? Lionel's behaviour towards her was hurtful but so familiar as to be quite unremarkable. It always had been, not just since she'd married Nick but well before that, stretching back as far as she could remember. A fact of her life. The last conversation about the lost glasses had been unpleasant but only averagely so, nothing out of the ordinary.

'No, not Grandpa Lionel. He's been no worse than usual.'

'Is it something to do with me then, Mum? Are you upset with me? Cross or something?'

'Why ever would you think that, Pips? Of course not.'

'I know you've never been that keen on Jamie.'

'Rubbish. I like him very much.'

'And me telling you last week that we were thinking of getting married? I just wondered whether that had upset you.'

'For goodness' sake! What put that into your head? I'm pleased for you, Pipsqueak. Honestly.' She'd tried so very hard not to convey her feelings about Pippa's good-natured but rather dozy boyfriend. Clearly she'd failed. She thought of her own parents' displeasure at her announcement that she was getting married.

'If I sounded a little bit surprised about it when you told me, it was only that you're still quite young. It's a big step for both of you. But really, I'm pleased to see you happy, and if you're sure that you've found the right person . . .'

'I am. I have.'

'That's wonderful, then.'

'I thought it couldn't be about Jamie and me. That would be stupid. But then, with you not returning my calls so soon after me telling you about our plans, I thought maybe you were upset and avoiding speaking to me. Silly, I know, but then . . . you never do this – go quiet like this. Never. You always answer my texts or calls straightaway, sometimes almost before I've even sent them. Back comes the message, ping. Unless you're in a meeting or something, of course. But ages and ages and nothing . . . That's unheard of for you, Mum. That's why I've been worried about you. And then when I went to see Dad and he didn't even seem to know where you were, or wouldn't say . . .' She paused.

There was an audible intake of breath, a small catch in her voice – a small voice, almost a whisper: 'Oh Mum!'

She'd ploughed her way through one thing after another before finally getting there, suggesting anything and everything but that. So unimaginable to her that she really hadn't even let it enter her head till this very moment, when, with a sudden flash of insight, it had dawned on her that her parents might be in serious trouble. She'd been so certain, thought Celia, about the unshakeable stability of their marriage. As, of course, Celia had been herself.

And now again, slowly, hesitantly, as if it was difficult to say, let alone think: 'Not you and Dad, surely?'

Celia caught a little sob at the end of the line.

'Have you had a row or something?'

Celia struggled to control her own voice. She wasn't sure what to say.

'No, Pips. Not a row.'

They hadn't had a row; it was the truth.

'Where exactly are you, Mum?'

'I'll tell you if you promise not to tell your father. I need a bit of space, a bit of time to myself.'

There was a long pause. 'I suppose so. If you don't want me to.'

'I'm with Anne in St Albans. She's letting me stay for a few days. I'll come back home after that, really I will. I just need a couple of days on my own, that's all. I need time to think.'

'Can I come and see you?'

It would be so lovely to see her, a comfort to have her close, to share her grief with her daughter, her darling girl. She longed for it, imagined her sitting cross-legged on the bed, holding her hand, hugging her, the two of them crying together. But it wouldn't be fair. Not yet, when it was still so ugly and raw, when she hadn't even talked to Nick yet, when inevitably she'd be pouring out all her fury against him and bringing Pippa over to her camp, when she hadn't even heard his side of things. She was still thinking clearly enough to recognise the wrongness of that.

'No, I think it'd be better not to, Pips. I need to see your father first. But I'll call you as soon as I get home. I'm OK, honestly. You don't need to worry about me. I promise I'll be back soon and we can talk then. And in the meantime, I'll keep the phone switched on, so you can get in touch if you need to.'

'But –'

'Give my love to Jamie. Tell him how pleased I am about you and him.'

'I will, Mum, but –'

'Bye, Pips. I'll call you in a day or two. I promise.'

She pressed End Call before Pippa could say any more, then fell back on the bed, sobbing. She reached for a handful of tissues, to wipe her stinging eyes, her dripping nose, her face that was now wet with tears, but instead she found herself absurdly stuffing the tissues into her mouth, biting them, her teeth clamping down viciously on the wads of paper. When she started to gag she spat them out but pulled more out from the box, ripping them up into shreds and throwing them onto the floor and then, when they'd all gone, she tore at the box itself, shredding the bits of cardboard, pulling it to pieces.

When there was nothing left to destroy, she looked around her, at the mess on the bed, the scraps of paper and cardboard like cheap confetti strewn across the carpet. This is it, she thought. This is what it feels like to be utterly abandoned, to have lost one's way. So very quickly, and with such ease, she had come to this.

She'd had troubles in the past – the normal worries people have about the children and their problems, that dreadful trip to A&E with Dan when he was ten, the awful summer after house prices collapsed and Nick was made redundant, the terrible, heartbreaking phone call from Lionel about Marje, when without any warning her mother had suddenly collapsed and died. But this was different; this was being cast adrift, rudderless, with no compass, no map, no companion, no one to share it with, all on her own.

In times of difficulty, she had always turned to Nick. Her troubles had been his; his had been hers. They'd sat together in the waiting room at the Whittington Hospital, waiting for news of Dan's surgery, crying together and holding hands. When she'd called him to tell him that Marje was gone, he'd dropped everything at work and come to be with her; he'd said all the right things, done all that she could have hoped for from the man she had married and made her companion for life. That Nick wasn't available for her now. That Nick had gone.

She sat on the bed staring at the mess she had created. What would Anne say, if she came in now and saw what she had done? Wearily, she hauled herself to her feet and began to tidy up, putting everything into a plastic carrier bag that she could hide and dispose of without discovery. To reveal the depths to which she had sunk would be too shameful.

When it was cleared away, she sat back down on the edge of the bed. All she felt now was a kind of cold blankness, an empty, bleak sense of what she had once had, which felt like it could never be reclaimed. With horrible clarity and, worse than that, no sense of fear, she imagined herself standing on the bridge over the Archway

Road and clambering up over the barriers, wondering whether you remained conscious as you fell, whether you felt the impact as your head bounced onto the tarmac and your skull shattered, as your spine snapped and the bones smashed into the ground, whether your organs remained intact or whether they ruptured, whether you would be recognisable when your family came to identify you.

There was a knock on the door. Anne waited a moment and then came in bearing a cup of tea.

'Are you OK?' She was looking worried.

'Yes, fine.'

'Feeling any better?'

'A little.' She didn't have the heart to say otherwise.

'Could you manage to eat something this evening?'

'Probably not.'

'I think you should try. A piece of toast, some scrambled egg or something? Even just a little warm soup. To keep your strength up.'

'Thank you, Anne. You're so kind.'

'I'll make us something small. If you don't feel like it, that's fine. You can just leave it.'

'You really are very kind.'

'I know you haven't wanted to talk about what's wrong, but if you change your mind . . .'

'It's something between me and Nick.' There. It was out.

'I'd guessed that.'

'That's all I really want to say.'

'If you need to stay here longer, there's always a room for you.'

Celia looked at her gratefully. 'I may have to take you up on that. I haven't decided yet. But it's good to know that it's possible.'

'Only if you need it, of course.'

'Thank you.'

A little later, Anne called up to see if she wanted to come down for some food. She didn't feel like eating but then Anne really had been so very kind. She put on her shoes and shakily made her way downstairs to the kitchen, to see if she could bring herself to try some of the light supper that Anne had carefully prepared. And, to her surprise, she found that she could eat something. Not much, but enough to satisfy Anne that she was trying. Enough to feel that by forcing herself to do something as basic as putting food in her mouth she might impose normality on herself, even if everything around her felt utterly abnormal and out of control. She would make herself eat, if only to take back some control.

Instead of going back up to her room after the meal, she was also persuaded by Anne to go for a little walk down to the cathedral and around the park.

The evening was fine and the town quiet, with just a few people taking their dogs out for a walk. It was dusk, the November night was falling fast and soon the footpaths would be deserted as darkness descended and the air became more chilly and uninviting. Celia zipped up her jacket. She pulled her soft woollen hat over her head and wrapped her scarf round her neck a few times; it was the fine cashmere set in smoky grey that Nick had bought her for her birthday.

Anne chatted as they walked. She chose to talk about neutral things: her work, the advanced training she was about to undertake on group dynamics, mutual friends from school days, the state of health of their surviving parents, holidays past and holidays planned. When the conversation risked entering dangerous territory, she skirted round it, or swiftly changed the subject. Celia could see why she was so successful in her work; she skilfully steered things in a direction that allowed Celia to forget, at least temporarily, whatever it was that had happened to cause her such pain. Celia even managed to laugh, at Anne's humorous account of how she'd recently bumped into Andrea Alsop, their old classmate, at a conference in Manchester. 'Still just the same,' she'd said. 'Impossible to get a word in edgeways. I heard every last detail of the previous thirty years of her life, with nothing spared!'

'Andrea Alsop! I'd forgotten all about her,' Celia said. 'Motor Mouth, we used to call her. We were terribly mean in those days, weren't we? We took no prisoners.'

'A grain of truth in it, though,' Anne said. 'She really does talk incessantly. And she didn't seem terribly interested in me, or anyone else for that matter. She didn't even ask me about you.'

'I'm glad in a way. You might have given her a false picture.'

'What do you mean?'

'Happy marriage, happy family, happy life. I'm not sure that holds true any more.'

'Oh Celia.'

Celia kept her eyes on the path in front of them as they walked. She noticed the uneven paving stones, the moss in the cracks, the grassy borders that had turned to mud from being trodden by numerous pairs of feet. She didn't look up as she spoke.

'Nick's been having an affair. For over a year. He's lied to me and he's been caught out.' She'd said it. Finally.

'I guessed as much,' Anne said quietly.

'I thought you might have. I'm all over the place. Completely thrown. I don't know what to do.'

'I'm appalled.'

'By me?'

'No, of course not. By him! What the hell does he think he's doing? He's a complete imbecile. You're everything to him.'

Celia was taken aback. For someone who worked professionally with people's feelings, Anne seemed surprisingly lacking in reticence in revealing her own. And though Annabel too had clearly been very upset for her, Anne's response was all the more powerful for being so out of character.

'I'm surprised at your reaction. I thought that since you probably come across this kind of thing such a lot, you'd take it more in your stride. Like you do with your clients. Calmly listen and not say much. I thought you'd perhaps suggest marital counselling or something.'

'I'm your friend, not your therapist. Right now, I just feel furious with him for hurting you! And desperately sad for both of you. But actually, counselling isn't such a bad idea, you know.'

'I'm not sure I could be counselled out of what I feel right now. Sitting talking to someone wouldn't change what he's done. He's utterly betrayed my trust for over a year.'

'I wouldn't dream of advising you what to do, Celia. Only you know how you feel. But I do think you should see Nick and talk to him. You're going to have to have it out with him at some point. You both need to work out what you're going to do.'

'Not yet,' Celia replied. 'It's too soon. I don't think I'm up to it. Maybe in a few days' time, when I'm feeling less wobbly. At the moment, I'm afraid of what he might say. I'm afraid of what *I* might say. I don't even know what I want to ask of him, or want him to do. Even if he promised never to see her again, I'm not sure whether that would be of any use.'

Celia stopped walking and turned to look at Anne for the first time. 'I'd like to stay a little longer with you, if that's OK. I want to give myself a few more days and then I'll go back home and see him.'

'Of course. Stay as long as you need.'

They turned and headed back towards Anne's house, both now quiet, lost in their own thoughts. They turned the corner, walked down the road and Anne opened the front gate. The house was dark; Anne had forgotten to put on the light in the porch for their return. She rummaged around in her bag for her keys.

'Where are they, now? They must be somewhere.'

Celia waited patiently. It was cold and she shivered slightly. Inside, it would be warm and secure. She looked back out towards the street and saw, in the distance, a car door open and a figure step out. Despite the darkness she knew immediately that it was him.

It must have been Pippa who told him, she thought. She'd broken her promise. And then she saw him walking towards her, moving with that same loping gait she'd known for all these years and would have recognised anywhere, that slightly awkward, ambling stride she'd often laughed at and always loved. She felt, at first, coldly detached, observing him and herself from the outside, as if they were both characters in a foreign-language film whose words and actions needed an extra effort of interpretation.

Then all at once she found herself shouting across the street, yelling at him, as he approached, loud enough to make passers-by turn their heads to look at what was going on.

'Don't come near me, Nick! I never want to see you again!'

Chapter 5

Once she'd calmed down, helped by Anne's gentle persuasion, Celia agreed to talk to him. She was shocked by the way he looked, as if he'd not been eating properly or getting much sleep. Truthfully, he looked his age, like the sixty-year-old that he was. In her mind's eye, lying weeping on Anne's guest room bed, he had been the Nick of ten years earlier, slim, upright, his hair still a mix of curly brown and grey, with his warm but slightly tentative smile, steady gaze and endearing way of holding his head to one side when he looked at you, the person she'd been in love with for so many years, the man that Marina Jones might plausibly have found so powerfully attractive. This Nick, standing on the pavement outside Anne's house, was distraught and haggard. He looked physically diminished; there was no tilt to his head, no smile on his face.

Sitting across from each other at the kitchen table, with Anne upstairs, they went through the story of what he'd done. There was his initial simple, carefully worded account and then, bit by bit, all the extra, painful details that she felt compelled to extract from him.

He had found Marina instantly engaging, he said, and had thought that she felt the same spark. He'd been having lunch with Bill at Sheekey's, she'd come into the restaurant on her own and Bill had suggested that she join them at their table. The conversation between them became increasingly animated and she began to focus her attention on him in a way that reminded him there was still a bit of life in him, a flash of youthful desire that he'd almost forgotten he had, and the thought that it might be reciprocated came as a pleasant surprise.

'I knew, even then, how stupid it was, still I couldn't help but feel pleased that someone as young as her found me attractive. Bill had seen it and was impressed. He even seemed a bit jealous. I could imagine myself telling you what had happened and us laughing about it together. I'd come home and tell you about this woman who'd flirted with me outrageously and you'd say, "Still a bit of life in the old dog yet!" or something cheesy like that. We'd both see it as one great big joke.'

'But you didn't tell me, did you?'

'No. Stupidly, I kept it to myself.'

Nick waited a moment to gauge her reaction – she sat stony-faced. He took a deep breath and continued. He'd obviously rehearsed what he was going to say, providing a narrative of events that, if not excusing his behaviour, might at least explain it. But when it came to it, saying these things wasn't easy. She knew him well enough to see the obvious signs of nervousness in him, the repeated sweeping of his hand through his hair, the uncharacteristic hesitations, the uneven timbre of his voice that made his words seem unnatural, drawing attention to the fact that his account had been pre-prepared, almost as if he was reading a story from a book or making a speech memorised from a script.

He'd thought little more of the whole thing until later that week, he said, when out of the blue he'd received a phone call from the woman. (Celia noticed that he did not use her name, referring to her only as 'she'.) On the pretext of wanting some information and advice for a legal case involving another local authority, she'd asked to meet him for lunch.

'Didn't the warning bells sound at that point?' Celia asked. 'You must have known that something was up –

that she wasn't just wanting advice. Bloody hell, Nick, you're not a complete imbecile!'

'I told myself that it was just a work meeting. I convinced myself that it was fine to agree to it. I meet people for coffee or lunch all the time, both men and women. So do you. Why bother mentioning it to you? We've never kept tabs on each other. We've always trusted each other.'

She laughed drily. Trust. Not a good word to use now.

He winced.

'I trusted you but I also trusted *myself*,' he said. 'I never looked outside our marriage.'

He groaned, clearly realising the absurdity of this. 'I can't understand how this has happened. I don't see myself as the kind of man who does this kind of thing.'

Nor did she. Nor *had* she. She had trusted him, absolutely. She wondered, now, why she never had been jealous of him with other women, or worried that he might look elsewhere. He was good-looking, though not in a very obvious way, and very charming – it was perfectly clear that others agreed with her on that score. But he was also quite diffident about himself, perhaps surprisingly so, given how good he was at things, how well respected at work, and the ease with which he made friendships, with women and men alike. That had been one of the problems in the relationship with her sister, Barbara, she'd come to believe. Barbara was so assertively successful and sure of herself, even as a young girl – a high achiever and very dismissive of hesitancy in others. Nick, like Celia a younger sibling, had a strong and persistent streak of anxiety and self-doubt. She could imagine that Barbara, aged twenty or twenty-one, wouldn't have offered him much support or succour, when he needed it.

Nick had always had a soft core, an almost feminine sensitivity to hurt, that Celia loved. Just as she had found something quite special in him, she thought he had found something special in her, beyond mere attraction or simple love, something that also satisfied a deeper need in both of them for safety and a shared sense of each other's value. He could trust – that word again! – that she believed in him and his worth. She'd repaid that trust with her own.

'But despite not being the kind of man who would do this kind of thing, you did,' she said bluntly now. 'And in spite of being someone who's always prided himself on being scrupulously honest, you told the most terrible lies. And you told them to *me*, of all people.'

'I didn't mean for it to happen,' he said. 'It wasn't like me. It isn't! I don't want to use the term mid-life crisis – it sounds too obvious – but it is something like that, I think. It's hard to explain. It was like stumbling slightly, tripping up on a little uneven bit of ground, thinking you could pick yourself up and carry on and then finding that you've fallen into an enormous hole that you can't clamber out of. Suddenly the idea of just dusting yourself off and getting up and walking away is absurd.'

'How did it happen? The "slight stumble"?' she asked, her voice thick with irony. He'd obviously worked up that metaphor in advance. She didn't find it remotely apt or convincing for something he'd walked into with his eyes wide open. It was no excuse for a whole year of lies and deceit. 'What happened when you met her for lunch?' she couldn't help asking. She both wanted and didn't want to know all the details.

He hesitated briefly, as if deciding whether to tell her.

'Well?' she said coldly.

Reluctantly, he carried on.

He'd arranged to meet up with Marina at a restaurant she suggested in town. He'd intended to talk about work, enjoy being in the company of a young, attractive woman and nothing more. He was intrigued to see whether she would flirt with him when they were on their own, as she had done the previous time in the company of Bill. That was all, he'd told himself, just interest and amusement and the possibility of an entertaining lunch that wouldn't be repeated. But they had drunk far too much Pouilly Fumé, he had allowed himself to put all his caution to one side and they had ended up going back to her place. By the time he acknowledged to himself what he had done, it was too late. And having done it once, the barrier breached, he was, he had to admit, then eager for the excitement of it again. It was more the feeling of being desired than his own desire, he said. It was too hard to resist. Each time he told himself 'Just one more time,' but each time he hadn't the strength to say no. It was weakness on his part, pathetic weakness – he acknowledged that.

And then all of a sudden a year had passed and he was still secretly seeing Marina regularly, meeting up during work hours at her flat, or early evenings before he came home, finding times that wouldn't be noticed by Celia, or by anyone at the office, that didn't disrupt his normal life or draw attention to anything being wrong. He'd settled into a comfortable pattern of deception that he stupidly shut his mind to, in the hope that it would all come right of its own accord.

'And what about the sex?' she asked, tight-lipped with fury. 'You haven't said much about that, have you? And surely that's much more to the point than anything else – mid-life crises, or anxieties about yourself, or other such lamentably pitiful excuses that men trot out in these circumstances? In the end it's all about sex isn't it? Presumably good sex? Presumably often? Presumably passionate? At lunchtimes, sneaking off from work, hurrying to her flat to squeeze in a quick fuck before coming back home to me.'

She waited for the words to strike home before continuing, her voice rising now as the reality of it hit her.

'And you still carried on sleeping with me all that time. Not that exciting, I imagine, after her! Not that often. But us, you and me! *Our* intimacy, yours and mine. You carried on making love to me, as if nothing had happened, for a whole year. Presumably to put me off the scent, going through the motions, to stop me from realising what you were up to.'

'No. Really, honestly, no. Not going through the motions at all. It's just that . . .'

'It's just that what?'

'It's different. After all these years . . .'

'Boring, I suppose? Predictable? Stale?'

'Not boring, absolutely not, but . . .'

Another look of anguish. An obvious hesitation.

'I can't lie to you, Celia.'

Again she laughed drily. 'You've managed to lie to me for a whole year without too much difficulty.'

She saw him flinch. She had struck a powerful blow. There was silence, while he searched for what to say next.

'What do you expect me to tell you? That I slept with someone I didn't really fancy?' He paused. 'The sex with her was good. It was different. It made me feel like a different person. Younger, more attractive. But it doesn't diminish –'

'It bloody well does diminish. It does. Not only does it diminish, it bloody well damages . . . it threatens . . .'

'I can't bear what I've done.'

'But you've done it. There's no going back.'

'I've already spoken to her. I've told her that you know.'

'And what's her reaction?'

'Shocked. Upset. Worried.'

'Have you told her that you're not going to see her any more?'

'Not yet.'

'Are you going to?'

There was a moment's pause. 'Yes.'

She noted the pause.

'Whatever I decide to do?'

Another pause.

Celia sobbed. 'Oh my God.'

'I'm so sorry. I'm so, so sorry.'

'Does Pippa know about this? About what you've done?' Celia asked. 'Did you tell her, when you spoke to her?'

'I couldn't bring myself to. I said we'd been having some difficulties. I said not to worry, we'd sort it out.'

'And what about Dan?'

'No. He's only back from the Lakes on the weekend.'

'I want them to know what a cheating bastard they've got for a father. I want to ring Pippa right now and tell her what a sodding bastard you are.'

Silence.

Then more quietly she said, 'I won't, though. It isn't the right thing to do. It wouldn't be fair on them, not till we've worked out what's going to happen next. Till we're clear what we want to do, whether we're going to go our separate ways.'

'But we're not going to do that, are we?' And now Nick's careful words, his rehearsed manner had deserted him. She could hear the shock in his voice. 'We can't. It's not you and me that's the problem. It's me. I'm the problem. But I can sort myself out, sort everything out, with your help. I know I can. If you can forgive me, of course. If anyone can rescue me – us – you can. You're the strong one. You always have been.'

She felt the pull of his words. He was nothing if not clever. He'd be aware that an appeal to her strength, a reminder of her importance to him, was what was needed. Was this a piece of astute argument, the words of a lawyer, making out his case, or an agonised attempt to save them both?

'We can work this out, can't we? After all these years?' he pleaded, and she felt the force of it, unplanned, unadorned, fearful, as if the reality of what he'd done had finally hit home.

'The way I feel at the moment, probably not,' she said simply. It was what she felt.

'Oh my God!' He put his hands to his head, in a gesture of despair. 'Whatever I've done, it wasn't meant to hurt you. It wasn't meant to damage us, or put us at risk. It was stupidity and weakness and lack of self-control and forgetting what's important and blindness and need and pathetic susceptibility to flattery and affection, and male egotism and all that kind of ridiculous rubbish. It was me being a complete prat, a stupid fool, an absolute idiot – reckless, dishonest, mad. I know that. But it wasn't meant to lead to this.'

And then he cried. He wept openly, unashamedly, his face contorted with grief. And Celia cried too, whether for him or for her, or for both of them, she wasn't entirely sure. He reached out his hand towards her, across the table, and she held it, unable to resist the comfort it gave her, or the need in him.

It was getting late; they heard Anne moving around in the bathroom upstairs, preparing to go to bed. They began to talk about practicalities, how best to get through the next few days and weeks, how to avoid saying too much to the children, in case something could be rescued from the wreckage. It was Nick who came up with the idea of Paris. He had inherited a small flat from his grandmother, which they rented out on short lets; it happened to be free. He would take leave from work, go away for a few weeks, give her some space to think about what she wanted, put himself at a distance from everything, from Marina and from her. Perhaps, after that, they might be clearer about what each of them wanted to do.

She picked up on the idea immediately, though not for him – for her. *She* would go to Paris for three or four weeks on her own. She could give him no assurances about the outcome, but equally made no demands on him about whether he stop seeing Marina or not; that would be for him to decide. If he were to end the affair, it would have to be on his own initiative, not as a panicky response to the threat of losing her. In a few weeks' time, on her return to London, they would meet again to take stock.

When he left, he tried to embrace her. It took all her strength to resist being drawn in close to him and feel the comfort of his familiar smell, his warmth, his hands on her back. She was engulfed by a sense of what she had lost, but brusquely waved him away.

'No. Just go,' she said. 'I'll come home to collect my stuff and sort things out while you're at work tomorrow. I'll ring Dora and ask her if I can work from Paris for the next few weeks – I can do most things from there by email. You speak to Pippa and Dan. Make up something to reassure them – you're obviously good at that!'

He started to remonstrate but took one look at her face and quickly stopped.

'I'll text you when I get to Paris to tell you that I've arrived safely and got into the flat, but other than that, I don't think we should call each other.'

He nodded. 'I'll try to end it with Marina while you're gone.'

She shrugged. 'That's up to you. It's for you to decide.'

'I know,' he said. 'I understand.'

She hoped he did.

Chapter 6

Celia was sitting in the tiny kitchen of the flat just off the rue Vieille du Temple in the Marais district of Paris. She knew it well. She was comfortable in this place; she felt at home. Over the years, sometimes with the children, sometimes without, Nick and Celia had spent many long weekends and short breaks here, in this old-fashioned, shabby, quintessentially French apartment on the fourth floor of a fin de siècle building on the corner of a bustling working street. She sipped the strong coffee that she had made in the small metal coffee pot. It did its work without any fuss, sitting directly on the gas burner, hissing and steaming away, producing a thick, rich brew that she had never been able to replicate in Kentish Town. Here she drank her coffee without milk; in London she wouldn't dream of doing so. London was London and Paris was Paris and somehow she found that the distance from her children, the office, her friends and, most of all, from her husband, had brought an unexpected calm. Sometimes she suddenly thought of him, and of the betrayal, got caught in a repetitive loop of dark fury about what he had done, her loss, and her fears for what would come next, and then there was an outpouring of grief that seemed unstoppable. But, increasingly, she started to notice that she was thinking forward, about herself and her life and how she might manage to survive if she were left on her own. It was a little shift of perspective that she found unnerving in its own way.

She was contemplating how to respond to the message on the answer phone that she had just picked up from Paul Legrand. A few days earlier she'd had a call from Yvette, Paul's sister, saying she'd heard that Celia was in town and would she like to come for Sunday lunch at the country home just outside Paris. She hadn't seen the Legrands for well over a year now but a meal en famille, with the extended Legrand family, felt like it would be difficult to manage, with all the explanations it might entail. Besides, going without Nick would have seemed all wrong. They were, after all, Nick's friends, first and foremost.

Paul and Nick had spent all their summers together, when Nick visited his grandparents in Brittany as a child. They'd been great pals. He told her about their adventures, doing all those things boys like to do – fishing or collecting frogspawn in the stream, going on cycling trips to the local village to buy an ice cream from the bar, or spending long hot afternoons at the seaside, digging for crabs in the sand. And then, later, as teenagers, they'd hitched up to Paris together and down to Provence, camping out on the beach, or staying in youth hostels, meeting girls, getting drunk, cooking their first meals in a single pot on a Camping Gaz, smoking their first cigarette, taking their first puff of weed. Yvette, too, had known Nick since he was just a little boy, though she had been younger, the annoying kid sister who trailed round after them, getting in the way. It was only when he was at university that he'd really got to know her properly, when Paul was at the Sorbonne and all three of them had begun meeting up in Paris in the summer and Nick was admitted into the big circle of hippie friends who hung around together on the Left Bank. Briefly – before Barbara – Nick had gone out with Yvette but it had fizzled out very quickly by all accounts, both of them realising that they were more like brother and sister than potential lovers. They had stayed friends, all of them, all their lives, their shared summers a bond that held firm into adulthood.

No, seeing the Legrands on her own wouldn't be such a good idea, Celia thought. Their strongest connection was with Nick, not her, and the questions about Nick would be uncomfortable and awkward. She wasn't sure that she'd be able to keep up the pretence that all was fine.

She had, however, already visited Nick's aunt Odile.

Odile was a slender woman in her early eighties, always stylishly attired in designer dresses or smart suits, never seen without her red lipstick and face powder. She had a measured style of speech and formal demeanour that were a cover for unseen depths, of which Celia was fully aware. She had led a full and eventful life, lost a lover in the war, been married twice and seen her only child die of cancer in his early thirties. Till she was sixty she worked as a civil servant, a fonctionnaire, in the Ministry of Finance, one of few women of her age to both rise up the ranks and maintain a successful career through marriages and child-rearing. She was an impressive and formidable woman.

'Celia, my dear,' she had said, opening the door of her apartment near the Champs Elysées and kissing her twice on both cheeks. 'I'm so glad to see you.'

She had welcomed her in and, once they were seated in the large elegant salon overlooking the park, she called Sylvie, the daily help, and asked her to make them both a pot of English tea, 'with milk,' she added, just to be sure.

'So,' she said straightaway. 'Where is my adorable nephew? Why isn't he here in Paris with you?'

Celia smiled to herself; Odile was sharp as ever, despite her advancing years.

'Does there have to be a reason?'

'You never come to Paris on your own. Nick wouldn't allow it! He loves to come here with you, showing off his

"Frenchness", his Gallic charm, don't you think? Even now, he feels it makes him stand out a bit. Gives him value in your eyes, or so I've always thought.'

'Perhaps you're right. It's true, we always come together.'

'And so?'

'Odile, you're impossible. You have a knack of getting straight to the heart of things.'

'Ah, I thought so.'

Celia sighed. 'Nick and I are having problems.'

'The naughty boy. What has he done?'

'It could be me, you know.'

'No, never you. I know you too well, Celia. You're an innocent in these matters, an ingénue. And anyway, it's always the man. In my experience, that is, and, as you know, I've had quite a lot of experience of men.'

'He's been having an affair.'

'Pooh! Just that? Well, that's a relief. I was worried for a moment.'

'What do you mean, "just that"? It's serious!'

'Men of his age often have affairs. They need to – how shall I put it? – fulfil their urges. They're like bottles of champagne – the cork's pushed in and it needs to pop out, or the whole thing will explode. Let him have his little affair and then welcome him back to your arms. That's the attitude I took with Didier, my second husband. We made our little accommodations and it all worked out fine. The mistresses were second fiddle – I always knew that. It was just the sex, nothing more. Marcel, of course, was faithful. Perhaps that was the problem! I stopped finding him fascinating.'

'You French have a very different attitude to these things.'

'A healthier attitude, Celia,' she said. 'We have no illusions. We don't expect so much and we don't lie so much either. So long as it wasn't thrust under my nose, I was happy to let Didier enjoy himself. It's only when it gets more serious and the other women make foolish demands that it becomes more of a problem. Is this the case with Nick?'

'I don't know. He says he wants to end it with her but it's hard to tell what he really wants. She's young and I'm sure she's beautiful . . .'

'My dear, they always are.'

'He's in a terrible state.'

'He loves you very much, Celia. He wouldn't want to lose you. Of course he's upset.'

'But he's lied to me for over a year. It's not just a meaningless little fling. He's been seeing her and pretending to me that everything's fine. The sex is bad enough but the betrayal of trust is much, much worse.'

'Hmm. He has been a very silly boy. He should have talked to you sooner, or been more – how shall I say? – discreet, so that you didn't find out.'

Celia laughed. 'You really are impossible, Odile! I can't believe how easily you take these things.'

'Oh no, my dear, I'm not saying it's easy. Just sensible. Perhaps we French are just more realistic about human nature and want to avoid all the fuss and bother that goes with your way of doing things. If you are scandalised and outraged and feel betrayed, then you're forced to do foolish things like separating or getting divorced, when no one really wants that, neither the man nor the woman.

But if you have less grand expectations of always being faithful, for ever and ever, if you understand that that's just a make-believe, fairy-tale world, then perhaps you can accept a little misdemeanour here and there, and you continue to love each other in something like the same way as before.'

'So, if I followed the French way of dealing with these things, I'd forgive him his little "misdemeanour" and welcome him back with open arms, would I?'

'You'd put up a fight to keep him, not just hand him over to your rival by withdrawing from the field of battle. You'd be the nice, charming wife that he adores and pretty soon he'd tire of the younger woman and you'd be the winner.'

'You make it sound like a military campaign!'

'Ah, Celia, my dear, it is!'

'I'd love to be able to see it that way, Odile, but I'm not sure I can. If I coldly made all the calculations about the best thing to do, perhaps I'd come up with an approach such as the one you advise. But that doesn't take into account my feelings. Nick and I haven't had a continental-style marriage, such as you describe. Our relationship has been based on things you'd probably call "fairy tale" – faithfulness, trust, honesty and so on. It's like a beautiful piece of porcelain, a lovely, priceless object, that's been dropped. Now it has a massive great crack in it that can never be repaired – glued together and touched up, maybe, so that it doesn't show, but however expertly it's done, I'll always know the crack's there.'

'Then I feel sorry for you, Celia. I fear that you and Nick have a very hard time ahead.'

'Yes,' Celia said, simply, 'perhaps.'

What Odile said was true. Her view of marriage might help Celia practically to live with the realities that had opened up, to continue with a life that not only she and Nick but also the children and their friends depended on. Maybe she would just have to say goodbye to the old, romantic notions she had about Nick and their relationship and learn how to accept something less special, something more ordinary and cheap? Live with the crack in the pot. Over time, perhaps she would be able to appreciate its beauty again, even with its flaw? Maybe even value it more? She thought of the Japanese concept of wabi-sabi, the idea that beauty has little to do with perfection and stability but rather with their opposites, imperfection and transience. If the French could live with weaknesses and faults in their marital relationships and the Japanese could make defects part of their whole aesthetic, then perhaps, in time, she too could find a way of transforming what now seemed ugly and spoilt into something good again.

'Can I speak to Nick about this?' Odile asked. 'If you think it would help and if he'll talk to me, of course. He may feel too ashamed of himself.'

'I'm sure he'll want to talk to you,' Celia replied. 'You've always been very important to him. I'd like you to, in fact, Odile. He's been completely thrown by all of this. He's brought it on himself, of course, but it doesn't stop me from worrying about him.'

'Have you been phoning each other?'

'I told him I didn't want to. But actually we have talked once or twice. He'd like me to speak to him more. He wants me to tell him I'm coming back to him, but I'm afraid I can't do that.'

'I'll try calling him, then maybe we can talk again.'

Celia thanked her and moved to leave. This time, at the door, Odile took her and gave her a hug. Celia felt her thin arms around her, surprisingly strong in their grasp.

'I want to see you and Nick happy and together again,' she said.

Celia fought to hold back the tears. 'So do I,' she said, 'but I doubt that's going to happen. That's *your* fairy-tale ending!'

In the lift going down, and on the metro, she thought about Odile's response to her situation and whether she should try to follow her advice. Even if she did, was Nick really ready to give up whatever he was getting out of his relationship with that woman? She wondered whether he would be willing to sacrifice her for the sake of their marriage. And what if he made that sacrifice and she still found herself unable to forgive him? Her grief sometimes felt like hatred. She wasn't sure how that could be turned back into anything approximating love.

She was so absorbed in her thoughts that she missed her station and had to jump off the train at the next stop and go back the way she came.

When she got back to the flat she went straight to the answerphone. Four messages. One brief one from Nick, asking her to call, a mildly anxious-sounding one from Dan, wondering if she was OK, and a rather more obviously upset one, from Pippa, asking if she could come over the following weekend to see her. And then a simple message, in French, from Paul Legrand, saying he'd heard that she was in Paris and would she like to meet him for a coffee tomorrow? First Yvette, whom she'd already turned down, and now Paul. The Legrand family were clearly keen to make contact with her. She felt that maybe she would like to see him but what was behind the call?

Perhaps Nick had rung and asked him to talk to her, on his behalf? That wouldn't be such a surprising thing for him to do. She could imagine Nick asking his old friend to act as an intermediary on his behalf, or even just to check that she was OK and not in danger of doing something silly. Nick knew how much Celia liked the Legrands and he might well hope that they could step in and help in some way.

Sitting in the kitchen, sipping her coffee, she wondered what to do. She would ring Pippa first and finally agree to her coming over to Paris – perhaps the time had come to tell her something of the truth of what was going on; she needed to know. Dan's and Nick's calls could wait till later – Dan's because he didn't seem too concerned, Nick's because she simply couldn't face talking to him. And then there was Paul Legrand. She weighed it up and finally decided that she would agree to meet him. Why not? Much easier than the far more daunting option of facing the whole family at their leisure on a Sunday in the country, where it would be hard to escape the questions and harder still to make a polite, early exit. Paul could hear the whole story from her, then tell Yvette and Henri and the others all the gory details and save her the trouble. And perhaps, knowing Nick as well as he did, he might have some insight into what had happened and how they could extricate themselves from the mess. Before phoning Pippa and before she could change her mind she picked up the phone and dialled his number.

Chapter 7

Paul Legrand was not a particularly good-looking man. He was, however, one of those men who had clearly grown into his body as time had gone on, starting out as an awkward, shy youth, all too aware of his physical flaws, and then, in later life, developing the confidence that comes from doing his job well, earning not insubstantial sums of money and discovering that women are attracted not just to a handsome face but to other things too. He was in his mid fifties, with a slight, slim physique, a full head of springy, silver-grey hair flecked with black, and a strong sense of style that made the most of his limitations.

He walked into the bar, wearing a dark coat and a grey felt hat, and looked around the room, searching for Celia. Within moments, his eyes alighted on her and he wove his way between the tables towards her. He took off his hat. Four kisses, two on each side. Placing both his hands on her arms, then straightening his own to hold her out for his inspection, he looked her up and down, smiling, and said, 'You're as beautiful as ever, Celia. Not a day older than last time we met!'

Celia managed a polite laugh, despite her despondent mood. 'Nonsense, Paul! You don't look too bad yourself. You've kept in good shape.'

'Ah, we are getting older, both of us, but it's what's inside that counts. The spirit. That's what shines through.'

She was reminded of his tendency to come out with philosophical comments like this that teetered on the edge of triteness and all too often tipped over. Nick and she had laughingly commented on this in the past.

'I don't know what you've heard, Paul, but I'm afraid there's not much shining going on in this spirit! It feels pretty bashed and battered.'

'I'll own up, I have heard something. From Nick. He emailed to say you would be in Paris on your own. He put it simply. "I've fucked up," he said. "I may be losing Celia."'

'Yes,' she said coldly. 'He's right on both counts.' And once again, the saying of it made it seem like the reality it was rather than the bad dream she wished it were, and she found that she couldn't stop the tears.

'I'm sorry,' she said. 'I'll pull myself together, I promise. I won't make a scene.'

He handed her a clean white handkerchief. She was astonished that anyone still carried these crisp little laundered squares, extraordinary remnants from a long-lost world. It was as if he had stepped out of a black-and-white film, where a man comforts a woman in distress in the most conventional way the director can think of conjuring up for the viewer. Any moment now, he would be taking his coat off and wrapping it round her shoulders, or placing it on the pavement as she stepped out of the café into the rainy street. Despite all her troubles, she wanted to laugh out loud.

He signalled to the waiter and ordered coffees and two glasses of water, insisting on a plate of macarons as well, though she told him that she really wasn't hungry. She had not felt like eating much since the evening of Bill and Judy's party, forcing herself to consume food for survival rather than savouring it for pleasure. But when the pink, green and yellow Ladurée cakes arrived, lined up in a tidy row on the plate, they looked so delightfully, childishly bright and cheerful that she couldn't do anything other than agree to eat one.

'So, why are we here, Paul?' she said finally. 'Has Nick asked you to persuade me to stay with him?'

He smiled. '"I've fucked up. I may be losing Celia. Can you help me?" No. Not at all. It was my idea to meet you, entirely my own. I have no other motive than as a friend. When Yvette told me you were in Paris and then Nick emailed and I found out why, I thought you might need someone to talk to. A bit of support. Pur et simple!'

'Yvette clearly thought the same. She invited me out to La Celle les Bordes but to be honest I couldn't face it – the whole Legrand clan, Yvette and Henri, the children, the grandchildren, your mother, your aunt, you and Véronique – Véronique's still your partner, isn't she?'

'Oh no!' He laughed. 'Véronique and I didn't see eye to eye on children. Her female clock was ticking. So finally we agreed to part and, lucky girl, she quickly found someone else, a very nice, innocent, uncomplicated man who wants a family. We're very good friends, you know, me and Véronique and her new partner. He's much better for her than I would ever have been!'

'And presumably you're on your own now, leading a monkish life as a single man?'

'Now, now, Celia, your English irony doesn't escape me! I know how much you disapprove of me.' There was a pause. 'Of course I'm seeing one or two women but nothing serious. I'm having a rest from seriousness! After that, who knows?'

'Nick's aunt Odile was giving me the benefit of her experience – a lesson in the French approach to these things. She thinks I should pull myself together and not make a great big fuss about Nick's behaviour.'

'Nick's behaviour, was it really so very bad?'

'Yes . . . at least in my view. Having an affair for over a year without saying anything – in my view that's inexcusable, though perhaps not in yours.'

She was surprised by his reaction.

'No, I agree with you absolutely. He's been abominable! It's all about the contract you've made with each other. In my relationships, it's always been very clear. None of my exes ever dreamt that I would be faithful to them – I never promised them that. And, of course, I had to put up with their little affairs as well. Mostly that was fine. Occasionally, there was a small amount of jealousy, you know, even from me. I didn't much like it when Eloise informed me that she'd been sleeping with my business partner, Jean-Luc. That was a step too far! But then I hadn't exactly been a saint myself. For you and Nick, it's different. You have been a different kind of couple in a different kind of marriage. What Nick has done is quite unacceptable!'

'Thank you for saying that, Paul. Not everyone seems to understand.'

'You deserve better, Celia. You've been a fine, loyal and, may I say, a very beautiful wife to him. He should not have thrown that away.'

They talked on for a bit and then Celia looked at her watch, made some excuses about having work to catch up on and emails to respond to and rose to leave.

'Shall I phone you to see you again before you go back to London?'

'That would be nice,' she said.

On the metro back to the flat she kept a close eye on the stations; she mustn't miss her stop a second time. But she felt churned up, just as she did after her conversation with Odile. Paul had endorsed her feelings of anger but also reminded her of how very special her relationship with Nick had been, her fury and her love for him – and the sadness at the loss of it,– two sides of the same now tarnished and seemingly valueless coin.

Back at the flat, she tried to banish these thoughts, focusing all her attention on her work, furiously tapping away at her keyboard, to distract herself with all those emails she'd put off for the past few days. There was a complicated one from Dora, her boss, with a string of tricky questions about a book due to be published in the spring, where the author was proving to be more awkward than usual about everything from the title, cover and blurb to the last bits of editing that Celia had been holding out for. The email was a little sharp in tone. Was she imagining that, or was there really a note of irritation breaking through in Dora's departure from her typically effusive style? Clipped sentences and bullet points were not usually her preferred linguistic choices. She wondered whether Dora was just feeling the pressure, or beginning to lose patience with her for being away from her desk for so long.

Despite trying to focus on the details of the new book and the urgent decisions that needed to be taken, it was hard to keep her mind on track, to avoid constantly coming back to the conversation with Paul and the indignation that he had given vent to on her behalf. He had definitely seemed to take her side. His support had been wholehearted. That had been a surprise. She always expected men to stand up for each other, to understand each other's motivations and needs, particularly in affairs of the heart, or sexual misdemeanours. Paul, in particular, would sympathise with Nick, she'd been sure. He was experienced in these things. But if even Paul felt that Nick had behaved badly, then forgiveness for him seemed out of the question. Her anger threatened to harden inside her, into a cold, flint-like fury that she found rather frightening.

Over the next couple of days something more urgent loomed, however, which took her thoughts in a different direction. She had agreed that Pippa should come over for the weekend and soon she was going to have to confront the problem of breaking the news to her about Nick and Marina. She didn't worry so much about Dan; he was wrapped up in his own world, off doing things with his friends, enjoying London life. He'd always been phlegmatic about his own ups and downs and she felt sure that, upset though he would be, he'd take it all in his stride. He was one of those sturdy, straightforward boys who seemed to have a steady and uncomplicated inner life. Pippa, however, would be devastated, of that she was certain. She adored Nick; Celia had always been her confidante and her friend but Nick was the captain at the helm of her fragile little boat, steering her through the choppy waters of childhood and adolescence with a confident, measured hand. What's more, Pippa was also worryingly immersed in the romantic idea of her parents' marriage; she loved to recount to her friends the story of their meeting, the young lovers clinging to each other against the odds, the family furore, the happy-ever-after ending of their wedding and life together. Pippa had been thrown by the discovery that all wasn't well. She was going to be even more upset when she found out about what Nick had done.

She was arriving on the Eurostar on the Friday, taking the afternoon off work so that she could get into the Gare du Nord by early evening. Celia decided that she would bring her straight back to the flat for a meal, rather than take her out to one of the bistros in the Marais. She knew that Pippa loved those atmospheric, quirky little restaurants tucked away down narrow streets, but if there were to be upset and tears, the flat would be a better place for them to be played out than in a crowded Parisian bistro, in full view of other people.

Friday. Celia couldn't settle to anything. She cleaned the flat and pulled out the sofa bed, making it up with the slightly damp spare sheets from the linen cupboard – at least they'd be aired a bit by the time Pippa arrived. Then she went out to the market.

It was a crisp early November morning, the sun was out and the market was pleasantly busy, with tourists ambling past stalls to browse the produce and choose speciality foods to take home, middle-aged Parisian women buying daily fruit and veg from banks of wooden crates, or ripe cheeses from the farmer's van, young bohemians sitting smoking on the bench round the old lime tree, or drinking coffee in one of the several bars. Celia still had little interest in food but the stalls looked beautiful, the produce displayed with a refinement and artistry that lifted her spirits. She needed to provide a meal for Pippa, so she selected some expensive sausage, a soft goat's cheese from the van, a punnet of green olives, some implausibly large tomatoes and a fine-looking crusty pain de campagne. At the last minute she added in a bunch of pink dahlias; they would brighten up the kitchen and look welcoming when she and Pippa opened the front door of the apartment.

In the afternoon, she went to the Musée d'Orsay, to pass the time before Pippa's arrival. It was a favourite place, one of the museums she never failed to visit on a trip to Paris, but she drifted round aimlessly, hardly taking in the paintings, her mind focused on the evening and the conversation she would have to have with her daughter. She had decided to try to keep it simple and stick to the facts – avoid saying anything negative about Nick, keep her own emotions in check but nevertheless tell something of the truth. She rehearsed the words she would use, thinking of all the different possible formulations: your father's been having an affair, he's got caught up in something he didn't intend to, he's been sleeping with, making love to, having sex with, bonking, fucking, screwing, shagging . . . She wondered whether, when it came to it, she would really be able to keep her anger with Nick under control. 'Your father has met another woman and we're now both working out how to deal with that.' If she said these neutral words to herself often enough, maybe she'd be able to say them effortlessly when the time came and her daughter was sitting beside her, listening in shock to her account of it all.

And then what? Would Pippa side with her? She hoped so, though she knew that this wasn't a sensible thing to wish for. Everything she'd ever heard about marital problems told her that being civilised about the other person was key to the children's ability to survive the fallout. She ought to be civil about Nick, whatever her true feelings, if only for Pippa and Dan's sake. She wished she knew what Nick had already said to them.

She wandered through the galleries and found herself standing in front of a painting by the American artist, James McNeill Whistler, a portrait of his mother in muted shades of black and grey. Celia was arrested by the image of the woman. She looked to be in her sixties, not so very much older than Celia herself but dressed in the garb of an old person, in a plain black high-collared dress, with just a cotton and lace cap on her head and a delicate trim of lace at her wrists. Sitting calmly, with her hands in her lap, in a simple, bare room, Anna Whistler appeared to be the epitome of quiet, maternal stability. Her face, in profile, was placid but strong, her dark clothing and the bland, colourless surroundings emphasising the purity of her expression. Was this a woman who was in turmoil over her husband's behaviour? On the brink of a separation? Did she ever think with a shiver of excitement of the touch of another man's hand on her starched black dress? She thought not. Mrs Whistler was enviably at one with herself. James McNeill Whistler, her son, had captured her essence as he saw it and the portrait had become an iconic image of filial affection and respect. The tears were coming again now and would be unstoppable, she knew, if she continued to stand looking at this painting, so she quickly moved on. But trying to concentrate on other pictures was impossible; everything was just a blur of shape and colour, gilt frames and hushed figures posed in front of canvases in stances of awe. So she gave up trying to distract herself and left the gallery, in search of something else to do to pass the time before Pippa's arrival.

She walked back towards the apartment and passed The Red Wheelbarrow bookshop, on rue St Paul, where she stopped briefly to talk to the owners. Dan had done a stint working for them part time during his gap year and she always liked to go in to say hello when she was in Paris and buy a book – she'd been so grateful to them for taking him on. She came away with a copy of something she thought Pippa might like and then headed home. She would have a little rest before going to meet Pippa at the station.

Returning to the apartment, she found a little note, slipped under the door and lying on the wooden floor, written on that squared paper that French exercise books are made of, a page roughly torn out and folded. It was from her neighbour in the apartment next door, Madame Fournier, telling her that a parcel had arrived for her. She had taken it in for safekeeping. On the answerphone was a message from Nick.

'Hope you're OK, Celia. Pippa is on the train. I gave her a lift to the station in the end. I thought I should let you know, I've told her about Marina. Thought it'd be easier for you if it came from me. At least you don't need to face that.' A long pause. 'I'm missing you a lot, you know.' Another pause. Then, 'This is hell. I want you to come home.'

She listened to the message once, went back to it again and then a second time. She wanted to hear his voice, just for the sake of hearing it, to remind herself of the sound of him. It was good of him to have talked to Pippa. He'd been brave, she couldn't deny that, and thoughtful about her, trying to save her from more grief. It couldn't have been easy for him. Was he repentant? Clearly he was feeling down. Just depressed, though, or more than that? In spite of everything, she felt worried about him. He'd looked so terrible in St Albans. There was one thing he'd chosen *not* to say in his phone message, though. The fact that he hadn't mentioned it meant that he almost certainly hadn't yet broken with Marina. She felt her anger boiling up again. Did he really expect her to come running back to him without hearing this news?

She wiped the message from the phone. She would not have to listen to it again, nor would she answer his call. Let him suffer! He deserved it!

There was a quiet knock on the front door. It was Madame Fournier.

'The package, madame,' she said. 'It was a special delivery, so I said I would look after it for you.'

Madame Fournier stood waiting eagerly, as if hoping to be invited in, to discover what this little parcel contained.

'It looks important,' she said. 'I had to sign for it, too. Usually that means something valuable. Otherwise they just leave it outside the door.'

'Thank you, madame,' Celia said. 'It was very kind of you.' She took the parcel and then closed the door firmly.

A small package, neatly wrapped. She recognised the handwriting straightaway and tore open the brown paper. Inside was a tiny black box. She opened it, unclipping the clasp at the front. Nestling on a padded silk bed was a pair of silver earrings, almost identical to ones that Nick had given her, many years previously. A long time ago, she had dropped one of the pair somewhere and had often mourned its loss. She looked at them, so beautiful, so familiar, yet not quite the same. Oh my God! She opened the card tucked into the lid.

'A token of my love. Nick.'

She stared at it, at the small, surprisingly neat handwriting, at the simple words. Nick's normal loose, illegible scrawl had been reduced and tidied to fit the limited space. She closed the card and returned it to the box, then picked up the earrings one at a time, feeling their cold, silver smoothness on her fingers. She put them on and went to the mirror in the bedroom to see how they looked: straight on, in half profile one way, in half profile the other, close up, at a distance. They really were beautiful. Then she went back into the hall, took them off and returned them to their soft, cushioned bed, to lie there silent, uncommunicative, side by side. She closed the box, which shut with a loud snap.

Six o'clock. The bells rang out from the church of Saint-Denys du Saint-Sacrement. Just enough time to get to the Gare du Nord and be standing at the gate when Pippa's train came in. She put the box into the drawer of the table in the hall, pulled her coat down from the stand and grabbed her scarf.

Outside it was dark. Looking back up to the apartment, Celia saw Madame Fournier at her window, lit up against the black sky, watching her. Quickly the woman pulled her shutters closed and was gone. Celia buttoned her coat and stepped briskly forward, hurrying towards the metro to reach the station in time to greet Pippa and face the new difficulties that this would bring.

Chapter 8

The weekend was over; Pippa had caught her train home. Celia returned to the apartment feeling very much alone, though the visit had gone as well as could be expected. They had talked a lot, cried a lot, discussed the future, sought to come to terms with this new situation. At first, Pippa had railed against both Nick and Marina. She couldn't believe how her father could have behaved in that way; it was so out of character, a horrifying betrayal. But then, towards the end of their first evening together, somewhat hesitantly, she suggested that perhaps eventually Celia might be able to get over this. She wondered whether, in time, she and Nick might be able to pick up the pieces. In the end, might not Celia find a way of forgiving him?

'These things happen to all kinds of people. Sometimes they surprise themselves and forgive each other, you know. They stay together, perhaps even become stronger.'

'Not so easy, Pips. Certainly not when he's still seeing her.'

'Is he? I thought it was all over.'

'Is that what he told you?'

'Not quite. But that's the impression he gave. He's pretty devastated, you know. He looks absolutely awful.'

'As bad as me?'

'Actually, you don't look so dreadful, you know, Mum. Strange though it may seem, you appear to be coping better than he is.'

'Oh.' It was the first time she'd thought of that possibility.

'He's done this to you but, in a way, you're tougher than him.'

'Am I?'

'I think so. He's lovely, and brilliant with me and Dan, a rock and all that, but when it comes to the two of you, you're clearly the boss.'

'I am?'

'Definitely. He relies on you, totally.'

'Not totally, Pippa. He's been doing his relying elsewhere.'

'OK, fair enough. I see that. But, when it comes down to it, in the end, that's just sex, isn't it?'

'PIPPA!'

'Sorry, Mum. But it's true. He doesn't love her or anything. He can't. He just can't!' Her eyes were filling with tears.

'Maybe he can. Isn't that the problem? Something we're all going to have to adjust to, most of all me.'

'I don't believe it.'

'You may have to.' Her words sounded harsh, even to her own ears, but then what was the point in pretending that everything was going to resolve itself neatly when that really didn't seem very likely?

'I think he'll leave her and if he does, perhaps you'll be able to forgive him,' Pippa persisted.

'Just like that?'

'In the end. Not straightaway, maybe, but eventually, once you've got over it. For your own sake as much as for his. You love each other! Lots of people your age who're married don't even *like* each other! With loads of my mates, their parents aren't even friends. They bicker all the time or hardly speak. They just kind of co-exist. But you two . . . You must be able to find a way of putting this behind you, surely? People do, all the time, you know, people who're a lot less fond of each other than you and Dad.'

People do, all the time. That's what Annabel had said too. Why not her, then?

'It's really not so simple, Pippa. What if you found out that Jamie had cheated on you?'

'He did.'

'WHAT?' Celia had heard nothing of this till now. She wanted to kill him, her now-to-be son-in-law. How could he? She wanted to stab him through the heart with a sharp blade.

'He got drunk and slept with Olivia at a party when I was over here for the weekend with you and Dad.'

'When was this?'

'Last spring. Don't you remember, we split up for a few weeks and then got back together again? I don't see Olivia any more but Jamie and I are fine. It was just one of those things. So you see . . .'

She was shocked by the revelation about Jamie. But perhaps more than that, it was a surprise to discover how Pippa hadn't told her at the time; she'd dealt with it all on her own. There was a keen little pang of grief. She hadn't been needed. But then again, it obviously wasn't of overwhelming significance to Pippa. She'd got over it and moved on. Jamie had made a mistake and she'd managed to forgive him. Why couldn't she do the same? Nick's betrayal was bigger, that was true, but in the end didn't it just come down to the same thing –sex, a fling, a bit on the side, call it what you will. And if Nick were willing to give up Marina, then maybe they could find a way through this eventually and return to normality, or something approximating it. And maybe nothing could be worse than losing him altogether. She'd been hurtling headlong towards the end of her marriage but maybe now she should apply a brake. Wait and see. Find out what Nick was going to do and then discover whether she could live with that. Maybe she couldn't but it would be a good idea to wait and find out.

She promised Pippa that she wasn't going to do anything rash or sudden. She had come to Paris to get some distance from things; she'd wanted time to think. She'd give Nick some space to work out what he really wanted as well. And then they'd see. Maybe, as Pippa said, they'd find a way of surviving this. Maybe, just maybe, sometime in the future, he could be forgiven.

After the intense discussions of that first night, they went to bed exhausted. At two or three in the morning, Celia heard her door open. It was Pippa, tiptoeing in, saying that she couldn't sleep. As she had done so often as a little girl, she asked Celia if she could come and sleep in her bed. Celia pulled back the duvet and Pippa climbed in beside her. Celia lay awake for a while till finally she heard the soft, regular in and out of her daughter's breath. And then, at last, she too fell asleep.

The next morning, over a late breakfast of croissants and coffee, they revisited it all again, going over the same ground in ways that yielded few fresh insights. But after that, they'd managed to put everything to one side and went into Paris to make something happier of their time together. It was a conscious effort of will for Celia to be more cheerful and, surprisingly, to some extent, it worked. As they walked arm in arm up to Sacré-Coeur, she found, with relief, that she could put her grief temporarily on hold. They stood looking out over Paris from the viewing platform at the front of the cathedral, then wandered back down through the narrow streets, stopping for a coffee in a bar before descending into the metro to head for the Musée Marmottan Monet. In the evening, they went to a favourite café on the Left Bank. That night, Pippa started off in her bed and they both slept remarkably well.

The following day, they got up early to go to the Sunday-morning flea market at Porte de Vanves, where Pippa fell eagerly on the vintage-clothes stalls. Celia chipped in to buy her a rather pricey patterned silk dress with a designer label, a beautiful second-hand grey leather bag and a fashionable t-shirt for Jamie. She bought nothing for herself but took pleasure in Pippa's enthusiastic search in among the jumbled piles of bric-a-brac and racks of clothes, and her excitement at her ultimate success.

On the Sunday afternoon, Pippa left her at the gate to the platform at the Gare du Nord and caught her train home, looking a little less worried than when she'd first arrived but still, when her daughter turned back to wave a last goodbye, Celia thought she caught in her face her underlying anxiety. They had both worked hard all weekend to keep it at bay. A text from the train, 'Love you mum!', before Celia had even got out of the station, was perhaps further proof of this.

Walking home through the narrow streets, she felt empty and alone. Shopkeepers were bringing in their stalls, sluicing down the pavements outside their shop fronts, sweeping up, putting out rubbish bags, pulling down the blinds. Women with children were dragging them by the arm, in a hurry to get home. Men were grouped around high tables at bars, gulping down a quick coffee, or a shot of anis, before heading back to their girlfriends or wives. Already, dark and difficult thoughts were crowding in and, with no one to share the hours with, Celia knew she was at their mercy. She feared them and she feared herself, remembering with horror the scenes on the bed at Anne's and how low she was capable of sinking. She was in no hurry to get back to the empty flat, so she wandered around for a while, finding a false security in the streets and the people, the strangers, that she passed. She stopped at a café and ordered a glass of red wine. In public, with other people, she would be forced to maintain a semblance of control. Then, when a heavy man with large jowls and an overly red face came to sit opposite her and started to try to engage her in conversation, she quickly drank down the last of her wine and left.

Back at the apartment, Celia went to lie on her bed. Although it was already quite dark, she didn't bother to pull down the blinds. She looked out from the bed at the rooftops. Clouds were scudding across the purple sky. A flock of birds – starlings, were they? – wheeled past, changing direction as they turned to settle in a stand of trees behind the church. Higher up, the lights of a plane could be seen tracing a silent path, drifting in and out of cloud, before slipping gradually out of sight. Across the road, on the same floor of the tall tenement building opposite as her own, a light went on. A young woman came into a bedroom, took off her coat and flung it on a chair. A man came in after her and she reached out towards him. Celia got up to pull down her blind and shut out the scene, but then paused. As she stood in the darkness of her own bedroom, as if in the dimmed light of a cinema, her window framed the action like a screen. She watched as the man slowly unbuttoned the woman's shirt. He traced his hand down her cheek, touched her neck, let his fingers travel slowly down her front. He stood back and looked at her, as if appraising her, taking her in.

She took her arms up above her head and undid her black hair, shaking it theatrically down onto her shoulders. She reached behind her back and unclasped her bra, letting it fall to the ground, allowing him to see her naked breasts, then stood there for him, stretching her back, arching it so that her neck and head were flung back in a pose of abandoned pleasure. He came towards her again now, first touching her breasts, then bending down to bury his face in them. They kissed, locking together so that their bodies pressed tight against each other. She reached for his belt, undoing it clumsily, feeling for his zip, and then he lifted her towards the chest of drawers, sitting her on it so that her skirt was pulled up around her thighs and her legs opened wide in invitation.

Oh my God, all this in full view, from her vantage point across the road. It was both extraordinarily erotically charged and utterly dreadful. Celia pulled down the blinds; she couldn't watch any more. She'd seen too much already. It was shameful to look, voyeuristic. And yet it was hard to stop, hard to deny herself the chance of seeing how it all ended, how much more there would be, how soon it would be over, what they would do in the climax of their passion and then afterwards, in the intimacy of the post-coital space. The real thing, not the cinema version. Other people, that woman and that man, and the sex they had, unique to them, entirely absorbing to her, reminding her painfully, excitingly, of the sex she'd had in the past. She wondered whether hers and Nick's had ever been this good, but also whether theirs, that couple in the room opposite, was really that great either, or just a very good act – whether, in a week's time or maybe two, he might be sneaking off with another woman, a work colleague or her best friend, and whether she might be meeting an ex and end up in bed with him once more for old times' sake. Or perhaps later that same night even, when her lover had gone to sleep, she would be giving herself the pleasure that she'd pretended to have when she had arched her back and let down her hair, and wrapped him in her open legs, with all the look of someone in the full throes of erotic bliss.

Celia went to the kitchen, poured herself a glass of Bordeaux and sat at the table, sipping at it slowly, swirling it in her cupped hands. Unable to concentrate on anything more substantial, she picked up the magazine she had bought at the news stall outside the Gare du Nord and flicked through the pages, skimming through the latest fashions, stories about healthy living and good skin, features on work/life balance, holidays with your girlfriends and how to keep your man happy. She toasted a small slice of bread and ate it with just butter and a slice of Brie. Her evening meal. Alone.

Later, when she peeped out from behind her blinds, she saw that the curtains in the apartment opposite had been closed. One storey above, an old man was stirring a pot on the stove in his kitchen; one storey below, a teenage girl with headphones was dancing to a musical soundtrack that no one but she could hear. The ordinary, the mundane. Lives that one could witness without any sense of guilt or embarrassment, but, she had to confess, without any real interest, compared with the intensity of the scene she had observed earlier.

Nine o'clock. Was it late enough to climb into bed, listen to the radio, doze off and fall asleep, shut out her thoughts, her sadness, at least for a time, till the inevitable moment when she would wake in the night, fearful and troubled, having had bad dreams, worrying about Nick, wondering about Marina, unsure of what the next few weeks and months would bring in terms of fresh suffering?

She went to the bathroom and brushed her teeth. She pulled a comb roughly through her hair and cleaned the make-up off her face. She was just about to get undressed when the phone rang.

'Celia?'

It was Paul Legrand.

'I'd like to talk to you. Can we meet?'

'Tomorrow evening, perhaps? Or Tuesday?' she offered.

'I'm free now, if you are. I could come over to your place.'

She hesitated, not sure what to say. She wouldn't tell him that she'd been getting ready for bed, had already brushed her teeth. 'How about Au Petit Fer à Cheval? The brasserie just round the corner?'

'Have you eaten? They do decent food there, don't they? We could have a light meal.'

'Of course. That would be lovely.'

'Shall I come and fetch you on my way?'

A moment's hesitation. 'No. Let's meet there.'

'In about half an hour?'

'Fine.'

She put down the phone and went back into the bathroom to put her make-up on again. It felt a bit foolish, just for an hour or two, but she was in need of the protection it offered, covering up more than just her ageing skin. 'You look a bit grim without your make-up,' Pippa had said over breakfast and she knew that the past two weeks had taken their toll. People usually commented on her youthful looks but now she needed that bit of artificial assistance to maintain the illusion that she was getting by OK.

A pair of black, well-cut jeans, a grey jersey top and a thin crêpe scarf that Nick had always admired. She looked herself up and down in the mirror. Not too bad, she thought. Passable. If Nick were there, he would say, 'Fine,' and she'd berate him for that. Fine was never quite good enough.

Paul clearly had something on his mind. 'I'd like to talk to you,' he had said. She wondered why. He was in touch with Nick; maybe he'd heard something from him that he felt she should know? Nick's intentions regarding Marina, perhaps? A message from him, offered via his old friend? It was possible, on the other hand, that Paul had been talking to Yvette and Henri and come up with a new angle on her troubles that he wanted to share with her. Or maybe he wanted to discuss something else entirely – to ask her advice on a book deal for a friend, or put her in touch with a Parisian publisher who was looking for contacts in the UK. Perhaps one of his new flings had asked him to intercede in some way on her behalf? He'd come to her with such ideas before, so it would come as no particular surprise to discover that he'd been persuaded by some ambitious young woman to ring her at nine o'clock on a Sunday night in order to broker an introductory meeting before her return to London.

Of course, there was another possibility that she finally had to consider as well. He had been very attentive that day in the café. And his hand on her back . . . not just her imagination, surely? The blood rushed to her face. You fool, she thought. What she'd seen through the window that evening had aroused her and now here she was playing out some silly fantasy in relation to a man in his fifties who wasn't the slightest bit interested in her.

At the brasserie, the owner greeted her with a handshake, rather than kisses on the cheek. 'Like the English,' he said, laughing. He recognised her from the many occasions she'd come in for a drink with Nick.

'Your husband, Monsieur Cabuzel? He's not with you on this trip?'

'No,' she said.

'Such a nice man! Charmant! Vraiment! I always say that to my wife, after he's been in here. A true gentleman, one in a million. They don't make them like that any more, do they?'

'No,' she said and smiled sadly.

'Busy in London?'

'Yes.'

'Well, give him my good wishes and my wife's too.'

'I will.'

She sat down at a table next to the window and ordered another glass of red wine – her third, she realised – while she waited for Paul. He was late, or rather, looking at her watch, she was a little early. She had a moment to reflect more on her situation. After Pippa's visit, she felt able to think about things a bit more clearly. Her first reactions after finding out about Marina had been extreme – excusable, perfectly understandable, but nevertheless, extreme. Now, after nearly two weeks in Paris, she was beginning to feel a little calmer. Pippa's view of it all was also something of a surprise. She'd imagined that her daughter would take exactly the same stance as she did, entering into her fury with Nick wholeheartedly, unable to forgive him, but in fact Pippa seemed much less troubled by his infidelity than the effect it had had on both of them, and if anything, was even more worried about

Nick than about Celia. 'You're tougher than him,' she had said. She'd described him as 'devastated'. For the first time since she'd been away, Celia yearned to be with him again. He needed her. What the hell was she doing here in Paris, when she should be back in London trying to piece things back together? Maybe Odile was right; she'd taken off her helmet, unstrapped her shield, set down her sword. Perhaps she needed to get back onto the field of battle and fight for her marriage. Why should she allow some stupid young woman to ruin all of their lives? People talked of marriages made stronger by coming through tests and trials. Perhaps Nick and hers might be one of those? She'd sleep on it overnight but if she felt the same way tomorrow, she'd give him a ring at the office and tell him to come over to Paris to see her, at least for a few days.

At that moment Paul appeared, opening the heavy, glass brasserie door and bringing a gust of cold air with him, along with a few russet leaves that blew in from the beech tree outside. She watched him unwrapping the scarf from around his neck and putting his dark wool coat on the stand by the entrance. He ran a hand through his hair to make sure that it wasn't standing on end, then came over to her side of the table, kissed her twice on both cheeks and sat down.

'Have you ordered?'

'Not yet.'

'Steak frites?'

'Just a small salad for me. Niçoise.'

He lifted his arm to call over the waiter and placed their order.

'So.'

'So.'

She wondered what was coming next.

'I've been worried about you, all on your own in the flat.'

'I've been all right. Pippa came for the weekend.'

'Was that OK?'

'Curiously, yes. In a way she was less upset than I thought she might be. Less angry about Nick and what he'd done, more worried for both of us and concerned about the consequences for the whole family.'

'Ah, that's children for you. Only interested in how it impacts on them. Selfish little organisms.'

'No, it's not so much that. She's fearful for us. I think she came partly to make sure that I wasn't going to do anything silly. To check up on me. She's seen what it's doing to Nick, too and she's worried about him. She says he looks absolutely terrible.'

'And you feel sorry for him?'

'No . . . Yes. Of course I do, on one level. I know he's in a complete state of turmoil. I still love him. What should I say?'

'You're confused.'

'Yes. Completely. Absolutely.' She sighed. 'Confused.'

'You're not sure whether to go back to him?'

'I want to, but I don't know if I can.'

She felt herself being drawn into the same conversation she'd been having over and over again, first with Anne and Annabel, then with him and with Pippa, but most of all with herself, every waking moment of every day. She was tired of it all and not sure that she wanted to go through it again, specially now, when she thought she might have made a decision of sorts.

'I've had an idea,' Paul said. 'Something to take your mind off all of this.'

It was as if he'd read her thoughts, realising that she was backing away from more talk, wanting to avoid more forensic dissection of her feelings.

'Yvette and Henri are going walking in the Alps next weekend. They've borrowed a friend's chalet. They're taking a big party. I suggested that you might like to come along too. It would do you good.'

'Are you going?'

'Of course!'

She loved the Alps. The mountain air, the views, that sense of losing yourself in something vast, a reminder of your own insignificance in the grand scheme of things. The sublime. Good old-fashioned food for the soul. Perhaps it *would* do her good.

'They're leaving the children behind. Adults only. And they've invited Charles and Madeleine Roux. You know them, I think?'

Charles and Madeleine. She hadn't seen them in years. They were charming people; she'd love to meet up with them again.

'Let me think about it. I've had an idea that I might see if Nick could come over to Paris for a few days but, if not . . . Can I let you know later in the week?'

'Of course. There's plenty of room in the chalet. You can just decide at the last minute and join us if you are able to. You could drive down with me on Thursday evening, or, if you want to come a bit later, there's a good, fast train to Annecy and I could come and pick you up from the station.'

'Thank you, Paul . . . for thinking of me. It's kind of you.'

'I want to be of help to you . . . and Nick, of course.'

'You're a good friend.'

'I hope so.'

When she got back to the flat and had taken off her make-up and brushed her teeth for the second time, she picked up the phone. It would be late in London but with the hour's time difference, not too late to ring Nick. Sunday night. He was usually still up at this time, watching the end of the TV news, then sorting out a few things before work the next day. He might be in the study, checking his work diary, sifting through papers, reading a few emails. Perhaps he'd be flicking through a sheaf of documents for a Monday breakfast meeting, or scribbling down a note to give to Mary, his secretary. At some point soon he'd be putting the kettle on for his cup of tea, always the last event of the day, the final bedtime ritual.

Now that she'd decided, she wanted to speak to him straightaway. 'We should talk. I've had a bit of space to think things through. I want to see you. I thought perhaps you could come over here. Stay for a few days, or a bit longer, depending on how things go . . . How does that sound to you?'

The phone rang a few times, then clicked straight through to the answerphone. Nick wasn't at home. She pictured the house. The TV was off, the study was dark, the kettle had not been switched on, the bedtime tea hadn't been made. She hesitated for a few moments, then put the phone down, without leaving a message.

Five minutes later, she rang Paul.

'I've decided to come on the trip to the Alps,' she said. 'I'll take you up on your kind offer of a lift and come down in the car with you on Thursday.'

'Superb!' he said.

Chapter 9

At ten o'clock the next morning the phone rang.

'Celia? It's me, Nick.'

'Oh.'

'Did you call me last night? Someone rang without leaving a message on the answerphone.'

'Yes. It was me.'

'I thought it might have been. I'm sorry I missed you.'

'I was phoning to ask whether you wanted to come and join me here for a few days . . .'

'Of course. That's great!'

'. . . but I've changed my mind.'

'God, Celia!'

'Where were you last night?'

Silence.

'Ah. I see.'

'It's not how it seems.'

Silence.

'I've talked to her. I've told her it's got to end. But . . .'

'But what?'

'She's in a terrible state. I'm worried about her.'

Silence.

'It's harder than I thought. She's not taking it well.'

'Whereas I am?'

'I'm trying to end it with her, I promise you. I'm doing all I can. But it's taking me a bit of time. It's not that easy.'

Silence.

'Celia? Are you still there?'

'Yes.'

'I'm doing everything I can. Honestly.'

'Like staying over at her place last night, for instance? For God's sake, Nick! It seems simple enough to me. You've got to stop seeing her before I can even think about us being together again. I can't even contemplate it while you're still sneaking off to see her. You must understand that. Surely you get that, don't you?'

'I do. I really do. But . . .'

'But you're still sleeping in her blasted bed! What am I supposed to say to that?'

Silence.

'Look, I've decided to spend a few days in the Alps next weekend with Yvette and Henri and some of their friends. I'll call you when I get back.'

'I hope things'll be sorted by then.'

'So do I.' She paused. 'I need a pretty clear signal from you, Nick. An absolutely clear one, in fact. At the moment it all seems pretty fuzzy to me. Not clear at all.'

'It'll be clear,' Nick said. 'I promise you.'

'I'll ring you in a week's time.'

'Enjoy the Alps, Celia. Give Henri and Yvette my love!'

Without saying anything in reply, she put the phone down.

She stared blankly at the phone for a while, then roused herself. She'd need to begin to sort out her plans for the weekend. She made a list of what she'd have to take with her. Looking in the wardrobe in the bedroom, she was pleased to see that there were some thick woollen sweaters, a warm jacket and a pile of fine silk thermal underwear.

There wouldn't be much snow in November but it would still be likely to be cold, high up in the mountains. The nights in particular could be bitter.

She took out one of the neat little scoop-necked thermal vests and held it up to her face to smell it. It brought back that time when she had gone to the Alps with Nick when the children were small. Nick's mother, Celeste, had come along to look after Pippa and Dan, taking them to watch the ice-skating, dressing them up warmly for expeditions into the village, while she and Nick spent the days on the slopes. He was better at skiing than her – he'd grown up taking holidays in the mountains and had had his first experience on skis at just five or six years of age – but despite that, she'd managed to hold her own. They'd been several times before the children came along, and bit by bit she'd developed in confidence till she was happy to try quite difficult runs and ski right through till the end of the afternoon, with just a short break for a sandwich and hot chocolate in an Alpine café. This time, however, they were more cautious; they didn't want to get back to Celeste too late and find her exhausted by the demands of the children and, anyway, Celia felt rather less tempted by the thrills of a black run now that she knew she had two small people relying on her, eagerly awaiting her return. She was responsible for them and found herself taking things more gently, adopting a more careful approach.

On the last day, the weather had turned. The clear blue sky of the previous day was now heavy and grey, threatening to unpack a fresh load of snow onto the mountainside and add to the burden already resting on the roofs of the chalets and hotels. Celia had decided not to ski. She'd stay with Celeste and the children instead, while Nick had one final day on the pistes before their return to London. In the early afternoon, the children had a nap in Celeste's room and Celia, finding herself with an hour or so to spare, went down into the hotel lobby for a coffee and a quiet read.

There was another English couple who had sat in the bar with them in the evening sometimes, after they'd put the children to bed, sharing a good bottle of wine and conversation about the day's skiing. They were in their early to mid forties, older than her and Nick, but childless. The woman was attractive in a rather conventional sort of way – dyed blond hair, plenty of mascara and face make-up, expensive angora jumpers in pastel shades, chunky gold jewellery and a perfectly polished smile. She had the look of an actress or model, though in fact she was a businesswoman, running her own design company. Her husband, Max, was also good-looking but in a less ostentatious, obvious way, as if it came more naturally to him. He laughed a lot, teasing his wife gently, often catching Celia's eye to share some joke that his partner took in good spirit. Celia and Nick enjoyed their company; they were sophisticated and charming.

That last afternoon of the holiday, as Celia sat sipping her coffee in the hotel lobby, she saw Max strolling over towards her. He too had decided against braving the elements and was having a quiet day in the Lodge, while his wife, like Nick, had chosen to squeeze in another day on the slopes. He came skiing mainly for his wife, he said. It wasn't really his thing, though the mountains were. He loved the whiteness, the purity, the air, that sense of being taken out of your usual urban world and reconnecting with nature. The sublime, he'd said. They'd sat and talked for a while – the usual pleasantries, but made more enjoyable by his warm good humour. Then, just as she started to pick up her book and keys, and gesture that she should be going, he reached out and touched her hand. He told her that he loved the way she turned her head when she talked, and her eyes and her smile. He said that the room lit up for him when she walked in. He knew it was foolish but he had to tell her. He honestly didn't expect her to do anything about it, or even say anything, but just wanted her to know. It should have been hideously awkward and embarrassing, but it wasn't. She felt a sudden rush of excitement, as if she were skiing downhill incredibly fast, her heart pounding. He walked with her to the lift and went up with her. In the lift, as soon as the doors closed, he pulled her towards him and kissed her. When the doors opened, he stepped out with her, into the silent corridor. At the door to her room, she hesitated for a moment and then shook her head. A silent no. He raised his hand to stroke her face gently, just once, then turned to go. She wanted to call him back, but she didn't. It would have been crazy, a moment's madness, a betrayal of Nick. Wanting was one thing – doing, quite another.

Back in London, she had told Nick about it. He'd been shocked but not altogether surprised.

'I could tell that he fancied you a mile off,' he said. 'He couldn't keep his eyes off you. But coming on to you like that, that's pretty damn cheeky, if you ask me. I'd've thought he'd have had more sense.'

'Yes. I don't know what he was thinking.'

'He picked the wrong person, didn't he?'

'What do you mean?'

'You'd never have taken him up on it. He should have got the hots for someone more likely to respond.'

'Yes,' she had said.

Nick hadn't said anything more and the conversation had moved on to school runs and practical arrangements for work the next week. But for days afterwards, intense irritation with him competed with sudden yearnings for that moment at the hotel-room door when she had said no. Why did Nick feel so very sure of her, when she had been on the verge of quite a different decision – so sure of her innocence? He seemed far less troubled by her account of the episode than she would have liked him to have been. And yet, of course, he was absolutely right. He had judged her perfectly; she had not acted on impulse and had remained true to him, as always.

I should have slept with Max, she thought now. I should have pulled him into the hotel room, closed the door behind us and fucked him. I wanted to but I didn't. I should have taken those chances when I had them. Then perhaps I wouldn't be where I am now.

She pulled a suitcase out from under the bed and packed the pale-pink ski jacket and thermal underwear, leaving the rest till later. Just then her mobile phone rang. She could see from the number that it was Dora. She'd better answer it.

'Celia, my love! How are you?' Her voice sounded cloyingly concerned. 'Just wanted to check that you're OK. I know you've been keeping up with work – I've been following a few of those email threads you've kindly copied me into – but it's you I'm worried about, my lovely. Just wanting to know that you're fine.'

'I'm surviving . . . just about. Glad to be away from the house for the time being. Thank you for being so understanding and letting me work from here.'

'Oh, no problem, my sweet. You know what we're like at Atlas – a caring little family. Though, of course, we're keen to have you back. There's so much going on with *Armed Combat* and that awkward cow Ffion, as you're only too well aware. It's the last time I agree to publish anything by that woman, however marketable she is! I swear to you, she's not worth the trouble. It'd be good to have a meeting with her, face to face, as soon as possible. When do you think you'll be back in the office?'

'I was thinking of next Tuesday, if that's OK, Dora. I can't stay here for ever, can I?'

'Certainly not! Come back and face the music, that's what I say. Have it out with that naughty husband of yours once and for all and get on with your lives. Read him the riot act and then milk his guilt for all its worth. That's what I did with Dominic and it's worked a treat. He bought me the beach hut in Dorset to appease me, so I did quite well out of it in the end. And look at the two of us now – all hunky-dory, as if nothing had happened. Like two turtle doves.'

'Thanks for the advice, Dora.'

'No problem, my pet. Trust me, he'll be eating out of your hand again soon, if you play your cards right. Don't be too hard on him, is what I say. You could lose him that way. The other woman always manages to provide a nice cosy retreat from an angry, aggrieved wife. If you're too tough, you'll just push him straight into her arms.'

'I can hear someone at the door, Dora. I've got to go.'

'OK, my lovely. I'll expect you in work tomorrow week. We do need you back then, you know. It's time to pull yourself together now.'

'Of course. I understand.'

Dora, the great giver of marital advice. Celia couldn't bear another minute of it. To be fair to her, though, she'd been understanding enough up to now about Celia's absence. But her patience was clearly wearing thin. When it came to the needs of the company, she'd only be prepared to take so much and her views on Celia's best course of action with Nick seemed to be much more about getting her back at her desk sharpish, than anything else. The days in Paris were definitely drawing to a close.

Celia sat down and emailed her straightaway, confirming her plans for returning to work; the last thing she wanted was to compound her problems by antagonising her employer. She also dashed off an email to Ffion Wyn-Jones, inviting her to a meeting eight days hence. She copied Dora in, hoping that she would be reassured by evidence of her intent. Finally, she emailed Nick with a simple message announcing her plan to return to London in a week's time. She would get the Eurostar early on the Monday morning, aiming to be back by late lunchtime. She would go straight home and suggested that he try to get back from work early that evening, to allow them to have a meal together and leave time for a proper talk. She said nothing about Marina, hoping it was obvious that she expected, by then, he would have found a way of ending it all. The possibility that he wouldn't did, of course, enter her mind, but she tried to dispel the thought. It was painful enough to deal with what had already happened, let alone face the prospect that, in the end, he might find himself unable to do what was necessary to save their marriage.

Chapter 10

Thursday came quickly. At around 3 p.m., Celia heard a car horn beeping in the street below, and hurried to put together her bags and close up the flat. At the last minute she went back in to pick up the cashmere scarf that Nick had given her and grabbed the little box with the earrings, which she slipped into her coat pocket. She wouldn't wear them while she was away but nevertheless it didn't feel right to just leave them sitting in a drawer.

Paul had left the engine running. He was looking out for a traffic warden, vigilant in case one suddenly appeared, brandishing his ticket book, ready to impose an instant fine. Anyone caught parking in this quartier at this time of day was at risk; he would know that. Despite this, he jumped out of the car as soon as he saw her and gave her two quick kisses on each cheek, before helping her to put her bags in the boot.

And then they were off, the smart black Audi coupé weaving its way through the tiny streets, with Paul finding cut-throughs to avoid the endless traffic lights and hold-ups that were an inevitable part of Paris life. Paul's concentration on the driving made conversation almost as stop-start as the traffic but finally they hit the Périphérique, with a sigh of relief that they had made it before the start of the rush hour and could count on an easier passage out of the city. Finally it felt as if they had started their journey proper.

'So. A weekend in the Alps. Looking forward to it?'

Celia thought for a moment. 'Yes, actually I am.'

'You sound surprised.'

'The last few weeks have been so ghastly – I haven't really been looking forward to anything. Following that clichéd advice about trying to take one day at a time.'

'A long weekend, walking in the mountains, it will do you good. You should try to put your worries on hold.'

'I will, if I can. I'm completely exhausted by the constant churn of my thoughts. I need a break from it all. In fact I really need a break from myself, even if it's just for a short time. Pity I can't leave myself behind! I'm hoping that being with other people and doing things together, I might become a bit less self-obsessed.'

'You're entitled to be self-obsessed. But, as you say, time out is no bad thing. Perhaps it'll give you a fresh perspective on your situation?'

'You've been so kind, Paul. So understanding.'

'Not kind. Selfish. I want my friends to be happy – that makes *me* happy. I'd like to see you smiling again. No altruism at all, you see! Just pure self-interest.'

'Have you heard from Nick?'

'After his email to me, he phoned and asked me to keep an eye on you to make sure you were OK.'

'He did?'

'He was worried about you.'

Celia wondered why this news made her spirits sink. 'He told you to make regular contact, to come and see me?'

'No. That was my idea. I promised him that I'd ring you from time to time and check up on how you were managing. But I thought you'd need some company and, anyway, I like seeing you. I assure you, it's no burden for me. I'm not fulfilling a duty, I promise.'

'That's nice to hear.'

He suggested stopping somewhere for a meal on the way to the chalet. Perhaps it would be nicer to have a break, rather than driving non-stop for five hours or more and arriving tired and hungry? Celia agreed. She was surprised to discover that he'd already booked them into a restaurant he knew, a smart hotel restaurant in the countryside.

'It's renowned for its cuisine,' he said. 'Well worth making a little detour for.'

'What if I'd suggested pressing on and driving straight to Annecy?' she asked, laughing.

'I'd have cancelled the reservation of course, but I think you've made a very wise decision. It really is spectacularly good food!'

From the window of the car, Celia looked out at the scenes of French life speeding past. First the ugly sprawl of the suburbs of Paris, with their high-rise flats and drab warehouses, their bright posters advertising Danone yoghurt or bottles of Perrier, their tiny gravelled parks with a bare minimum of shrubs and flowers, their malls with the compulsory Mr Bricolage do-it-yourself stores, Carrefour supermarkets, petrol stations and Decathlons, the McDonalds sitting incongruously alongside conventional roadside brasseries, friteries, selling sausage and chips, and kebab or couscous cafés. Leaving Paris behind them, soon they were driving past flat plains of ploughed up and fallow fields stretching to the horizon, a reminder of the sheer size of the country, as compared with the more compact neatness of the English countryside. Finally, the motorway began to wind and bend, pushing its way through a more undulating landscape towards the mountains. Now habitations were more widely spaced out, there was lush green vegetation on the hills and thickly forested areas that threw dark shadows across the road.

Dusk fell and, in the warm car, with the Bach sonata that she'd chosen playing on the CD player, Celia felt her eyes growing heavy. She'd been sleeping badly over the past few weeks but now, she realised, she felt relaxed enough to slip into an easeful rest. She reclined her chair and dozed.

When she awoke, she lay still for a while, trying to work out where she was. A moment of confusion, lying in an unfamiliar car, with darkness outside and the headlights of oncoming cars flashing past, suddenly illuminating the interior with acid-sharp beams. She looked towards the driver. Paul. Of course. It was only an instant of disorientation, coming to from a deep sleep, but it threw her into a state of panic. What the hell was she doing, driving through France, sitting next to another man, on a journey that was taking her further and further from Nick? She tried to calm herself. Paul's eyes were fixed on the road. He was wrapped up in his own thoughts and unaware that she had awoken, oblivious of her agitation. He looked easy in himself, like many men who enjoyed being behind the wheel, taking as much pleasure in the journey and the handling of the car as the arriving. A difficult thought suddenly came to her. Why, when she had said to Nick that she was going to stay with Yvette and Henri, hadn't she mentioned Paul? She couldn't explain it to herself, except to say that she didn't think it was necessary, not worth telling him, but that didn't seem to capture it fully. She needed a few moments to collect her thoughts, breathe deeply, calm the rapid beat of her pulse.

Rather too quickly, Paul turned to look at her.

'So you're awake. You've been asleep for over an hour. Feeling better?'

'Yes, I think so. A bit muddle-headed, I'm afraid. Woozy.' Would he see through her dissembling and notice her agitation? 'I really must have been sleeping heavily.'

'Don't worry, you didn't snore, or say anything in your sleep.'

'That's a relief.'

'Almost there. I turned off the motorway about five minutes ago, so it's just another five or ten minutes.'

'If it's smart, will I need to change?'

'Not at all. You look fine.'

Fine. Not good enough, she thought. Fine never is. Well, what did she expect? Men were all the same in that respect, unless they were looking at you in that different way, when they took in everything about you, noticing every last detail of your hair, your clothes, your mood, because there was something more going on, whatever you might call it – attraction, chemistry, lust. Paul's fine said it all. It would have been quite good for her morale to think that he fancied her, even just a tiny bit.

'You look more than fine, of course. That top suits you,' he said. 'Très chic. You know us French men. We notice these things.'

She felt herself blushing and hoped he hadn't noticed that.

'You may be feeling – how do you say it in English again? – down on the dumps, but you look great all the same.'

'In,' she said, laughing.

'In?'

'The dumps.'

'Ah, there you are. My English is shit! I knew it!'

'No, it's almost perfect. Flawless. So it's very charming when you make the odd mistake.'

'Thank you for being so generous.'

And then they were there. He was pulling into a car park and they were getting out of the car, him resting his hand lightly on her back, guiding her up the dark path, towards the lights of the hotel, opening the hotel door for her, with a sudden whoosh of warm air, helping her out of her coat and talking in rapid French to the young woman who greeted them, directing Celia towards the bar, ordering two Kirs with chestnut liqueur, something she really must try if she'd never had it before, pressing her to eat the olives stuffed with anchovies and the smoked-salmon canapés before he made himself sick on them and spoiled his meal, laughing at the mess she made when one broke into pieces in her fingers and scattered dark oily crumbs over the bar, ushering her at last into the dining room towards the small, beautifully decorated table that had been chosen for them.

The Kir had gone straight to her head.

'This is lovely,' she said.

The food arrived, rather more slowly than one might have anticipated in a restaurant of this quality, but each course was superbly presented, set out on angular black or white plates and full of unusual flavour combinations that shocked the palate and provided plenty for them to talk about. Was that aniseed or something else? How could a tomato consommé taste so tomatoey yet look so colourless and clear? What wizardry allowed the chef to put such fiery pepper into the sauce and still make it infinitely subtle and refined?

By the time the dessert arrived, it was getting late. Paul poured the dregs of a bottle of Châteauneuf du Pape into their glasses.

'Can you drive after all that wine?' she asked.

'Sure. I haven't drunk very much.'

'Oh.' She suddenly realised that, unusually for her, she'd drunk the lion's share.

'Could we stay here overnight instead and finish the journey in the morning?' she asked.

He looked up at her abruptly and caught her eyes in a steady gaze. What was he thinking? He looked deadly serious, as if weighing her words carefully, trying to read her meaning. There was no smile.

'Of course, if that's what you want.'

Did she?

'Yes.'

'I'll ask them if they have a couple of rooms free, then.'

'OK.'

She waited while he went off to speak to the woman at reception. There was nothing wrong with this, was there? It was sensible to stay the night, now that it had got so late. Better to arrive refreshed in the morning than struggle on with the journey. She'd drunk far too much and could sleep it off, rather than turn up the worse for wear. They would ring Yvette and Henri to tell them that they'd been delayed. Yvette would probably be greatly relieved that she could just go off to bed, rather than having to wait up for them. If they'd had a good day's walking in the mountains, and another planned for tomorrow she and

Henri might well be jolly pleased for an early night. It was all very sensible. And two separate rooms. All perfectly innocent.

And then, butting in, annoyingly, infuriatingly direct and clear, that other voice that she really didn't want to hear, not now after such a lovely meal, the first time since the revelations about Nick that she'd been able to enjoy herself and forget the car crash her life had become. You idiot. You fool. It's got nothing to do with being sensible, has it? Quite the reverse. Nothing to do with Yvette and Henri. You've been angling for this all along, pretending that you weren't but just waiting for it to happen. Ever since that meal in the brasserie. And now you're about to make a complete fool of yourself – utterly embarrass yourself in front of a man whom you like very much and respect as a friend, who'll either be appalled or feel desperately sorry for you, for your idiocy. Nick's friend. You must be completely mad. Life is complicated enough at the moment, as it is, without adding this. Getting revenge or restoring your sense of your own attractiveness or looking for a bit of instant affection or the effects of too much wine, or something equally shallow. You need to get a grip.

She got up out of her chair to go and find him to tell him that she'd changed her mind. Perhaps it would be better for them to get to the chalet that night after all. He was walking back into the dining room and caught her arm as she stumbled slightly towards him.

'Careful,' he said. 'You've drunk a bit too much. Don't fall. They've only got one double, so I think we should head off to Yvette and Henri's tonight after all.'

Was it the sudden sense of disappointment or the pressure of his hand on her arm that made her say no?

'Let's stay anyway.'

He was looking hard at her again.

'Are you sure? Is that sensible?'

'Sod sensible. I've had enough of being sensible. Look where it's got me.'

'Sensible, in your situation, might be . . . well, sensible.'

She laughed. 'You're right. Of course. Let's get our coats and drive on.'

And now she had the pleasure of witnessing the look on his face.

'What's it to be?' she said.

'I think you need to decide.'

'I'm tired. I'm quite drunk. I've had a terrible time, a really awful time. And I've had a great evening. It's simple. Let's stay.'

'No regrets tomorrow?'

He really was a very nice man. It made him all the more appealing.

'No regrets,' she said firmly, though she wasn't sure if that was a promise to him or to herself.

Chapter 11

The next morning she woke early, to find him still asleep beside her. She'd hardly slept at all herself, only finally dozing off just as dawn was breaking, a light, fitful, unsatisfying sleep, full of lurid half-dreams that brought no proper rest.

It felt strange to be lying next to a different man. His body took up the space differently from Nick's, his face turned in towards the centre of the bed, his arm hooked behind his head, one leg pulled up towards his body, the other straight. The sheets were thrown off on his side and she felt some relief to see that he was wearing his pyjamas, smart black ones, not the everyday, homely kind that Nick wore, so typical of an Englishman's bedtime apparel. He smelled different – a salty smell that was not unappealing and reminded her of the sex they had had the night before. Different. His grey and black hair was ruffled, his face in repose rather more lined and weathered than it appeared when he was awake and fully clothed. He drew air into his nose and blew it out softly – not a full-blown snore but a rhythmic pattern of breaths that created its own unique sound. Different.

The sex had been neither a wondrous revelation nor a complete disaster. He had been attentive and thoughtful and, surprisingly, given the passionate, highly charged start of it all, it was not over too quickly. At one point, after they had already stripped most of their clothes off and she was left just in her underwear, he had asked to put on a side light so that he could watch her as she removed the last remnants of her clothing. He wanted to see the whole of her, he said. She hesitated for a moment, then went ahead and took off first her bra and then, slightly more awkwardly, her pants. What would he think of what he saw? Though she had aged quite well, she knew that her body wasn't what it had been and feared that he might be disappointed. She couldn't disguise the droop of her breasts or the lack of tautness of her stomach and thighs. She wondered if he expected pubic hair or not, a neat triangle, or contemporary styling, perhaps, or nothing at all. If he was disappointed, he didn't show it, but the pause, the sudden doubting of her own attractiveness and the glare of the side light dragged her out of the moment and made her question what on earth she was doing and whether she should call a halt right there and then. And then he came to her and kissed her again and let his hands brush lightly over her nipples and knelt down so that his face was touching her breasts and she smelled his salty skin and the scent of his hair and felt the thrill of the difference in the way he used his hands on her body and felt pulled again towards the sex itself and away from the dulling and disturbing questions that it raised.

Borne up on waves of pleasure one moment, dragged back and beached by difficult thoughts and self-consciousness the next, Celia found that the sex was less all-consuming than it might have been. I can see that this *could* be good, she thought, if I could abandon myself to it. But I can't. My fault, not his, for imagining it could be so simple to forget Nick and spend a night with another man.

Afterwards, they talked about it. Again, this came as a surprise. Paul had sensed her hesitation, her drawing back even as she seemed so intensely involved. She explained it and he seemed to understand. How could she expect anything other than this? After all those years with Nick, and given everything that had happened. If they made love again, if there was a next time, perhaps it would be different, maybe better. Would there be a next time, did she think? She was taken aback that he even asked. They skirted round the subject tentatively, neither wanting to make demands or commit to an answer. No regrets, they'd both said the night before.

'I don't know. It's been good for me – to feel wanted by you, to be close to someone, to imagine that I might be able to be with someone other than Nick. But I also feel guilty as hell. And very ashamed that, of all people, it's you. Nick's friend. Is it just an eye for an eye? Me getting my own back on him? I don't think so. I really did – *do* feel attracted to you but I shouldn't have dragged you into all of this. It's not fair. It's messy.'

'I shouldn't worry too much about it. He's behaved badly to you. Why shouldn't you have some pleasure of your own, even if there's a bit of good old-fashioned revenge mixed in? You've got a right to that, you know? It's natural in the circumstances. Tomorrow you can think about what to do, whether you want all this to be forgotten, a silly little drunken moment that we can both pretend never happened.'

'And Nick? Should I tell him?'

'Why would you do that, if not to hurt him? That *would* be a nasty kind of revenge, don't you think? It wouldn't do my relationship with him much good either. He trusts me.'

'Lie to him, then?'

Paul sighed. 'It's been done before. A small lie to save a bigger hurt.'

'Maybe that's how it started between him with Marina.'

'Of course, if it continued with us, then that would be different. You'd have to tell him.'

That was a further surprising thought. She said nothing.

Finally he suggested sleep. From the speed with which he fell silent and his body went still, Celia could see that he wasn't overly troubled by doubts or concerns about what the future might hold. Maybe it was just a male thing – an ability to cut off from the consequences, some biological drive towards action and procreation that took precedence over neurotic self-analysis. Or perhaps he'd simply had enough sexual adventures for him to take it all in his stride. He was experienced in these things. It was less of a big deal for him. Perhaps he saw this, and her, as just one more in a string of similar encounters. Insignificant. Inconsequential.

He was still asleep, so Celia carefully got up and went to the bathroom. When she came out, she quietly tiptoed round, looking for her bag, trying to find her mobile phone. She hadn't looked at it since the previous afternoon, just before Paul had come to collect her. She had deliberately switched it to silent to shut out anything coming from London that might interfere with her determined efforts to forget everything while she was away.

There were two missed calls and a text-message alert, all from Nick. Suddenly she felt sick. She opened the text message.

'Been trying to reach you. Have finished with Marina. Absolutely final. She's distraught. Horribly difficult but it's done. Need to see you. Missing you dreadfully. Can you come home straight from the Alps? A flight back from Lyons or Geneva instead of Paris, after your weekend? We need to try to sort all this out. We need to talk. Nick.'

'Message from home?' Paul was lying watching her.

'Nick.'

'Important?'

'Yes.' She hesitated and then, without looking at him, 'I think I need to go home.'

'Right now?'

'As soon as I can.'

'Do you want to tell me what's happened?'

'Nick's finished with Marina.'

There was a moment of silence between them, nothing said. What he might be thinking or feeling she couldn't really guess and, for the time being at least, it wasn't her main concern.

'I suppose you feel that you've got to go, then.'

'Yes.'

'Now, or after the weekend? Could you stay for the weekend and go after that?'

She had brought her passport with her. She could pick up what she'd left in the apartment another time – there was nothing she couldn't manage without. Going straight back to London was entirely possible.

For the first time, she looked at him.

'I'd like to go now, if possible.' She wanted to apologise to him but she didn't know quite what to say. In the end she just said simply, 'I think I need to get back.'

'Of course,' he replied. 'I'll help you find a flight. Maybe from Geneva? You might be able to get something this afternoon if you're lucky.'

She burst into tears. Not for the first time she said, 'Thank you, Paul. You're so kind. Many men would react differently.'

He smiled but without much conviction. 'As I've told you before, I'm not kind at all. I'm really a selfish old bastard, you know!'

She wanted to go over and hug him but she knew that wouldn't be a good idea.

While she showered and dressed, he was making phone calls, seeing what could be arranged, and by the time she was ready and packed he had organised a flight from Geneva, leaving at one.

'Will we have time to get there?'

'If we leave straight after breakfast. I've called Yvette and told her that the plans have changed and that I'll be joining them later today, without you.'

At breakfast they sat in silence, each wrapped in their own thoughts. He managed to eat a croissant or two; she just had a black coffee. He patted her hand.

'It wasn't nothing, you know,' he said. 'It was something.'

'I know. It was something.'

'But no regrets,' he said.

She wasn't quite sure if it was a statement or a question.

'No regrets,' she replied.

'And will you tell Nick?'

'Probably not. I'm not sure.'

In the car to the airport they were quiet. Later, as they stood at the gate to the departures area, he said, 'Keep things simple. Don't tell Nick. Get on with your life again. That's my advice. All this will fade and you'll go back to normal again.'

'And you?'

'I'll never breathe a word, I promise you. I'll go to the chalet, I'll have some wonderful walks in the mountains,

I'll breathe the fresh air, I'll eat well, drink far too much and come back to Paris, and then, pretty soon, I'll undoubtedly meet a very nice, attractive person – perhaps almost as attractive as you – and I'll start a new affair. And next time we meet, you, me and Nick, I'll have a charming woman on my arm. We'll have a meal together and it'll all be just as it was before. You'll go home and the two of you will laugh at my philandering ways and wonder if I'll ever find someone to settle down with.'

'And will you?'

'The best ones always seem to be already taken.'

Though they both smiled, there was little enthusiasm in it.

They hesitated over a kiss goodbye, standing awkwardly facing each other, before he finally took charge of the situation and kissed her politely on each cheek.

'Tell Nick to call me and tell me how things are going. I'd like to know.'

'I will.'

And then he'd turned to walk away and he was gone.

Celia made her way through passport control and security then found the nearest toilet, went into a cubicle, pulled the seat lid down so that she could sit and, as quietly as she could, gave vent to her feelings. She was going to see Nick again. He'd made the break with Marina. She still loved him. The surge of relief when she read his text was proof of that, wasn't it? The urgency to go home had relegated everything else to a secondary place in the scale of things. She was longing to get back to something like normal life, to try to make things work with him again, if she could. But what had just happened with Paul – for all his wise advice, could that really just be put to one side? It complicated things. It had been a stupid thing to do, a really stupid thing, she knew that. And yet, she *didn't* regret it. It had been tender and warm. And she couldn't pretend that it hadn't been exciting. Dangerous, unsettling, taking her out of her habitual sense of who she really was, but exciting. Now she was closing the door on all of that. There would be nothing more. Ever again. No chance to discover where it could lead. When next they met, as Paul said, there could be nothing more than polite friendliness at best. More likely, there would be the kind of stiff formality that comes from fear of revelation. They would be like strangers. She thought of him lying next to her in the bed, his arm cradling his head. This is what silly adolescents do, she thought. Get tangled up in foolish, complicated situations and find themselves in a mess. Not middle-aged women like me, who should know better.

But she thought that she *would* probably put it behind her. In time the night with Paul would become a distant memory, the sharpness fading to something quieter, more muted, less disturbing and raw. In time, when they met, perhaps they'd even find themselves relaxing their guard and treating each other, once more, simply as friends.

She looked at her watch. She would need to make her way to the gate and catch that plane. She pulled free a short stream of toilet roll, blew her nose loudly, flushed the paper away, then came out of the cubicle and washed her face. She put on some fresh foundation and a quick dab of lipstick. It made her feel more normal, more like her usual self. She smoothed down her hair and then, almost as a reflex action, felt into her coat pocket to check where she'd put her London house keys. Her hand touched the box with the earrings. She'd forgotten about them. She opened the lid and looked at them, lying on their bed of satin. In turn she gently eased the fine wire clasps into her ears. She looked at herself in the mirror. When Nick saw her she would be wearing them. He would take this as a sign. Should she take them off, or leave them on?

She took hold of her suitcase and handbag and headed off to catch her flight home.

Chapter 12

'I couldn't do it,' she said.

She was sitting with Annabel in the kitchen of her house, a week later.

Annabel groaned.

'Christ, Celia!'

'You do understand, don't you?'

'Yes, of course I do. You're very principled. And that's a very good thing. I admire you. I always have. But hell's bells, it's not what I'd have done, in your shoes, not if it had been me. For goodness' sake, Celia, you shouldn't have said anything at all to him about Paul.'

'I tried not to. I really didn't want to. But we'd promised to be honest with each other. We agreed that the only way we could make it work from now on was if we trusted each other. There'd have to be no secrets.'

He'd come to meet her at Gatwick and, rather than going straight home, on his suggestion they'd stopped off at a National Trust place en route, for something to eat and a walk round the gardens. Neutral territory, away from their normal environment, a chance to talk. They'd wandered through the formal planted gardens without saying much, commenting only on the surprising amount of colour for the time of year, the immaculately kept beds, the neatness of the box hedges and the loveliness of the old red-brick walls, the trellises supporting gnarled old apple trees and the well-established honeysuckle. It was easy to imagine that everything was as it had always been, save that they walked without looking at each other, without touching, without smiling, without any evident pleasure or affection.

Then, finally, as they stepped beyond the old walls, out through the gate and onto the woodland path, into the shadows cast by the tall beeches and birches and oaks, he had turned the conversation towards the subject at the forefront of both of their minds.

He told her that, in ending it with Marina, he'd made it clear that this was absolutely final. He'd hated seeing her suffer but he'd known it was the only way. 'Nothing is more important to me than you,' he'd said to Celia. 'I have to try to win back your trust.' He'd repeated to her his awareness that he'd behaved like a fool. He swore that it would never happen again and when he said it, she believed him. She made no promises herself but by the time they got back in the car and headed for home, something had shifted, a small but subtle change. What she felt was just sadness, not anger but a softer kind of grief.

Back at the house, he'd sat on the bed while she unpacked and they'd talked some more. She slept in the spare bedroom that night. The next day they moved round each other carefully, avoiding tricky conversations, unsure of where to put themselves or what to say, trying, not very successfully, to get on with normal routine things, fearing that one false move from either of them might send them off in their separate directions for good. That night, once again, she slept in the spare room.

The next morning, since it was a Sunday and showed no signs of rain, he'd suggested that they might go out somewhere nice for the day. They'd driven just north of London to Rickmansworth and walked along the Chess Valley footpath, stopping only for a simple pub lunch in a village just off the track. In the car, on the way home, they'd both been quiet, tired from the walking and each lost in their own thoughts. She'd enjoyed the day with him, despite everything. It was a reminder of all that they had in common and of happier times. She felt calmer than before and looked back at herself as she was at Anne's – stuffing tissues into her mouth, weeping – with a sense of wonder that the pain she had thought both unbearable and infinite had in fact begun to lessen at last.

She cooked them both a light supper of pasta and salad, and just before he began to clear the plates away she told him that she had made a decision. She made no promises, gave no guarantees, but said that she would try to make things work. They agreed that honesty was essential. No more lies, no more secrets. Trust needed to be restored. They had to be entirely open with each other, if their marriage were to stand any chance of recovering. She needed to know that she could believe in him again.

'And that's when I told him about Paul,' Celia said to Annabel. 'I couldn't not. It's a fresh start – it couldn't be built on a lie.'

'Blimey.' Annabel was silent for a moment. 'What happened?'

'Nothing at first. Just silence. Shock. I don't think he believed it, initially. He didn't really take it in. Like you, he imagines I'm thoroughly principled, self-controlled, reliable. He's always regarded me as something of an innocent. I don't think he ever dreamt I'd be capable of doing something like that.'

'After his behaviour, you had every right . . .'

'He said that himself. He used those very words. "I suppose after the way *I've* behaved, you had every right . . ." But I could see that he was appalled. We sat looking at each other and at first I thought, "Jesus, what have I done?" and then I thought, "Serves you bloody well right for what you did to me."

'Then Dan phoned in the midst of it all to say he'd heard I was back in London and could he come round, and five minutes later there was an excited call from Pippa saying she was so glad I was home and how about her coming too and us all having a family meal together. I had to put them both off. I was tired, I said. "I need to talk to your father some more," I said. "Maybe in a day or two's time." So Pippa said, "Of course. That's cool. We'll give you some space." I could tell from her voice that she thought everything was going to be fine.

'When I put the phone down, he started up straightaway. Why Paul, he wanted to know. Why not some stranger, or someone from work? Why did it have to be one of his oldest friends? That felt unfair. Like pure revenge. And then, why go and tell him? Why put the knife in? I reminded him that we'd promised to be honest with each other. Up to a point, he said. Up to a point.'

'He's got no right . . .' Annabel said. 'After what he did to you.'

'No, he hasn't. But how he sees it is that there he'd been, struggling to end it all with Marina, and while he was dealing with the horrors of that, trying to put everything right, according to him, I was getting my revenge with his best friend.'

'Still, what he did is far worse. He brought it on himself. He really doesn't have any right to . . .'

She wondered what rights either of them had now. A few months ago she'd have been more certain. Though resolutely atheist and untrusting of any external moral framework, she'd had a strong 'faith', if that's what you wanted to call it, in their private world. She'd believed in it. She may not have been bound by a morality provided by any god, but nevertheless she'd had an unswerving moral compass where relationships were concerned. She'd happily looked at other people and passed critical judgements on them. Betrayal, fidelity, honesty, truth, principle: they were all easy words to use. They'd tripped off the tongue; they'd never been called into question. She even remembered her own private conversation with Nick, a few years back, when Annabel had disappeared off for a short period with that ghastly bloke, Patrick, the man she worked with. Celia had strongly disapproved and been greatly relieved when Annabel 'saw sense' and returned to Charlie. But now she wasn't so sure any more. What Annabel saw as Celia taking her usual principled stand didn't feel quite like that. She'd thought of herself as doing what would work to save her marriage – an act of pragmatism from a very poor liar, trying to put all the mess behind her. Telling Nick had seemed like the *best* thing to do in the circumstances, not necessarily the *right* thing to do. But was that all there was to it? Might it have been that she was also really trying to test Nick's love for her, looking for proof that it could survive a test from her, in the same way that she had been expected to survive the battering he had given her? If so, his reaction was troubling, but also, perhaps, in some way, gratifying. She'd hurt him; he was, it seemed, capable of being hurt by her, and that, it had to be admitted, brought some satisfaction.

'So what now?' Annabel asked.

'We met up with Pippa and Dan yesterday and put a brave face on it. We said it wasn't going to be easy but we were trying to see if we could get back together again. I said not to break open the bottles of champagne quite yet, but I could see that Pippa in particular thought it was a done deal. Lots of big hugs for each of us and plenty of smiles. Neither of us had the heart to disillusion her. And anyway, what would we have said? That we'd decided to try to patch things up but then I'd told Nick that I'd slept with Paul, his best friend, the man she'd known since she was a little girl?'

Annabel sidestepped this. 'It'll be OK in the end, though, won't it? Once Nick gets over the initial shock, he'll understand what that was all about, the fling with Paul, don't you think?'

'Maybe. We haven't slept with each other yet, though. Probably not a very good sign.'

Annabel fell silent. That wasn't something she was willing to contradict.

'Have you talked to Paul?'

'How can I?'

She'd thought of ringing him, but it didn't seem like an option. Nick would have every right to see that as part of a continuing betrayal, if he ever found out. And anyway, it didn't seem fair to Paul. It might send out the wrong messages. Was she going back to Nick or wasn't she? She seemed, so clearly, to have made her choice. She couldn't expect any support from him now. She'd burnt her bridges.

'So what now?' Annabel asked again.

'No idea.'

'Can I do anything to help? Get Charlie to talk to him, maybe?'

'I can't see that it'd make any difference.'

'Don't forget Charlie's dealt with stuff like this himself, that time when . . .'

'Yes, I know.' She reached out and put her hand on Annabel's. 'You know what Charlie's like, though. He'd find it excruciating talking about it, specially with another man.'

'He'd do it for you, Cee.'

'That's sweet of you. And I'm sure he would. But I'm not clear what good it would do. Rationally I think Nick knows he's not being fair to me. But it doesn't stop him feeling angry and hurt. And I'm not sure that I'm willing to weep and lash and prostrate myself, mea culpa and all that. I'm still too hurt.'

She refrained from saying that, in any event, she couldn't really see Nick taking Charlie's advice very seriously, fond though he was of him. The rules by which Annabel's marriage worked had always been something of a surprise to both of them, Nick often joking about the lack of balance in the marriage. Charlie, at least to an external eye, seemed very much under Annabel's thumb. He was a lovely man, but no match for Annabel.

They talked on till late into the afternoon. Just as Annabel said that she thought she'd better be getting back home to feed Buster and take him out for his walk, the doorbell rang. It was Celia's father, arriving unannounced.

Celia hadn't seen him in weeks. Since the lost-glasses conversation she'd rung him a few times, just to check that he was OK. She'd staved off having to meet him, with stories of a sudden flurry of work in Paris for a French publishing house and, when she got back home, complaints of a frenetically busy schedule on her return. Seeing him now on her front doorstep, she was all too aware that she had neglected him.

He managed a polite greeting to Annabel before she left, then plonked himself down in an armchair in the living room in an ominously aggressive way.

'Something's up,' he said sternly. 'You haven't come to see me for far too long and you haven't called on the phone either. Something fishy's going on and I want to know what it is.'

Even now, at eighty-two and with a bush of coarse white hair, he had a rugged, strongly defined face that, in anger, could transform whatever he looked at into stone. If he wanted to, of course, he could turn on the charm; Celia's friends usually found him delightful company, witty and genial. With Marje, Celia's mother, barring the occasional normal marital spat, he had been soft as warm butter, and Barbara had never found him anything other than loving. But Celia, for reasons she'd never fully understood, had always borne the brunt of his irritation and Nick, for rather more comprehensible reasons, had always been held by him in utter disdain.

'Is it that husband of yours?' he said. 'Is he leading you a dance?'

'Daddy, please. Don't be silly.'

'I've never trusted the man. Not after what he did to Barbara.'

'I know, Daddy, but please don't do this. That was years ago.'

'So what's up?'

She'd been dreading this conversation. At some point she would have to tell Lionel that her marriage was in jeopardy, and she would have to give at least some indication of the reason why. But now definitely wasn't the time.

'Everything's fine. I've just been busy, that's all.' She attempted a cheerful smile.

'I want to say that I feel neglected, Celia,' he said. 'I think maybe you've forgotten that I'm nearly eighty-three and I'm not going to be here forever. I'm slowing down.'

'I know, Daddy.'

'And with Barbara off in the States, I rely more on you now.'

'I know, Daddy. I'm sorry. It's been a tricky few weeks.'

'There are things I need to talk to you about.'

'Oh.'

She realised that for all his usual grumpiness and air of throwing his weight around, he was looking thinner than usual, a bit more frail. His old brown cords were hanging baggily around his legs.

'You're not ill, are you?' she asked.

'Dr Caldicott has told me she wants to see you.'

'She does? Why's that?'

'She wants you to come along with me for my next appointment.'

'Has she told you why?'

He paused. 'She thinks I should do a Power of Attorney. Thinks it'd be a good idea. Sooner rather than later.'

'You've always resisted that, Daddy. You've wanted control of things. And you've managed your own affairs brilliantly.'

'Not for much longer, though, apparently.'

'Oh,' she said again. There was a pause. 'Is something wrong?'

'I've been struggling a bit with . . . things. She's done a few tests. My memory's not quite what it used to be. Going a bit down . . . hill.'

'Oh, Daddy!'

She saw that his eyes seemed to be misting over.

'It's been harder than you might realise since your mother died, but I've just got on with it. I like my independence, as you well know. Can't abide other people taking over, mollycoddling me, interfering with my affairs. Seems now that's all going to have to change. I'm going to need some help. And you've drawn the short . . . straw.'

She hesitated. It was tempting to comment on this but now definitely wasn't the time.

'Not at all, Daddy. Of course I'll come with you to Dr Caldicott,' she said. 'Fix an appointment with her, any time after Thursday morning. I'll make sure I'm there.'

'And what about him?'

'Who?'

'That husband of yours.'

'What about him?' She took a deep breath.

'You're not going to tell him about my doctor's appointment, are you? Not yet. I'd rather he didn't know.'

'No, Daddy. I won't tell anyone. Not till we've spoken to the doctor and found out more about what's going on.'

'I'm sorry to be such a nuisance,' he said gruffly.

She thought this might be the very first time he'd ever apologised to her. At least, it was the only occasion she could actually remember. It brought a lump to her throat.

'Don't be silly. I should have been making more time for you.'

'I haven't wanted to intrude. The two of you, you lead such full lives. You always seem so busy, happily caught up in your own affairs. You don't need a foolish old man like me trailing around after you.'

She said nothing. She couldn't bring herself to speak. Had she done so, she would have burst into tears. She just patted his hand.

He pulled himself up out of the armchair. 'I'll call when I've made the appointment. Give my love to Pippa and Dan when you speak to them.'

There was, of course, no mention of Nick.

When he had gone, Celia went back into the living room. Outside, night had fallen. She didn't turn on the lights or close the curtains, but just stayed there in the darkness, hoping that Nick would be delayed coming home. She needed time to try to pull herself together. She had to regroup, before the next bombardment started.

But instead of coming home late, Nick was, in fact, rather earlier than expected, and when he came in he found her sitting on the floor propped up against the sofa, hugging her legs and rocking backwards and forwards, slowly, slowly, rocking, rocking, slowly, slowly.

Chapter 13

'I've been thinking,' he said, coming to sit beside her on the floor, without even taking off his jacket. He was close to her, their bodies in symmetry, touching at the hips, backs straight against the sofa, like small children watching a favourite film on TV. Tentatively he put his hand on her leg. 'We can't go on like this.'

There was a long pause. He was looking ahead at the floor, rather than towards her, whether through nervousness or guilt or fear, or something else, she couldn't tell. Is this it? she wondered. Is this the end?

She thought of all those books she had published and their endings, schlocky fictions where passions flared and adulteries were spawned, where men got their comeuppance, women their revenge, or strange twists of fate intervened to take things in entirely unexpected directions. Then there were the more 'literary' fictions, the ones she felt more proud of shepherding into print, usually written in the first person, in voices that were quirky, playful, wittily postmodern in the way they subverted the conventions, but nevertheless mining the same themes, albeit in rather edgier ways.

Fairy tale, Gothic horror, tragedy or edgy contemporary romance – it was one thing to read the constructions put upon men and women's torrid relationships in fiction, quite another to be living them yourself. The ending that was coming for her would be real. Perhaps it wouldn't even be an ending at all, just some kind of interim event, randomly emerging, unshaped by an author's vision, messy and confused, liable to be done and then undone again, unknowable in its consequences for their future lives. What Nick said right now might be of momentous significance in the grand scheme of their lives but then again it might not. One of them might get run over by a bus, or die of a heart attack, the next day, the next month or the next year, and that might be their defining moment, their joint tragedy, not this tacky mid-life episode of sexual misadventures. Equally, what was happening now might be a single period containing their only adulteries or the first of many, the start of a different phase in their marriage, a temporary separation, or maybe the end of their marriage altogether.

'I set this whole thing going and now it's got out of control. I started it all,' he said finally.

She turned to look at him. His face, in the gloom of the darkened living room, gave little away. Nick Cabuzel. Her husband. The man she'd given her heart to in her twenties and lived with ever since. Not a bad or vicious man. Not wilfully selfish or uncaring. Foolish, capable of self-deception and doing things that he later regretted, insecure and flawed just like anyone else. Not a storybook hero – definitely not quite the hero she'd once thought he was. Still attractive to her, though, but in a quieter way. Grey-haired, his face more lined, less wiry, a little slower in his movements but still the same man. She was suddenly overcome with affection for him. He'd treated her shamefully. And yet . . . he'd reacted badly to her admission about Paul. And yet . . . it had been a stupid thing for her to do. Just because he'd hurt her, did she have to behave in the same, foolish way?

She put her hand on his leg. Another symmetry. The closest they had been in weeks.

'About Paul . . .' he started. She waited for him to continue. 'I hate what you did. I feel sick at the thought of it – him touching you . . . him being with you. I felt betrayed by you when you told me – I *feel* betrayed. But I have no right.'

No right.

'It's no more than I deserve, for the way I've treated you.'

There was another pause. She said nothing, waiting, unsure of what she wanted to say, which of her thoughts she should give voice to.

'Of course, you may want to go on seeing Paul. I don't know how you feel about him. Perhaps you've decided to give up on me, after everything I've done to you, now that you've found someone else? If that's the case, if you care for him, I need to know.'

This she could answer simply, without requiring time to reflect. 'It's over,' she said. How clichéd that sounded. 'It happened. But we agreed before I left that it would never happen again. I'm very fond of him . . . I *am* attracted to him,' she said. It felt important to be honest now. 'But I wouldn't have been looking at him in that way if it hadn't been for you and . . . Marina – if I hadn't felt so appallingly hurt and betrayed by you . . . It wasn't a sensible thing for me to do, perhaps, but I haven't been feeling very sensible these past few weeks.'

Now he turned towards her. They looked at each other, their faces matched, both serious, uncertain.

'I understand what happened with Paul. And I'm relieved that it's what it is and no more. What I did to you is far, far worse, I realise that. So is there any chance that we could put all of this behind us and start again?'

Only just visible in the darkness, she saw his face close to hers, his eyes on her, a penetrating gaze. 'I'd like to try,' she said. 'I don't want to give up on us, not after all these years. We've been happy together. We've had a good marriage – that must be worth something. We'd have to take things slowly, though. Bit by bit. Carefully. I'd like to try.'

She touched his face tentatively with her fingertips, feeling the contours of his cheekbone, his nose, his lips, his chin. And then gently, carefully, she took his head in both hands and pulled him towards her, so that she could hear his breath and feel his rough stubble on her own skin, and she kissed him, cautiously, not passionately but tenderly, letting her tongue pass softly over his inner lip, reminding herself of the familiar feel and taste of him.

And then all at once they were grasping hold of each other, and taking off their clothes and touching each other, not slowly, not bit by bit, not carefully. The same pleasures as she remembered, the same set patterns and moves, the same taste and touch, the same sounds, the same man. A sense of coming home after a long time away, of things being reassuringly unchanged but odd little things that you'd forgotten all about suddenly coming into focus as you unlocked the front door and stepped inside; a painting on the wall that you'd forgotten, the quality of the light in the kitchen; a comforting smell of home that went unnoticed when you were there but exploded with memory when you returned. Security and danger, domesticity and desire, innocence and guilt, friendship and love, the physical and the spiritual, all collapsing into something complicated and yet, confusingly, more whole.

Sheepishly, when they were done, they collected together their clothes from around the sofa and the floor and began to put them on, woolly socks, plain white underwear, everyday clothes that looked anything but sexy lying strewn all over the carpet. They smiled at their foolishness, behaving like teenagers, unable to control themselves.

'I feel happier than I have for a long time,' Nick said.

Celia nodded. 'Me too.'

'I hope we can make this work.'

'Yes.'

'A fresh start, putting all this behind us.'

His face was bright, hopeful. She could see how much this meant to him. But she wasn't sure she was ready for something quite so neat and simple, as if all that had happened was a silly little falling out with each other, a lovers' tiff. 'I'll try. I promise I will,' she said. 'But my trust in you has been damaged – it may take some time to rebuild. I need your absolute assurance that you won't see Marina again. Not under any circumstances. Never. Never, ever. I need to know that categorically. I must be sure that it's over.'

'I can promise you that. It's over. That's definite. She knows that. A bit late in the day, I know, but now, at least, I've made that perfectly clear to her, and most importantly, to myself.' There were tears in his eyes. 'I got in too deep, Celia, and then didn't know how to get myself out of it. I've been a bloody fool.'

'You have. You certainly have.' She stroked his face. 'I'll make us a cup of tea,' she said, leaving the room quickly to avoid the risk of joining him with her own tears.

Chapter 14

Dr Caldicott's surgery was in the same house that the previous GP, Alistair Caldicott, her father, had occupied for fifty-odd years, on the better side of Park Road, right next to the cricket pitch and just a short walk from Celia's old family home. The original Dr Caldicott had retired some time back and, when his daughter, Caroline, finally took over, she had renovated the place straightaway, doing away with the flat upstairs and bringing in two new partners, a practice nurse, a podiatrist, an osteopath, a counsellor and all the other smart trappings of a thoroughly modern surgery. Still, the outside of the house had remained largely unchanged, with its red-brick Victorian façade, gravelled path and scattering of ungainly rose bushes, which were, as ever, in need of a good pruning and proper care. For Celia, the exterior alone brought back childhood memories of being brought to see Alistair Caldicott, the rather formal, austere man in a white coat who stuck a thermometer painfully under your tongue and felt your glands with brusque, impolite assurance. Mostly it was high fevers, tummy bugs or measles that brought her there but she also remembered that more worrying episode of hospital investigations, when she'd appeared in his consulting room with a set of symptoms that everyone mistook for the early stages of leukaemia. It had all turned out, thankfully, to be a false alarm, but for Celia the doctor's surgery was tainted with those memories of nasty blood tests, rough physical examinations by Dr Caldicott, and her mother's palpable fear.

They parked on the other side of the road. They were in good time and Lionel wanted to wait in the car, rather than going across to the surgery to sit in the waiting room.

'You just catch germs from the other patients,' he said. 'Dangerous places, doctors' surgeries.'

She humoured him, knowing full well that it probably had more to do with wanting to forestall the moment when Caroline Caldicott might confront them both with a whole series of difficult truths.

'It may be years, you know,' Lionel said.

'Yes, Daddy. It's probably nothing to worry about at the moment.'

'All my friends struggle. We all laugh about it, as if it's one great big joke, how we search for names, forget the titles of books and can't remember the films we've seen.'

'It's normal. I'm just the same. Nick too.'

'Forgetteries, that's what we've started calling them. Silly fools, all of us. We haven't got memories any more, we say among ourselves, just forgetteries. A retreat into comedy, I suppose, to keep the tragedy of what is happening to us at bay. But it doesn't seem so very funny to me any more.'

She smiled. 'You're still sharp as anything, Daddy. You never miss a trick. You seem absolutely fine to me.'

'Ah but not always. You're not around me enough to notice. I've been slowing down. I get a bit confused sometimes.'

It was true that she'd seen very little of him recently. And it wasn't just the problems with Nick that had kept her away. She knew she should spend more time with Lionel but the way he was with her, and she with him, they constantly seemed to rub each other up the wrong way. No matter what she did or said, he found fault with it. She'd often wondered whether he really liked her. He must love her, deep down, mustn't he? After all, she was his daughter. Blood of his blood, flesh of his flesh and all that.

But did he really *like* her? Probably not. And, while she was following that rather difficult train of thought, why not admit it? Did she actually like *him*? She could lose her temper with him at the drop of a hat. No one could provoke such instant fury in her as her father. Whether the two were connected or not, she wasn't sure. Did her crossness provoke his petulant behaviour towards her, or was it the other way round? Chicken or egg, chalk and cheese, pots and kettles, spilt milk – all those old proverbs seemed well worth trundling out when it came to her and her father and their fractious relationship!

This past week, though, since her return from France and that conversation at the house, he'd been sweeter with her than she'd ever known him and she'd found herself responding in similar vein. When she'd mentioned this casually to Pippa, she said that she'd noticed it too. 'He's always been lovely with everyone else and grumpy as hell with you – and Dad, of course,' she'd said. 'Like he's really cross with you for some reason. Bears you a grudge or something. But he seems to have softened a bit now, doesn't he? He's been quite nice. Stopped being so mean to you.'

Celia had smiled wryly. 'It's taken him well over fifty years but he's finally managed it,' she'd said. 'A lifetime's work!'

In the warm car, Celia patted Lionel's hand.

'Let's see what Caroline – Dr Caldicott has to say. She'll probably be very reassuring.'

'Perhaps. We'll see.'

'Afterwards, will you let me take you out for lunch, Daddy? We could have a meal together and a chat.'

'That would be nice.'

There was a moment's silence, then, 'How's that husband of yours?'

'Can't you call him Nick, Daddy? After all these years.'

A long pause.

'Nick, then. How is he?'

'He's fine. Working quite hard. Not loving the job any more but it pays the bills so he'll keep going a bit longer. We're actually thinking about both taking a bit of time off work, unpaid, if we can, over the winter. We'd like to have a trip somewhere. Maybe Australia and New Zealand. Just the two of us. It's not fixed yet . . . just an idea. We'd like to travel. Have some time on our own.'

Lionel was quiet.

'Only if you're OK, of course. We'll see what Dr Caldicott says and then decide. We wouldn't go if you needed us here.'

There was another long pause. She wondered what was coming next. Annoyance at the suggestion that she might even contemplate leaving him on his own? Complaints about her inadequacies as a daughter? Lionel looked down at his hands.

'Your marriage has been a success,' he said. 'A great success. I know that. It's been a surprise to me. I thought he would hurt you, like he did Barbara. I didn't think he could be trusted. But he . . . Nick . . . he's turned out OK, hasn't he? He's not the bounder I took him for. He's made you happy. You've lasted the course together.'

Celia looked straight ahead, scarcely trusting herself to breathe.

Lionel carried on. 'My relationship with him . . . it's not been very good. I haven't behaved well to him, have I? Not my finest hour, I'm afraid.'

'Oh Daddy!'

He cleared his throat. 'Let's go in, then, and get this over with!'

Afterwards, in the restaurant, his favourite brasserie in Highgate – Lionel insisting, as always, on a proper lunch, rather than just a sandwich – he managed to delay the inevitable conversation with endless distractions, fussing over which table they would take and where his coat should go, whether they'd have the set menu or go à la carte, complaining about being too warm, and then showing his irritation towards the waitress for the draught caused by the constant opening and closing of the door. In other words, Celia thought, my father as I've come to know and love him. She couldn't help but notice the waitress raising her eyes skyward and gesturing towards them, as she whispered to the other girl at the till. Lionel managing to work his usual charm, she thought.

But finally, after the plates for the starter had been cleared away, Celia managed to turn the conversation towards what had been said in the doctor's surgery.

'It's not so bad, you know, Daddy. She was quite positive really.'

He shrugged.

'She said that the progress of these things was unpredictable – that you might have years and years of being pretty much fine.'

'She also said it might go apace.'

'Not necessarily, though. That's the worst-case scenario. The best isn't so bad.'

'Forgetfulness, muddle, needing more help with my . . . my things . . . my affairs, someone to keep an eye on me, making lists, writing things down, sticking those . . . those things . . . those damned sticky things on my walls. Not so bad, eh?'

He was red in the face, furious or about to cry, she wasn't sure which. For a while she said nothing. Then, 'I'll help you, Daddy. If you want me to be there, I'll be there for you.'

There. She'd said it. If you want me to be there.

He didn't reply. So that was it. There it was. His silence said it all.

'It's OK, Daddy. I get it,' she said, calmly enough. 'Don't worry. You don't have to say anything. I understand. I'll call Barbara tomorrow. I'll tell her she needs to come back for a while, to sort things out.'

'No, no, no!' Now he was getting upset. He was going to create a scene. 'No.'

'I can't see any alternative, Lionel. If you don't want me to help you, I'll need to call Barbara. Someone needs to take charge of all this. Work out what needs doing.' Her voice was rising. 'I know that you'd rather have her do it than me. I know that. You don't need to explain. It's always been like that and I understand, Lionel, really I do.' She realised she was calling him by his first name again. Distancing herself from him and his bloody . . . his shitty . . . She felt that dryness in the back of her throat, the tears welling up in her eyes. His stupid . . . his –

'No, Celia, please. I want to talk to you . . . I want to tell you . . . to explain to you . . . before it's too late. I want to tell you something I've not said to anyone, not your mother, not Barbara, not anyone. I'm not sure I even admitted it to myself until recently . . . not until . . . well . . .'

He hesitated.

'Daddy, please. This isn't necessary. You don't have to tell me anything. I think I know all I need to know.'

If he was going to apologise, it wasn't going to make any difference now. It should have come a long time ago.

'It's important,' he said. 'I need to tell you. I haven't been very fair to you and I want to explain why.'

She didn't think she could bear to hear what he had to say. He hadn't been very fair to her, he'd said. True. He'd been incredibly unfair. Always making it clear that he liked Barbara best. Not her. As a child she had had a secret set of fantasies. She'd imagined that she'd been adopted, or that she was the child of Marje's affair with another man, or some other ghastly secret that might explain how she felt within her family, a reason for Lionel's behaviour towards her, his distance from her. She knew that many children had similar fantasies. Occasionally, however, these implausible fears popped up even now, in her adult consciousness – not something she really believed to be true, but nevertheless bubbling up from some deep boiling well of anxiety, taking her by surprise with the heat they generated. She'd never shared these feelings with anyone, not even with Nick, so foolish had these imaginings seemed to her. Now, if Lionel was going to start on explanations, a bit of her was afraid. What if her worst imaginings turned out to be true? In that case, she really didn't want to know.

But Lionel seemed determined to continue. 'I've never been . . . quite as I should be with you. We both know that.'

'Please, Lionel, don't! There's no point in crying over spilt milk and all that. Water over – or is it under? – the bridge.' Why did those stupid proverbs always come to her at times like this?

'You might not want to know but I need to tell you. For me, if not for you. I've got to that stage in my life where I want to tidy things up . . . leave a clean balance sheet. No loose ends.'

So Lionel's needs would have to come first once again. Of course, his desires were paramount. So be it. She sat back in her chair. Perhaps she'd lay her stupid fears to rest at last. The waitress appeared with their second course and fresh cutlery. Cheerily she poured them water from the bottle of sparkling on the table. Celia half thought she should ask for a glass of wine after all, or even half a bottle. She might need it. Lionel started on his fish but she left her vegetable tart untouched for the moment, letting it sit there going cold.

'It's hard to know where to start,' he said.

She said nothing, just fixed her eyes on the tart.

'You know how much I loved your mother . . .'

This was clearly going to take some time.

'And you know how happy we were when Barbara was born.'

Oh God. How much more of this?

Then Lionel suddenly stopped abruptly. He was looking over her shoulder. She turned round to follow his gaze. There was Judy coming up rapidly behind her, hurrying towards their table.

'Celia. Fancy meeting you here! Not your usual haunt, is it? But I'm so glad to see you! And looking so much better than last time we met . . . at Bill's party –though I shouldn't mention that, of course. Not a good night. But here you are, on top form again. Back to normal! You looked so dreadful that evening. And Mr Brown . .

. Lionel. How very nice to meet you again after all these years. And youthful as ever, if I may say so.'

'You remember Judy, don't you, Lionel. She's an old friend of ours from the early London days. You know, Judy and Bill.'

Lionel hesitated, a little flustered, but made the right noises.

'I hope things are better between you and Nick. Bill tells me, from Buntings talk, that things have been sorted, once and for all. She's got a new job, out of London, starting quite soon, so Bill says. I'm really pleased for both of you.'

Shit. What did Judy think she was doing? In front of her father. She looked at him; he seemed to be focused on his plate of food, prodding at a piece of sprouting broccoli. She stared hard at Judy and hoped she'd get the message.

She seemed to have realised because she quickly swung into a brisk, cheerful sign-off. 'I'll leave you both to your lunch. That tart looks too delicious to allow to go cold! Courgette, red peppers and leeks, is it? I should try that next time I come here. I always go for the fish, like your father, or the steak frites. That's always top-notch. Let's meet up for a coffee soon and talk. It's great that you're back in the swing of things again, Celia. I'm so glad.' She bent down to kiss Celia on one cheek. 'Ring me this week to fix something up.'

She looked at her father. Had he noticed? He didn't say anything. Quickly she picked up her fork and started on her tart.

'Judy's right, this *does* look delicious,' she said. 'I'm going to tuck in before it goes cold.'

'Look here,' Lionel said firmly. She held her breath. 'I don't want to talk any more about Dr Caldicott. We've done enough of that for one day. You can speak to Barbara about it if you want to, though I'll tell her myself when she gives me her weekly call tomorrow. And tell that husband of yours if you must. I can't be foolish about all this and pretend it's not happening. But I'm going to try to follow your advice and look on the positive side of things. As the doctor said, it could be years and years before I go completely doolally.'

They finished their meal, with her steering the conversation towards other things – updates on Pippa and Jamie's wedding plans for the summer, the ever-busy Dan, discussions of books just published and the demands on Barbara resulting from the complicated building works that had just started on her loft apartment in New York. He seemed to have forgotten the urgent need to tell her something. For the time being at least.

Then suddenly, just as they were leaving the restaurant, and quite out of the blue: 'You and him, you are all right, aren't you?'

'Me and who?'

He hesitated. 'Nick.'

'Of course, Daddy. We're absolutely fine.'

'Oh good. I just wondered. Something or other that woman – what's her name again? – said in the restaurant back then made me wonder.'

'It was nothing, Daddy. Just Judy being Judy. Really, I promise, we're absolutely fine.'

Chapter 15

'I saw Judy in Café Rouge up in Highgate today. Lionel and I had lunch there after seeing Dr Caldicott.'

'Mmm.'

Nick had listened carefully to her account of her father's illness. He'd been both kind and generous in his offers of support, which was particularly good of him, she thought, given how badly Lionel had treated him over the years. 'We'll have to help him as and when he needs it,' he had said. 'Like we did with my mother.' Nick's father had died young, leaving his mother, Celeste, in grief, depressed and dependent on him for support. It had involved several years of Nick going back and forth to Kent to see her, until she finally met Arthur and found a new stability in his companionship. Nick had been admirably attentive to her needs during this period, the loving only son.

Now Nick had started on the sudoku. His head was bowed and he was staring intently at the square of numbers. 'How is Judy?' he asked after a few moments.

'Good, I think. She wasn't very discreet, though.'

'In what way?'

'She seemed to forget that Lionel was there and started banging on about you and me.'

He looked up.

'It's OK. He wasn't very quick on the uptake. I think he was too busy trying to remember who she was and fretting about that. He clearly didn't quite recognise her. But it was silly of her. She made it perfectly clear that we'd been having difficulties.'

'She can be a daft cow sometimes, can't she.'

Celia managed a small laugh. 'A well-meaning daft cow.'

Nick had the pen in his mouth and was frowning. His lips moved slightly as he continued to tot up the numbers.

'She mentioned something else, though,' Celia said, '. . . that she probably shouldn't have.'

'Oh yes?'

Celia hesitated slightly.

'She said that Marina had got a new job and was leaving London.'

Silence. The pen fell still.

'Did you know that, Nick?'

'No.'

'So it's news to you?'

'Yes.'

There was a pause.

'How did Judy know?'

'Bill told her.'

Celia tried to read the expression on his face. It was blank, unfathomable.

'Does it upset you, Nick?'

Another silence and then a hasty, 'No.'

'Shall we talk about something else?'

He nodded.

She offered to cook and made them a simple dish of pasta and spicy tomato sauce that they ate quickly at the kitchen table – both had work the next day and emails to deal with before bed. He washed up the pots, scrubbing vigorously with the brush. He didn't look up and didn't say anything.

But then he came over towards her as she was clearing the last things off the table and wiping it clean.

'I think it's for the best,' he said. 'No chance of me bumping into her, or of Bill or the others inadvertently mentioning what she's up to, taking the lead in some big case or other, and upsetting me or upsetting you. It'll be easier to put everything behind us if she isn't on the scene any more.'

'But it's a shock?'

'A bit.' He was being truthful and she was glad of that. 'It makes it more final, more real. I'm glad about that, though, honestly I am, for lots of reasons, but most importantly because it cements the fact that we're firmly back together again. But I can't say I don't feel any sadness at all. That wouldn't be true.'

She nodded. 'I understand that.' And then in response to his worried look, 'Really, I do understand. I never expected any of this to be easy for you.'

'I feel most sad for her, actually. I think about what it's done to her. She's moving out of London, leaving her job because of me. I can't help but feel guilty. I feel like a complete shit.'

'She went into it, knowingly,' Celia said. 'She was the one who –' and then she stopped herself. Airing all her resentments against this woman probably wasn't such a good idea, however much she wanted to rail against her for going into it with her eyes wide open, knowing that she was sleeping with someone else's husband, a married man. Surely she'd forfeited the right to sympathy

'I wish I could turn back the clock,' Nick said.

'So do I. But you can't. So you may as well concentrate on the future. Both of us need to do that. And her absence will help. As you say, no chance of either of us bumping into her. Easier for all of us, her too, probably.'

'Yes.'

He came up and held her close to him and she allowed him to do so. This was their best chance of winning through, she thought, if she could be the person he turned to, even at a moment like this – most of all at a moment like this. Nick's aunt Odile was right. She mustn't just throw down her sword. She'd fight for their marriage, even if it meant that she needed to put her pride to one side and keep her mouth shut about her feelings towards Marina. Better to bury all of that than constantly upbraid him with his guilt and sour any attempts at a fresh start. She reminded herself of all that she had ever loved about him and of the support he provided for her. That was not to be lightly discarded. She would try to focus on the positives, rather than getting mired in corrosive, ugly resentments.

'Thank you for being so understanding about Lionel,' she said, turning the subject away from Marina. 'It means a lot to me. He's been pretty unpleasant to both of us over the years. I wouldn't blame you if you wanted nothing more to do with him.'

'He's your father. I've known him for so long now. I can't say I like it but I've got used to his ways. I reckon he's fonder of you than he lets on.'

'Maybe,' she said. 'Though, up till now, it's never really seemed that way. But today, at the café, he seemed a bit different – softer. And there was something he wanted to get off his chest . . . something he seemed to want to tell me. Then Judy waltzed over and the opportunity was gone.'

'An attempt at reconciliation?'

'We'll see,' Celia said. She knew Lionel well enough to doubt that anything he was planning to say would be free of complexity and hurt for her.

Chapter 16

It is December. Five weeks have slipped by surprisingly quickly and Christmas is almost upon them. They have plans for a quiet time together, just the four of them, with Lionel joining them for Christmas Day. Lottie and Jamie will go to their own parents; Barbara is going to spend Christmas with Nigel's family in New Hampshire. Celia has picked up her work again and is hurrying to complete the signing of a contract for a new book with the dreadful Ffion Wyn-Jones before everything shuts down for the holiday period; Nick is preoccupied by a problem involving a close and trusted colleague who has decided to take the Council to an industrial tribunal. But they have managed to make time to spend with each other and have settled back down into a routine that is, in the main, event-free. Event-free is good after the past couple of months that have been anything but. Sometimes they find themselves tiptoeing around each other, careful not to take anything for granted, avoiding awkward subjects. Occasionally, one or the other reacts more sharply than is necessary and then backs down quickly, afraid of provoking something that could get out of hand and threaten the delicate peace that has been established. Marina is never mentioned and Paul Legrand also has 'Warning: Keep Out' signs posted all around his name. But as Celia tells Annabel, they are, generally speaking, by and large, for the time being at least, not to tempt fate in any way, of course . . . happy again.

So much so, that when Nick tentatively suggests that they might have their usual New Year's Day party, Celia agrees. Why not? An act of faith in the future together. They'll invite the usual crowd – Mary and Evelyn, Bill and

Judy, the Websters, George Parker, Annabel and Charlie, naturally, Pippa and Jamie, Dan and Lottie. Then there's Lottie's mother, Mrs Campion, who is delightfully bonkers. They've taken to inviting her in recent years and she has become quite a fixture, much appreciated by Annabel who describes her as 'a hoot' and by Judy who bemoans the fact that her own children's partners have no relatives quite as entertaining as Alicia Campion to bring in tow to festive occasions. But they won't invite Jamie's parents, whom they really haven't got to know in the same way, though she's always wondered why not. Perhaps because Jamie hasn't shown any signs of wanting it, though the wedding will probably change all that. She'll ask Annabel's children, Daisy and Alex, of course, and maybe George's daughter, Liza, and her fiancé. Pippa and Dan will like that. She'll have to invite Lionel, and maybe she should ask Auntie Vera, though she's unlikely to accept – too old and doddery to cope with all those people, so she always says. She wonders whether to invite Lois and Howard Glassman, who've never been to their New Year parties but would undoubtedly fit in well. They'll probably have other plans, of course. People like the Glassmans often do. They give off an air of being tremendously popular and having a fantastically busy social life, though Lois was so friendly when they'd met that evening at . . . With everything that has happened Celia hasn't followed up on her suggestion of a lunch date, so this would be a very good way of making an overture towards her. She'll brush aside her shyness – so very foolish at her age – and give Lois a ring.

She should really invite Anne, of course, but she's not sure she wants to. It seems terribly unfair on poor old Anne, she knows, but having fled to her in St Albans, she rather associates her now with those awful days just after Nick . . . She'll invite her another time but not for the New Year party, where her presence would be a bit like the Ghost of Christmas Past, putting a dampener on their spirits, dragging them back to the events of the autumn. She really doesn't want to be reminded, not at her party. Forward, that's where she needs to be going.

Nick leaves it all to her. 'You're so good at these things,' he says. 'I enjoy watching you planning, orchestrating everything, making sure that it's just right. I'll take instructions, of course, when the time comes. Very happy to collect stuff from Waitrose, if you give me a list.'

'The drink's your forte, though – those innumerable trips to French caves and chateau wineries with your grandfather in the summer holidays!' She knew he'd be pleased.

'I'll buy in the booze, then – a good crisp Crémant de Loire, perhaps, and a nice Bordeaux – but the grand plan and the cooking, that's your territory.'

She doesn't mind taking charge. In fact she's grateful for the fact that he'll leave all the arrangements to her. She's always enjoyed the planning of parties and the New Year's Day party in particular. Perhaps it was reading *Mrs Dalloway* in her first year at university that did it. There was something so supremely graceful about Clarissa Dalloway's deep, intense commitment to the idea of a party, her precise focus on getting every element right – the flowers, the food, the crockery and polished cutlery, the starched linen, the cleaned and aired room, everything in a perfect state of harmony. And that despite the undercurrents of dissatisfaction and repressed feeling in her life, her doubts about her marriage, her sense of missed opportunities with potential lovers, the narrow constraints of her wifely role, the backdrop of war. She wonders whether Virginia Woolf, so fragile in her own state of mind and febrile in her relationships, was projecting herself as Clarissa, the wife, mother, womanly figure who could dedicate herself so utterly to the organisation of a stupendously good party, whatever else was happening around her. Wish fulfilment, she thinks, for Virginia Woolf, given the fact that she ended up taking her own life. And perhaps an element of wish fulfilment for Celia, too. Another of her own little compensations for other failures. But she doesn't really mind that. A party provides her with a pretty decent illusion of being at the heart of her family, the giver of pleasure and contentment. A cracking good party will definitely restore her sense of self-worth.

'Are you sure this is such a good idea?' Dan asks when he speaks to her over the phone. 'Lottie and I were both thinking . . .' He hesitates. 'After all that stuff that's happened with you and Dad, do you think you feel up to a big party?'

'Things are going fine now, Dan. We want to do it. In fact, if we didn't everyone would wonder – our party's such an annual event.'

'That's OK, then. Just wanting you to know that I'd be cool with you missing a year if you wanted to. And I'm sure Pippa'd feel the same.'

'I appreciate that, Dan, really I do. It's sweet of you to think of us. But honestly, I think it'll be a good thing for your father and me to go ahead with it. It'll be fun.'

She puts the phone down and has a sudden, sickening moment of doubt. Maybe Dan's right. Maybe it isn't wise. But she's already started working out the menu and asked Svetlana, the cleaner, to come and help serve drinks and food and clear up afterwards. She's left the harbour and the wind is in her sails. She won't change tack now. It will be a good party; she'll make sure of that.

The day comes and everything is ready. The food is set out in the kitchen on the central island, swathed in foil and cling film; the white wine is cooling in a large tin bucket of ice on the floor. Svetlana has done the washing-up, tidied away the kitchen debris and daily mess into cupboards and, last, mopped the oak floor. Nick is upstairs having a shower. Celia stands, arms folded, surveying it all with a detached observer's eye. It looks fine, she thinks. Better than fine. There is a quiet calm, which she breathes in, the stillness of the house before everyone arrives, the food untouched, the glasses unfilled; all is anticipation and expectation; no peanuts dropped and crushed under a shoe, no spilt cranberry juice, or petals of a flower disturbed, as yet, by a clumsy hand. In a few moments, Nick will come downstairs and compliment her on the way everything looks, the tall-stemmed lilies in the vases, the bowls of olives and cashew nuts, the impressive salmon, the large glazed ham, the plates of salad, the ranked rows of flutes and wine glasses. He'll kiss the nape of her neck or stroke her arm and they'll stand and wait for the first ring on the doorbell, preparing themselves for the start of it all.

'A good idea to go ahead?' he asks when he finally does appear, freshly shaven, smelling of soap, with a clean shirt and fresh pair of jeans.

'A lovely idea,' she replies. 'A celebration.'

'Of us?'

'Of us.'

'Our ability to endure?'

'To survive.'

He pours them each a glass of Crémant de Loire and they have just enough time to toast each other before the doorbell rings and Svetlana ushers Lionel in.

*

It *has* been a good party. Only the young people remain, going up to Dan's old bedroom with armfuls of beer. She can hear their laughter and is pleased to have them back again, a reminder of the best bits of their teenage years when the house was full of youthful activity, energy and noise.

Svetlana is clearing up the kitchen, drying glasses and stacking them back in their boxes; Nick is taking empties out to the bins and moving furniture back into its usual place. Celia sits down for a moment. It has been a good party.

Alicia Campion and George Parker seemed to be getting on particularly well and Celia wonders whether this is the start of something.

'Have you seen them boogying on down to the music in the living room?' Pippa had hurried over to tell her. 'I didn't know George had it in him. He has all the moves!'

Celia had reminded her that George was quite a hit with the girls in his youth. 'Highly fanciable, was George. Everyone had a crush on him. He looked a bit like Paul McCartney in his druggy, hippie, Maharishi phase,' she said, 'though you'd hardly think it now to look at him. Got a bit paunchy – though Alicia seems not to mind.'

Annabel and Charlie had been on good form, as had Mary and Evelyn. Those two had seemed quite oblivious to Celia and Nick's difficulties, despite having been at Bill's party. They hadn't mentioned it at all, or given any inkling of having heard any gossip. Perhaps they had left early and missed the anxious talk? Or were they just being typically tactful about Celia and Nick's feelings, careful to avoid intrusive questions? Celia had managed to avoid long conversations with Judy, who approached her several times with a look on her face that threatened unwelcome expressions of concern and the clear intention of speaking about the one topic Celia most wanted to avoid. But happily, Celia contrived to be terribly busy offering around drinks every time Judy appeared and finally Judy conceded defeat, giving way to the other calls on her attention – the sudden arrival of Lois and Howard Glassman, the announcement that food was served, the distraction of Alicia Campion's compelling and rather risqué account of ending up by accident at a nudist campsite, when holidaying with her sister in the Haute-Loire. 'It was rather fun,' she'd said loudly, 'looking at those naked men and their dangly bits, all different shapes and sizes.'

Lionel had stayed right through to the end. That had been a surprise, too. He'd seemed to enjoy himself and even thanked her as he left. 'A good party,' he'd said. Praise indeed. Pippa and Dan had, of course, been great with him. They'd done sterling work in making sure that his plate was filled, his glass topped up, and she'd noticed them coming over to have a chat with him when he looked as if he'd been sitting rather too long on his own. The biggest surprise of all had been seeing him in close conversation with Nick, towards the end of the party. At one point she'd even noticed him putting his hand on Nick's shoulder.

'What were you and Lionel talking about?' she asks Nick, as they are getting ready for bed.

'Very little, really. Just your average small talk. Fantastic, isn't it? Finally, after all these years, to manage to have a normal, unbarbed conversation with your father. Quite an achievement!'

'He's softened, hasn't he?'

'Yes. He's looking older, less sure of himself. I didn't mention his visit to the doctor. I thought I should steer clear of tricky topics. Keep up the spirit of cheer and goodwill and all that.'

'Wise,' Celia says, pulling back the covers and climbing into bed. 'Good party, Lionel said. So did several others. One of our best, according to George.'

They both laugh and don't need to say anything more; George and Alicia Campion, both rather drunk, had left the party together, much to the embarrassment of poor Lottie.

'Yes, good party.' Nick kisses her. 'And plenty more to come, I hope.'

'Yes,' Celia says sleepily, reaching out to touch his arm. 'Let's hope so.'

Chapter 17

'You're very brave,' Judy said, when they finally met up for lunch, at Marco's, the bustling little café just round the corner from Atlas Books. She had phoned the evening after the party with her thanks for another 'wicked' New Year's Day do. 'Amazing, under the circumstances,' she'd said. 'But we didn't get a proper chance to talk. Let's meet up sometime this week.'

Celia had tried to put her off with protestations of being madly busy at work and having to spend more time with Lionel but Judy had been determined. 'I'll come and meet you for lunch on a workday, if the weekends are tricky,' she'd said. 'You do take a lunch break, don't you?'

Celia had given in and suggested a place too busy to allow either a quiet tête à tête or a leisurely meal. Judy was always stubbornly assertive, but she had her own ways of quietly resisting. She wasn't going to let Judy have it all her own way. She knew that, for perfectly good reasons, perhaps, Judy wanted to hear the whole story of Nick's and her attempts at putting the affair with Marina behind them. She probably also wanted the chance to confirm that she'd known nothing about it and share with Celia her crossness with Bill for keeping the whole ghastly business a secret. Celia understood this; there was probably nothing wrong with Judy wanting to hear more, nor her desire to proclaim her own ignorance of the affair. Celia did not blame her, either, for hoping to be her confidante, party to whatever details Celia was willing to divulge. It was just that Celia didn't want to discuss it any more, not with Annabel or Anne, not with Pippa and Dan, least of all with Judy, whose energetic expressions of sympathy would be most likely to turn the heat up on her anger again, rather than helping to cool it down.

She arranged for them to meet on the Thursday. In the meantime, there genuinely *were* other pressing demands on her time. The new book by Isabella Girotti was at the design stage and they were working with a cover designer whose initial mock-ups were underwhelming, to say the least – clichéd images of Tuscan landscapes with cypress trees and undulating ochre hills coupled with a choice of font that would not have looked out of place on a cover from the 1990s. He'd come with high recommendations from a friend at another publishing house and a portfolio of modish covers under his belt, but this one, frankly, was well below par. Perhaps she hadn't briefed him well enough, or maybe she hadn't sufficiently taken into account the fact that he'd only ever done non-fiction before, rather than high-end literary novels. She was either going to have to ditch him and start from scratch, or he was going to have to make some pretty swift and radical changes.

Dora would not be pleased. Now that she was back at work and giving off strong signals that her marriage and home life were back on track, Celia was, unfortunately, also fair game for Dora's undivided critical attention. She was quickly reminded of the joys of Dora's idiosyncratic management style, where every detail was pored over and deliberated upon, and where decisions made one day were altered on a whim the next. Perhaps, if things continued to go smoothly at home, Celia might consider responding to that approach from her old colleague Michael Dodd, who had just set up a new independent publishing house and been keen to poach her. Why not? If Dora was going to be so difficult, micro-managing everything she did, and Michael's offer still held, why shouldn't she have an exciting new adventure at the end of her career, helping to give birth to Dodd & Co? Michael had promised her a free hand with the literary-fiction list, admittedly in return for a rather reduced salary while the venture was in its initial phase. Before all the problems blew up with Marina, she'd talked it through with Nick and reluctantly decided against – it seemed too precarious at this stage in their lives to lose the security of Atlas and a dependable salary – but now her mood had changed. If life was so bloody unpredictable, why not take a risk of her own and free herself from Dora's oppressive iron grip?

The children were also taking up her time and thoughts. Pippa had talked to her just before the party about plans for her wedding. She'd held off suggesting a date while things had been so awful between her parents, but now that they seemed to be back on an even keel, she and Jamie were hoping to make firm decisions about timings and start letting people know. The beginning of May was the favoured option. Celia had been delighted to hear that they had already been investigating venues and had come up with the idea of an old converted barn in Sussex – large enough to hold plenty of people but not overly formal and much less conventional than a typical hotel wedding. That kind of glitzy affair just didn't really appeal to either of them; their friends would appreciate something more quirky and cool. Nor, thankfully, did a big, expensive hotel wedding appeal to Celia or Nick and their purses, so Celia entered into the discussions with energy and genuine enthusiasm, promising immediate help with the printing and design of the invitations and assistance with the search for a good catering firm in the locality.

Meanwhile Dan, in a rare moment of neediness, was also, rather unusually, wanting her attention. Despite his air of independence and unflappability, he too had clearly been shaken by seeing the family set-up teetering on the brink of collapse and was now having his own little wobble. He popped over one evening to talk to her and Nick about the fact that he'd been thinking of giving up his job and travelling for a year, a round-the-world trip to South-East Asia, New Zealand and Australia, ending up in South America and the Caribbean.

'My God, Dan, I'd think twice about that!' Celia had said. 'Your job's been brilliant and you've always said how much you love it. There are no guarantees you'd find something anything like as good when you got back, certainly not in this economic climate.'

Nick was more cautiously positive in his response. 'It sounds very exciting and I can see the attractions. But would you go on your own, or would Lottie go with you?'

'I don't think she'd want to leave her job,' Dan said. 'She'd love to come too but she feels like she's just beginning to get her head round the teaching and she has a lovely class that she can carry on with next year, so I think she's decided against.'

Nick shook his head. 'In that case, I'd think hard before doing it. Being away from Lottie for a year, that's a real risk. If she's important to you, which I think she is, you need to consider that.'

Celia wondered if Nick was thinking of himself as he said it, warning Dan to take his relationship seriously, value it properly and not endanger it, but Dan did not seem to have noticed that angle. He just nodded. He was feeling seriously torn, he said, but if he didn't do it now, there might never be another chance. He blushed.

'Another year or two and Lottie and I might be properly hitched and wanting kids and then it'd be impossible. We've talked it through and she's cool about it. We've agreed that she'd come out and join me during the school holidays, so we wouldn't be away from each other for very long.'

'And the job?' Celia asked, anxiously.

'They haven't exactly promised, but they've hinted that there might well be something for me when I get back. It's a risk, but I think it's worth taking.'

'It sounds like you've decided already,' Celia replied.

Dan smiled nervously. 'It does sound like that, doesn't it . . . but actually I'm nervous as hell and I don't want to do something stupid that I come to regret. I want you to give me your blessing and tell me it'll all be fine.'

'We can't promise it'll all be fine,' Nick said, laughing. 'But of course we'll give you our blessing, won't we?'

He looked at Celia. She swallowed hard. 'Of course we will. And if you decide to go, we'll be there for Lottie if she needs us. I can't say I'm not worried for you, but as your father says, it sounds very exciting.'

Dan's face instantly brightened. 'Thanks so much! I'll go away and think it through before I finally decide, but you've been a big help, both of you.' He came and gave them a hug. 'I'm so glad you're OK again, you two. You make a brilliant team!'

On Wednesday evening, Celia looked in her diary and realised that she was meeting Judy the following day.

'Do you think I can put her off?' she asked Nick. 'I've got a really busy day. And anyway, I'm not sure I can face her.'

'It's up to you,' Nick said. 'But if it's because of me and you and wanting to avoid talking to her about that, perhaps it'd be better just to get it over with.'

'You haven't exactly been rushing to see Bill.'

'That's different. Bill and I aren't close in the same way. We "do" things, like playing poker or tennis. We don't talk!'

'Did you ever talk to him about Marina?'

'I didn't talk to *anyone* about Marina. I was too embarrassed and ashamed and afraid of being found out. I stupidly thought it was a secret that no one knew anything about.'

'A secret from everyone, except half of Buntings! Presumably Marina was less circumspect. She certainly told that Lavinia woman all about you.'

Nick placed his hands on her shoulders and looked at her hard.

'I don't think this conversation is going to take us anywhere helpful,' he said. 'So let's decide not to have it.'

She looked back at him, hesitating for a moment. It could go either way; it was in her hands to decide. She took a deep breath.

'You're right,' she said. 'Let's talk about nice things, like our daughter's wedding and our son's adorable sweetness with us. I'll follow your excellent advice and go ahead with seeing Judy tomorrow, though I'm going to make it quite clear to her that I don't want her raking through our affairs – that's our business, not hers!'

'You tell her!' Nick said, laughing.

It was a cold day, with a fierce, driving wind, and Celia was glad to get into the steamy warmth of Marco's Café. She'd met Judy just outside, the two of them approaching at almost the same time, from different directions. They sat down at a small, rather rickety wooden table in the corner, well away from the draughts of the open door and the long queue of people waiting for their takeaway baps, toasted ciabatta or polystyrene tubs of minestrone. Marco brought them over their food. Celia had chosen Marco's homemade ravioli with ragù, Judy a simple mushroom omelette and chips.

'A proper meal today, eh?' Marco said. 'Not just your usual sandwich?'

'I take credit for that,' Judy said. 'I persuaded her to meet me for lunch.'

'Good idea,' Marco said. 'These business people, always in a hurry, rushing in, grabbing their takeaway lunches and straight back to work. Not good for the digestion! A nice, slow Italian lunch everyday – a good plate of pasta – that's what she needs!'

Celia laughed. 'Tell that to Dora, next time she's in, Marco! Explain to her that she's working me too hard and she needs to give me a proper lunch break.'

Now that the food had arrived and Marco had scuttled off back behind the counter, quick pre-emptive action was necessary, Celia thought. She'd have to take the initiative and get in fast before Judy got going.

'Look, Judy, it's lovely to see you, but I want to say before we go any further that I'm not very keen to talk about Nick and me. I want to put all that behind us and talking about it constantly churns things up for me again. So let's just chat about other things. I'm sure we won't run out – Alicia Campion alone could keep us going all day!'

'She's quite a character, isn't she?' Judy said. 'Some people might think *I'm* a bit OTT, but she puts me in the shade!'

'Poor Lottie looked mortified at the party. Having your mother behaving like that must be quite a trial.'

'I like her hugely, though, don't you? She's got spunk. She'll be a great addition to your family, if Dan and Lottie decide to tie the knot.'

'He seems to be taking an awful long time getting round to it, if you ask me. They've been together for such a long time and now he's talking about possibly going abroad for a year – a kind of late-in-the-day gap year or something. Though he hinted that perhaps at some point after that they might settle down properly, even mentioned kids, so perhaps eventually . . .'

'You and Nick lived together for years, though, didn't you, before you got married? You weren't in any great hurry to make it legal. In fact, I seem to remember you being rather sheepish about the whole thing, as if it didn't fit with your radical values.'

'Well it didn't! Weren't most of us pretty negative about marriage as an institution in those days? It was jolly embarrassing when Nick and I decided that the piece of paper was worth something after all, so we kept it hush-hush, opted for a quick ceremony in the register office just down the road and a small family lunch in a posh restaurant off Upper Street. Done and dusted with hardly any fuss. I didn't even tell my work colleagues or invite a single one of my friends. I don't think even you and Bill knew, did you, till a good few months later? But nowadays, these young people seem to take weddings a lot more seriously. All Dan's close friends from school and uni have got spliced in grand style!'

'Celia . . .' Judy was looking at her intently. She was fiddling with the stack of paper napkins on the table, moving the wooden holder backwards and forwards in her hand. 'I know you said you didn't want to talk about you and Nick and . . . whatever's happened. Fair enough. I get that. Totally. I don't want to intrude. You're just trying to get your life back together again and you don't want loud-mouthed, bossy old Judy barging in.' She paused. 'But there is something I want to talk to you about, around this whole . . . business. I don't know whether I should . . . perhaps it's not right . . . but . . .'

Celia put down her fork. Suddenly she didn't feel very hungry any more.

'Christ, Judy! I thought I made myself perfectly clear. I don't want to tell you anything and I don't want to hear anything. I mean it.'

'OK. I'll stop.'

There was a long silence. Judy was playing annoyingly with a paper napkin, shredding it into little pieces.

'For God's sake, Judy. It's too late now – you've made it clear that there's something you want to say. Whatever it is, just get it over with and then we can go back to the normal chit-chat, about children and holidays and the terrific books we've been reading. Then after that, I can return to my desk and focus on my problems with my designer, and the delay at the printer's and my difficult author and my demanding boss and all those other nice, easy, uncomplicated distractions.' She was surprised at how her temper had flared, at how angry she sounded.

Judy sat quietly, not saying anything. She looked pale and anxious.

'I'm sorry, Judy,' Celia said eventually, rather more gently. 'I'm a bit fragile, that's all. You must understand that. I'm not usually so sharp with people, nor so melodramatic.'

'Of course. Absolutely. I don't know what I was thinking of.'

'But you do have something to say?'

'Perhaps another time.'

'If there's something . . .'

Judy sat forward in her chair. Celia saw that she was struggling to hold back the tears.

'It's just . . . I don't think you'd forgive me if I didn't say something . . . You'd feel betrayed, if you thought I knew and hadn't said anything. It may be nothing at all – just a silly rumour – you know how these things come from nowhere and disappear again – Chinese whispers and all that . . . If you heard it from someone else – or didn't hear it at all . . . At least this way you can talk to Nick and ask him straight out – clear it up straightaway . . .'

Celia pushed her plate of pasta away from her. She felt the colour drain from her face; her hands trembled.

'He's seeing her again – is that it? He's been lying to me and he's taken up with her again? Is that what you're about to tell me?'

Judy looked aghast. 'No, no. Oh my God, Celia, no. That's not it at all. He hasn't been anywhere near her, from what I've been told. Bill says she's been distraught, beside herself. He made it perfectly clear to her that it was over, finally, absolutely, once and for all. He told her that saving his marriage came before anything else. No, he's definitely not been seeing her.'

'Thank God for that!' Celia sobbed. 'That's the most important thing. Nothing else matters.' She laughed out loud and wiped away her tears with her hand. 'You had me worried for a moment.'

And then Judy told her. Just a rumour . . . something that one of the other women solicitors in the office had said to Bill's PA, who passed it on to Bill.

'It's probably complete nonsense,' Judy said. 'But I thought you should know.'

'Thank you,' Celia replied, her voice barely above a whisper. 'I'd better get back to the office now – I have a meeting at 2 p.m.'

'I'm so sorry to have upset you like this.'

'No, I'm grateful to you,' Celia said, clenching her teeth to stop herself from crying or shouting or howling like a woman in a Greek tragedy mourning the cruel intervention of fate or the vicious acts of the gods who used mere mortals as their playthings. She could so easily throw herself down on the floor in Marco's Café and howl and wail till she was hoarse and not stop to care that the businessmen and PAs, the computer analysts and designers, the shop assistants and bank clerks on their lunch breaks would see a fifty-seven-year-old woman tearing her hair and ripping her clothes and ululating at a table in the corner of the café, and wonder why.

Celia pulled her coat on and, outside the café, quickly kissed Judy goodbye. Without turning back to look at her, she half ran back to the office, where she was already late for her two o'clock meeting. She would need to go straight to the toilet, wash her face and put on some make-up, then hurry upstairs to the conference room where Dora and the designer would be waiting for her, looking repeatedly at their watches and wondering where the hell she was. After the meeting, she had already decided, she would ring Nick at his office, and then she would go straight home.

Chapter 18

Judy had been calling and leaving messages on the answerphone all afternoon and early evening but Celia, sitting face to face opposite Nick at the kitchen table in fraught conversation for what seemed like hours on end, had chosen to ignore her calls. Annabel too had been trying to make urgent contact, perhaps tipped off by Judy that all was not well. When Pippa phoned later that evening, however, she had picked up, interrupting a particularly painful exchange with Nick. She had forced herself to sound cheery, directing the talk back to the wedding, and Pippa, full of excitement about the planning, had been too self-absorbed to notice that anything was wrong.

In the early hours of the morning, with both of them exhausted and tearful, Nick had finally gone to bed and she had found herself sitting in the kitchen on her own. She had a sudden desire to speak to Paul. She pulled her mobile phone out of her bag and started flicking through her texts to find the last one he had sent her. She read back through all of them, a handful of simple, unemotional messages revealing nothing, just confirming arrangements while she'd been in Paris. Neutral, detached, bland. Should she text him and ask him to call? But what would she say? It would be irresponsible to involve him a second time in her troubles. She had no clear plan, or thought of what he might be able to do, but nevertheless, foolish or not, the urge to talk to him was there.

At last she went to bed, slept fitfully beside Nick, aware of his restlessness, conscious of her own, and after a brief period of intermittent dozing and bad dreams, woke up early to find that he'd already got up quietly and gone off to work. He had left a draft email printed out from his computer, propped up on the kitchen table. It had a Post-it note stuck to it, in an incongruous shade of fluorescent pink. It said, 'Couldn't sleep. Got up and wrote this. Won't send it till you've said what you think. Hope you got some sleep. XXX Nick.'

She read the first sentence of the email, then pushed the piece of paper away to the far end of the table, leaving the rest unread. She made herself a cup of black coffee. Could she face eating anything for breakfast? She thought not. She picked up the newspaper to scan through the front-page stories, but after a few minutes realised that she hadn't taken anything in, not a single word of it.

It was still only 7.40 a.m. There would be time for a quick walk over to Parliament Hill to clear her head before having to get ready for work. Luckily her first meeting with one of her established writers had been cancelled so she didn't have to be in till ten thirty. She went back upstairs and pulled on some jeans, a warm fleece and trainers, then grabbed her old duffle coat from the stand in the hall and went out.

At Parliament Hill, the tennis courts were deserted, the nets wound down, a layer of light frost coating the playing surface like icing sugar. A few men and women, most of them young, were running, breath from their mouths hitting the cold air like trails of warm smoke from a pipe. They wore shorts or tracksuits, had earphones and didn't look up at her or anything else, entirely focused on the job at hand, their early-morning exercise regime. They seemed not to notice the crisply frozen grass, the fine layer of mist hovering over the land, the thin, veiled sunlight appearing on the hill, slowly edging away the last shadows of night. Did any of these people have problems like hers?

As bad, or worse? Were any of them, like her, out there in the park after a sleepless night, grappling with sadness or grief, desperately trying to banish overwhelming despair? The pretty young woman with the ponytail and huge fluffy white muffs over her ears looked cheerful enough, as did the middle-aged man with the thinning hair and large paunch, wheezing slowly up the hill towards the viewing point at the top. The elderly woman in the padded khaki jacket walking her spaniel was smiling, as was the chap in the wellies with the Labrador who stopped to chat with her; they were obviously enjoying swapping tales of Bobby's and Toto's latest humorous escapades with puddles, pigeons and other dogs.

A couple jogging past caught her eye. They looked the same sort of age as Dan and Lottie and were running together, side by side, chatting to each other and laughing along the way. As they left the flat ground and started to climb the hill, the young man was clearly making better progress, more easily able to pick up speed and take the ascent in his stride but, within minutes of pulling ahead, he had stopped and turned to wait for his companion. Chivalrous, she thought. Caring. She placed their chances of a successful long-term relationship high, though of course, for all she knew, he might be having a secret affair with her best friend, and she might have already decided that he wasn't the one for her. The body language said different, but who could really tell? These things were so 'random', as Pippa and Dan and their friends would say, so impossible to predict. If she'd had to lay bets over the years, she'd have always said that the odds on her and Nick going through the marital misery of the past couple of months were extremely low. Yet here she was, walking on her own up Parliament Hill, aware that her marriage, once again, was in serious danger, that this might well be her future life: solitary strolls along paths she had always seen through his eyes as well as her own.

At the top of the hill, she stood for a moment, looking out over the skyline of London, stretched out below in the early-morning mist. She could just about make out the faraway outline of the city's old churches and new skyscrapers. A changing landscape. The Gherkin and the Shard were already stale, worn-out talking points, edifices that had become an accepted part of the city's history; now it was the Cheesegrater and the Walkie-Talkie that were the subject of fierce debate. She couldn't help wishing for a slower pace of change. She'd been coming up this hill and standing on this spot for all her adult life and most of her childhood, and the view had hardly altered at all during the greatest part of that time. Looking out over London had always made her catch her breath; there was that obvious sense of wonder at a whole city spread out before you but also a strong feeling of connection with its past, an intimation of something that endures well beyond you and your own lifetime, reminding you of your place in the scheme of things. From a distance, with the landmark of St Paul's just visible, you could imagine that that's what it would have looked like, more or less, give or take, not just in your own lifetime but for all those earlier generations who trod up the same path to the top of this same hill. Old certainties were important, weren't they? There was a lot of value in the familiar, a lot to fear in the new. Or perhaps that was just how she was feeling right now, scrabbling around looking for something secure to latch onto in her external surroundings, when her inner world was failing her so catastrophically.

She sat on the bench for as long as she could, before the cold really got to her, drilling deep down into her bones and making her fingers go numb. Then she got up and walked briskly back down the hill, past the tennis courts, crossing the main road at the traffic lights and then hurrying along Lady Somerset Road, till she reached home.

After showering, drying her hair, putting on her work clothes and make-up, choosing a scarf and earrings, sorting through the papers she needed to take into the office with her, there was nothing else for it; she really would have to read the damn email.

Wearily she went down to the kitchen. She sat down, reached across the table and drew it towards her:

Dear Marina,

I hope that you are well. I understand that you've left London and have a job in a new firm. I hope that's suiting you and that you're coping with things better than when I last saw you. As you're aware, I'm very sorry for the hurt I've caused, both to you and Celia.

I know I said we would not be able to have any contact with each other but I feel that I need to get in touch for a particular reason. I have heard some rumours via Bill and Judy and I would like to know whether they are true or not. If you say they are, then perhaps we should meet to discuss what to do.

As you can imagine I am feeling rather worried, so would appreciate a quick response.

I should say that I am emailing you with Celia's knowledge.

Nick

Did it do what was needed? In some ways perhaps it did, but it was too friendly, low key and lacking in any real sense of urgency; obviously feeling squeamish, he hadn't even been able to bring himself to say what the rumours were. Perhaps it was sensitivity towards Marina, or maybe an unwillingness to say it in print and so make it into a reality, she couldn't really say which.

She picked up a pen and found a sheet of blank paper in the drawer under the table. She started writing in a large, scrawling script:

Dear Marina,

Judy has told Celia there's a rumour that you are pregnant and are claiming it's mine. Is this true? If so, this is worrying news for all of us. I wonder how far into the pregnancy you are? We need to discuss your intentions and my situation in relation to any decisions you take. I feel that I have a right to be told what's happening and to be consulted about the best course of action. Celia is, naturally, like me, extremely worried about all of this. We would both appreciate a quick response from you.

Yours,

Nick

Better than Nick's own effort, she thought. More direct and firm. At least her version cut to the chase and stated the issues. His email suggested meeting Marina; hers did not, though in reality she thought that couldn't be avoided. Unless Marina got back to them instantly with a flat denial, there were going to have to be discussions, either with Nick on his own, or with Celia too, she wasn't sure which. It didn't bear thinking about, any of it.

When she'd told Nick Judy's news, he had put his head in his hands and moaned, like an animal in pain. She herself had cried profusely at first but then, when the tears stopped, she had got angry, sworn at him and repeated all the things she'd said when they'd first talked at Anne's kitchen table in St Albans, a rerun of all the hurt and blame. Late into the evening, they had gone through the implications, as calmly as they could despite the inescapable, rising sense of panic that came with thinking about what it might mean if Judy's stories were true.

'I can't force her to get rid of it, you know.'

'Of course not. It may be too late anyway. Given the timings she may well be too far advanced, even if she wanted to end it . . . or were prepared to take your views into account. What's her thinking on babies? Do you know?'

He'd groaned. 'She's in her late thirties. What do you think?'

'She's said that to you?'

'She sometimes hinted at it. Not often, just occasionally, when she was worrying about where our relationship was going. She reminded me that her biological clock was ticking.'

'For fuck's sake, Nick!'

'I know, I know. I was always clear, though, that whatever happened, I didn't want children. She knew that. It was part of the deal.'

'Doesn't mean to say that she wouldn't ignore that, though, does it? People break deals. If she wants children enough, perhaps she decided to override your wishes . . . just not tell you – or hope that it'd force you to go back to her. Who the hell knows?'

'No, she's not like that. I can't believe she'd use something like that to blackmail me emotionally. If it's true that she's pregnant, then it must have been a mistake, not part of a big scheme.'

'You're too trusting. There are plenty of women who would play that game.'

As she said it, she felt the irony of her words. She'd always been sympathetic to women in this situation; she'd supported a woman's right to choose; she'd marched under that banner in her twenties; she regarded herself as a feminist, for Christ's sake! And yet, now, with Nick, with Marina . . .

Nick was silent. He didn't point out the contradictions, though he was probably just as aware of them as she was; he knew her views on these things. Or maybe he was reflecting on how naïve he had actually been – looking back on events, perhaps, and trying to recall whether they'd been careless, whether Marina had been responsible for taking precautions, or he had been, how such a catastrophic mistake could have occurred and whether it was plausibly an act of will on her part. Whatever it was, Celia would rather not know.

'If she goes ahead, there'll be a child of yours out there in the world. Your flesh and blood. Just think about it. Either you'll have to promise never to see it, or have anything to do with it, and forget that it exists. Or you'll have to be involved with it – you'll have to *be* its father. And that will mean you being connected closely to her, too – making arrangements to see the child, going along to its first nativity play, its first concert, attending parent-teacher evenings together, picking it up from her house on weekends. And what about the holidays? They'd be with me, would they? You and me and the baby – who's actually got nothing to do with me, who's not *my* flesh and blood, whom I didn't want or ask for, who would remind me every day of the week of your sodding relationship with its mother, the woman with whom you cheated on me. We'd take it on those holidays, would we, the ones we were planning for our retirement, to New Zealand or the Far East or China? Good places to take a baby? A toddler? And that's just the start of it. We'd invite Marina and your baby to come along to Pippa's wedding, would we? To our New Year's Day party every year? To my sixtieth birthday? Bloody hell, Nick, I'm not sure I'm willing to do all of that. I'm not sure I'm willing to do *any* of that.'

'So what are you saying? That if she's planning on going ahead with the pregnancy, I should have no involvement. Is it as clear-cut as that?'

'I don't know.'

'A child of mine, like Pippa or Dan, a part of me no less than they are, but denied the chance to know me or for me to know it. A complete abdication of my responsibility as a father. Knowing that it's being brought up by someone else, without any relationship to me. That's pretty appalling, don't you think?'

'Yes, it *is* appalling. You're absolutely right. That's why it's all such a total disaster.'

'Do you not think we'd find a way to accommodate all of this?'

'What do you mean?'

'If it came to it, if she is pregnant, if she does have the child, wouldn't we find a way of making it work?'

'What do you think?' she had said.

'If it meant saving our relationship, yes. We'd have to make it work.'

She had remained silent at first and then finally asked him, 'Do you think we could survive all that?'

'I don't know. I certainly hope so.'

She hadn't replied.

Finally, exhausted and both needing sleep, they'd agreed that he'd have to contact Marina urgently to find out for certain whether the rumours were true. There was no point in discussing things further until they knew for sure; there was still the smallest sliver of hope that the rumour mill of the legal firm had been working overtime, with little truth in the stories that were doing the rounds.

Now, looking at the reworked email once more, she wondered what Nick would make of it when he saw it. Would he baulk at the tough tone, or recognise the sense in taking a firm line from the start? Whatever was decided, they needed to get something to Marina quickly; there was no time to lose. She folded it and put it into her bag; she would type it up straightaway when she got to work and email it over to Nick to reach him at his office as soon as possible.

She was just about to lock up and walk down to the Tube when the phone rang. She looked at the number on the screen. It was Lionel. She hesitated. The last person she wanted to speak to. She moved towards the front door but then, at the last minute, changed her mind. She'd better pick up.

'Celia? Thank God you're still there. I'm locked out. I went out to get the newspaper from the shop on Fortis Green Road and I forgot my keys. The newsagent has helped me find your number on my phone – you know what I'm like with these new mobile contraptions and what with being upset, I got flustered and I just couldn't remember how to find it. Anyhow, he's found it for me now and he's letting me wait here till you come. Can you bring your keys over, so I can get into the house?'

Christ. What next? She'd just about have time if she took the car, left it parked in his drive, and went straight into work from there, rather than coming back home first.

'Of course. I'll come over right now. But I won't be able to stay – I've got work today.'

'Thank you. I don't know how I did it. Bloody idiotic!'

'It's OK, Daddy. It's just one of those things that we all do sometimes.'

When she reached him, he was sitting on a stool in the corner of the shop waiting for her, surrounded by piles of newspapers and magazines, fizzy drinks and unpacked boxes of chocolate bars. As she took his arm to help him up she realised that he was trembling all over.

'Oh Daddy, you're really upset!'

'How could I be such a stupid fool?'

She gave him a quick hug.

'Is this what it's going to be like from now on? Me being a complete nuisance to you? Driving you mad? I don't want to be a constant worry to you, honestly I don't. You have your own life to lead.'

'This isn't so terrible, Daddy. Try to keep it in proportion. You just forgot your keys.'

He sighed. 'I suppose so, but I worry that this is just the beginning. There's only one thing we know for sure and that's that it's not going to get better – it can only get worse.'

She drove him back to his house and let him in, then told him she'd have to go.

'I'll be back around six, to collect the car,' she said.

'Can you stay to talk to me then?' There was a slight pleading tone in his voice that she'd never heard before.

'Sorry, Daddy. I need to get back home early this evening – I've got things I need to talk to Nick about. But perhaps on the weekend I can come over and see you properly?'

He looked disappointed.

'It's been a busy week. I'm snowed under. Tomorrow or Sunday would be best, really it would. I'll see if Svetlana has any time today to come and give you a bit of a hand with things – check that you've got what you need.'

He shook his head. 'I'm fine. I don't need help. Let your Svetlana get on with her usual work, rather than bothering with someone like me. Tomorrow, then. You'll come and see me then?'

'I'll come and see you then. In the morning, if that suits you. Say 11 a.m.?' As she reached the front door she called back, 'Write it down, like Dr Caldicott suggested, so you don't forget.'

'What was that, Marje?' he shouted.

'Oh, never mind.' She would call him the next morning, before setting out, to remind him, just in case.

It was only as she was opening the car to take out her briefcase that it registered with her; he had called her Marje, her mother's name. Dr Caldicott had been right to insist that she come along to his appointment; it was clear that he was beginning to struggle with things. She walked to the Tube station with a heavy heart.

Chapter 19

Nick had sent the email more or less as she'd drafted it, with just a slight softening of the rather brutal first line. Even she agreed that, given the circumstances, something a little kinder was called for. The negotiations over the wording had taken place in quick-fire Send and Reply exchanges while they were both at work, supposedly attending to business, so there had been little space for lengthy, agonised discussion.

The day at the office had been busy: Dora was in a rage about a typo on the second page of a new novel by one of her favourite authors and demanded an instant post-mortem meeting on what had gone wrong; Celia was still struggling with her new designer, whose second efforts still didn't make the mark; then, to cap it all, an author she'd been so delighted to attract to the Atlas list just a couple of years back had rung for a long conversation about taking her next manuscript elsewhere, to a bigger, more prestigious publishing house. Still, it was good to be occupied and focused on work issues, however problematic, rather than brooding on the more deeply troubling events at home.

But then, that evening, on Nick's return from work, she had to face it all again. He told her about the reply that had come back from Marina – a simple confirmation that the rumours were true, that she had left London partly for that reason, and that her thinking was that she would go ahead and have the baby, regardless of whether he might wish to play a role in the upbringing of the child or not. He told Celia that there was some more 'upsetting stuff' in the email and asked her whether she wanted to see it.

'What kind of upsetting stuff?'

He pulled his hand through his hair and groaned. 'Her feelings for me, how she'd like to see me, how she's still hoping that I might change my mind.'

'And have you?'

'What?'

'Changed your mind?'

Now he looked straight at her, holding her gaze.

'No. Of course not.'

'I don't think I want to read the upsetting stuff, thanks. It's all horrible enough as it is.'

He nodded. 'I just wanted you to know that I'm not hiding anything from you. You can see it all, if you want to.'

'I appreciate that,' she said, softly. 'I can see you're trying to do what's right, what's best.'

'She wants to meet me to talk.'

'You'll have to go,' Celia said. 'That's obvious. And it'll have to be without me, I suppose.' A pause. 'What are you going to say?'

He looked at her pleadingly, as if looking to her for the answers. Clearly, he had none himself.

'Will you try to persuade her not to go ahead with it, assuming of course that it's not too late?'

There was a long silence. He raised his hands and looked up to the ceiling in a gesture of despair, or perhaps rather as a final, last-ditch appeal to a God she knew he had long stopped believing in, to provide him with a path through these troubles. The God of his Catholic childhood would have been more likely to point a furious finger of judgement at him than offer him any comfort. Adultery and now the contemplation of the murder of an unborn child – both of these cardinal sins would have consigned him to a fiery pit that could hardly be much worse than the hell both of them were going through now.

Celia saw how haggard he looked, his face pale and thinner than usual, his eyes ringed with the dark marks of sleeplessness.

'I don't know what I should do. Look at it from Marina's point of view. She's in her late thirties, she wants kids, this is her chance and she might not get another. If it were Pippa in a similar situation, getting to the point where it might be too late for a family, what would you feel? Have I got the right to try to make her give that up, because it puts me into an awful bloody mess? But if she goes ahead with it, everything you say is true – there'll be a child of mine out there in the world. I don't want a child. I don't want all those parental responsibilities. I've been there and done that. I'm too old for any more of it. And you don't want it either. Why should you? You didn't ask for any of this. I get all of that. Completely. I get that it wouldn't be fair on you and that maybe you couldn't accept it. But I honestly don't know whether I could just walk away from some kind of connection with the child. Once it's born, it'd be there, growing up. I'd know it was mine.'

'I can't tell you what to do, Nick. And I can't tell you for sure what it means for you and me either. You'll have to go and see her and find out how determined she is to have the baby. Then, we'll see ...'

He nodded.

She hesitated, and then she said, cautiously, 'I'm not going to say anything to Annabel, or the kids, or anyone else just yet. I think we should keep this quiet till we know more. There's no point in upsetting the children or having people gossiping at the moment. I'll ask Judy to keep her mouth shut, though whether she will is anyone's guess.'

There was little more to be said. He went to the kitchen to make them some food, even though she said she wasn't hungry. She sat in the living room on her own, going back over what had been said, replaying the conversation in different ways and wondering if there could have been a different outcome. She thought not. Nick would go to see Marina. He would, more likely than not, have it finally confirmed that the pregnancy would go ahead. For his own sense of what was fair, he would probably end up agreeing to play some kind of role as father, and knowing him, probably he would become more deeply involved than he might like to think he would; his life would become ever more closely entangled with that of Marina. Could she accept that? As things stood at the moment, she thought not. He'd have to make his new family and she – and now she felt the tears coming and the solid lump in her throat – she might end up having to make a new life of her own.

She had a sudden impulse to text Paul and speak to him, to find out what he thought she should do. He could have been in the same situation as Nick, at some stage in his life, given his many relationships with women, perhaps well used to living through traumas such as these. It wouldn't altogether surprise her if Paul had an unacknowledged child somewhere in the background, from one of his various affairs. She felt that she needed to speak to him urgently, to tell him about it and to hear his views.

She'd text him sometime the next day, she thought, not there and then. She needed a bit of space to think first, to be sure that it was the right thing to do. She felt nervous about what she would say and apprehensive about hearing his voice again. She wondered what his reaction would be. And then, of course, what would Nick think if he found out? It almost certainly wasn't a sensible thing to do.

Nick called her from the kitchen. He had made them scrambled eggs on toast and a tomato salad, which they ate – or in her case failed to eat – in silence. Afterwards, she cleared the table and filled the dishwasher; he went up to his study without saying anything while she remained sitting in the kitchen, flicking through the newspaper, unable to take in even the boldest headlines.

Sod it, she thought, and got out her mobile phone. Before she could change her mind she had written the text and sent it.

'I'd like to talk to you. Suggest a time that's good for you. Celia.'

She put the phone on the table. Almost immediately there was the bleep bleep of a text arriving back. Christ, that was quick. Would Nick have heard? Surely not, in his study one flight up. He probably had the door shut anyway. No doubt he'd be busy emailing Marina to make the arrangement to go and see her, working out what he wanted to say to her. She picked up the phone, her blood pulsing fearful and fast. It wasn't from Paul at all, but from Dan, saying that he'd finally made his decision; he'd be giving up the job and doing the world tour. It was full of exclamation marks and excited 'wow's and 'thank you's for help in deciding. Celia hoped to goodness he was doing the right thing. She texted back straightaway, with something calmer and more enthusiastic than she was actually feeling, wishing him luck and asking him to drop round sometime for a chat.

Now she found her brain leaping forward six months. Dan would be halfway round the world in Thailand or

Cambodia, Pippa married to Jamie and off doing her own thing, Nick would be gone, established in a new life with Marina and his child, while she was left in the big empty house in Kentish Town all on her own, her children having grown up and away, deserted by her husband. She saw herself sitting in this same spot, at the kitchen table, with her happy family life having turned to dust. She began to feel dizzy, her skin cold and clammy, as if at any moment she might faint. She poured herself a glass of water and sipped it slowly, then splashed water on her face from the tap, to try to calm herself. She would have to force herself to avoid such thoughts, or go completely and utterly mad.

There was no response to her text from Paul that evening. When Nick finally came downstairs to say he was going to bed, Celia had turned her phone to silent. He'd emailed Marina, he said, but hadn't yet got a reply. There was a certain symmetry in this, Celia thought, Nick waiting to hear back from Marina, her awaiting a response from Paul. She almost told him but then, at the last minute, held back. The moment passed and another suitable one didn't seem to appear.

'I've suggested going over to see her, or meeting her somewhere in town, sometime tomorrow,' Nick said. 'Get it over with, rather than leaving it all hanging. That's if she's free, of course.'

Celia nodded but didn't say anything.

'We'll get through this, won't we, Celia?'

'Honestly, I don't know.'

'Are you coming upstairs to bed?'

'I think I'll sleep in the spare room.'

He hesitated a moment, as if to protest, but then just turned away and went upstairs without her.

The next morning, Celia woke in the spare room to the light flashing on her mobile phone. It was still quite dark outside, the winter morning barely shaking off the covers of night. She'd forgotten to close the curtains before getting into bed and she could just make out the shapes of the trees at the bottom of the garden, stirring in the wind. The rain fell steadily, angling in towards the house, missing the gutters and splashing onto the windowpanes. The pathetic fallacy. Rain pouring down in sympathy – or not. She thought probably not; sympathy seemed like the wrong word for the hostility of the world, its downright disregard for all that seemed fair.

She groped around on the bedside table and picked up her phone.

It was Paul. He'd only just got her message. Was everything OK? He could speak to her there and then, if she rang him back straightaway. Celia listened for stirrings in the house. She strained to hear sounds from the kitchen – Nick making an early-morning cup of tea, or going down to collect the Saturday *Guardian* from the doormat. She listened for movements from the next landing up, from their bedroom, the sound of the shower running, or of Nick opening the closets to pull out fresh clothes. She listened for the sound of the toilet in the hall. All was quiet.

She got out of bed and went to shut the door. Without switching on the light, she climbed back into bed, then scrolled down through the text to the Call button and pressed it.

He picked up immediately. At first hesitant, almost shy, they took a while to get through the preliminaries, the conventional 'how are you's that seemed so inappropriate and unnecessary when they both knew that she must have phoned for a very precise and urgent reason. She realised, with a sudden jolt of surprise, that he would have absolutely no idea why she had called and might be speculating about the possibilities. He might, of course, think that she was missing him and perhaps phoning because she wanted to see him again. She'd forgotten that while *she* wanted to talk to him about Nick and Marina, *he* might want to talk about him and her. And so it was. He started by telling her how terrible he'd felt after leaving her at the airport in Geneva; he said he'd been thinking about her a lot and had wanted to call but hadn't thought it fair to her or to Nick. He'd been worried about her but assumed that, somehow or other, she and Nick were finding a way through their difficulties. He talked rapidly, leaving few spaces for her to tell him what was on her mind. When she finally told him that Marina was pregnant, there was a deep intake of breath before he spoke.

'Is she going ahead with it?'

'We're not sure . . . but I can pretty much guess!'

'What about Nick?'

'He's feeling sorry for her and guilty and worried and not able to give me any clear answers. He says he doesn't want to lose me, absolutely swears that . . . but then he goes on to say he's not sure he can cut himself off from her completely if she has the baby. I can't help but wonder, whatever he says, if he still has feelings for her. A whole year he was seeing her . . .'

'And, given all this, what about you?'

'Oh God, what about me? I wish I knew. I thought you might tell me what to do, help me find a way through. I'm going crazy.'

'Shall I come over and see you? Would that help?'

'No, no, that would be silly . . . I'd like to see you, of course, but better not to.'

'I could cancel my lunch date with my friend Laurent, get on the Eurostar later this morning and be in London by early afternoon. We could meet up. If you like.'

'I don't know. What about Nick? What would I tell him?'

'It's up to you. Tell him or not, but I'd like to come.'

She could hear the sound of Nick's footsteps on the stairs and the door to the toilet opening, closing and being locked. He was awake and soon he'd be coming down to check on her, to see how she was. She would need to end the conversation quickly.

'Look, if you want to come . . .'

'Of course I do. What are friends for?'

They agreed that he would text her to let her know what time he'd be arriving, so that they could meet somewhere in town. She put the mobile back on the bedside table and pulled the duvet up around her body, turning her face towards the wall.

When Nick quietly opened the door to see if she was awake, she lay still. She sensed him there, in the doorway, watching her for a few moments, and then, when she'd waited a while, she finally opened her eyes and turned over. He had gone.

A little later, she got up, showered and dressed. By this time, he had already made his morning cup of coffee and his usual plate of toast and jam and had headed off to his study. She went into the kitchen, unable to face more than a cup of tea herself. She boiled the kettle, put the teabag in a mug and let it brew for a moment or two, then stood looking out of the kitchen window, sipping the tea slowly. Just as she was finishing the last dregs, Nick came downstairs and joined her.

'I've had a reply from Marina this morning. I'm going to go and see her this afternoon. I think I'll take the car rather than the train – it'll be quicker. Is that OK with you?'

She shrugged.

He came over to her and put his hands on her shoulders. 'You know this is the last thing I wanted. I want us to get back to normal.'

'I know,' she said and placed her hand tentatively on one of his. 'I know you regret all this. I know that.'

He looked at her. 'I hope we can get through this.'

She said nothing.

Afterwards, she wondered whether she should have said more, or said it differently, whether she was still in the frame of mind for punishing him, exacting a price for the pain he'd caused her. She asked herself whether she was really so unable to see how normal life could be picked up again, with such an impediment to their happiness, or whether she was simply in such a state of shock that emotion was marching forward and common sense stumbling, limping far behind. If she had understood her own feelings better, perhaps she could have offered him some reassurance that ultimately they would find a way through. But she couldn't. She didn't. Too many questions and no answers.

It was no good asking what others would do in the circumstances – what Annabel would do, or Dora, Mary and Evelyn, Alicia Campion, or the young people, Pippa, Daisy, Alex or Dan. No doubt they would all come up with a different set of questions and a different set of answers.

She felt that she had very little to draw on, compared with many of her friends, who, over the years, had had to cope with much more complexity in their love lives than her. But people's experience only seemed to hold true for them. It wasn't readily transferable. Annabel's everyday pragmatism got her through in her relationship with Charlie but, to Celia, it seemed full of gaping holes; she and Nick had often marvelled at how successfully they managed to plaster over the cracks and crevices that opened up with such regularity in their marriage. Mary, she knew, took a tolerant approach to Evelyn's occasional lapses; she'd once laughingly told her that Evelyn needed the constant excitement of a crush or flirtation but that she knew they would only ever be temporary and if she simply ignored them, they would never be a serious threat to their relationship. She had been absolutely right about that. Dora's cynical view of marriage as a financial arrangement might make good practical sense but it was not for her. And George clearly didn't have any answers; his divorce so many years back had been a brutal affair that seemed to have left him permanently scarred. As for Alicia Campion, she'd had such a string of men in her life that looking to her for any solutions would be unthinkable; she'd been lucky to get out of the relationship with Lottie's father with some financial security, but thereafter had managed to lurch from one dodgy man to another, losing her money and large chunks of her emotional stability along the way.

If any of these people were to advise her to stay with Nick, or leave him, to get relationship counselling, or reignite her affair with Paul, to stay in her home in Kentish Town, or go forthwith into a nunnery, she would listen with interest but be unable to follow their advice. In the end, they all took separate, different paths, and those paths seemed to have as much to do with their personalities and temperaments as with any deeper wisdom or knowledge. Couch it how they might, they acted from instinct, and, try as she may to search for her own justifications, or torture herself as she did about what was the most sensible course of action, she feared that she was exactly the same. Instinct prevailed – a hardwired set of emotional responses that rationality and pragmatism couldn't touch. Her silence and refusal to reassure Nick might not be the best way of handling things, but for the time being at least, that was all she could do. If meeting Paul at St Pancras was a stupid thing to do – as she feared it well might be – then she felt she had no choice but to be stupid.

Later that morning, as she was trying to distract herself with household chores – putting a load of washing in, tackling the enormous heap of ironing in the basket in the kitchen, doing a supermarket shop online, sorting out the post that had been accumulating on the table in the hall – the phone rang. It was Lionel.

'When are you coming over, Celia? You said you'd come and see me at 11. I've been waiting for you. It's after 12.00.'

'Oh God, Daddy! I'm so sorry. I completely forgot.'

'I wrote it down on my notepad. 11.a.m. '

'You're right, Daddy. It's just that I've been so busy, so preoccupied…' There was a little catch in her voice. If she weren't careful she would burst into tears. But she mustn't do that, on any account. 'I'll come straight over.'

She ran up the stairs to tell Nick. She wouldn't see him again before he set off to talk to Marina. For a moment they clung to each other, as if this might be their last chance to stand so close to one another, aware that the next few hours could change everything. She asked him to call to let her know when he'd be back. She didn't mention Paul.

Then she hurried downstairs, grabbed the keys to the small car from the hall table and drove, much faster than she should, straight to her father's house, where he would be waiting for her.

Chapter 20

Sitting in the car in Lionel's driveway, she got out her mobile phone to check for messages. A text had come through from Pippa, asking if Celia could pop over on Sunday evening to talk with her and Jamie about the wedding. There was another from Annabel, asking if everything was OK and suggesting a drink sometime the following week. And finally, there was a brief text from Paul, saying that he'd be getting into St Pancras at 14.39 English time and how about meeting at Searcys Brasserie in the station soon after that?

She looked at her watch. If she stayed an hour or so with Lionel, she would be able to get to St Pancras in plenty of time. She texted back to say yes. Then she rang Nick and left a short message on his voicemail telling him she'd be going on somewhere else after seeing Lionel. She didn't say where; he had preoccupations of his own and would be unlikely to ask. She had a moment's doubt, then decided that she'd already gone too far. She couldn't stop Paul coming – he was probably already on his way, on the train leaving the Gare du Nord – and she didn't want to complicate things even further by telling Nick. God, that was deceiving him, though, wasn't it? What would he think if he knew? But then she was only getting advice from Paul, wasn't she? That was fair enough, wasn't it, in the circumstances? Paul had insisted on coming. She couldn't say no. Now her anxieties shifted. She realised that she'd come out in a hurry, just as she was, leaping straight into the car to get to Lionel's, wearing jeans, a T-shirt, a woollen sweater and her duffle coat. Had she thought, she'd have dressed up a bit more. She was conscious of looking rather thin and wan, exhausted by the strains of the past few weeks. Searcys and Paul perhaps deserved rather better. But then she was only going to be talking to him, only asking for advice, so what did that really matter?

She got out of the car and rang on Lionel's bell. He came to the door quickly.

'Sitting out there in the car for a long time!' he said.

She blushed.

'Sorry, Daddy, I'm at sixes and sevens. A lot going on, I'm afraid.'

'Not like you to forget an arrangement. That's supposed to be my province these days.'

'I know. I feel awful. I really don't know how it happened.'

He examined her, with a penetrating gaze.

'You're not looking too good, my girl. Something up?'

Just for a split second she was tempted to tell him, to spill it all out. Perhaps he'd step up to the mark and play the role of loving father that he'd never quite managed up to now and she'd be glad to have shared it with him. But the reality was more likely to be that much more depressing, predictable one, involving Lionel railing against Nick and his shortcomings, and bombarding her with an endless fusillade of 'I told you so's.

'I'm fine, Daddy. Just a busy time at work and lots going on at home. Pippa's wedding and the discussions about Dan's trip have been taking their toll. You know how it is.' She wasn't sure whether he believed her or not, but he seemed happy enough to leave it at that.

He offered to make her something to eat. He'd already had an early lunch, he said – a cheese and tomato sandwich and some tinned fruit – but he could make something for her if she liked. She said she wasn't hungry and would get something later, but agreed to a cup of tea.

He took her into the kitchen. She hadn't been further than his hall and front room for a while and was shocked at the state of the place. Used plates were piled up on the worktops and dirty pans full of water spilled up over the edge of the sink, at all angles. A stack of old newspapers stood waist-high in a corner. On the kitchen table was a motley assortment of jars and cans: pots of jam, their sticky lids left off, a large empty jar of peanut butter, cans of tomatoes, some unopened, some used, their jagged lids gaping dangerously, a very ancient-looking jar of marmite, a loaf of white bread sweating unhealthily in a plastic bag. The floor looked positively alive with microbial activity – spills unmopped, odd bits of old vegetable peelings scattered near the unemptied bin, a large unidentifiable pile of something or other – who knows what? – near the cooker. The hob itself was deeply encrusted with burnt and reburnt food – it clearly hadn't been cleaned in months.

'Daddy,' she said gently, 'I really think I *should* ask Svetlana to come and give you a hand, if she has a bit of time.'

'I don't need it. I'm managing fine.'

'Nothing major or anything . . . just a little help every now and then, cleaning up and keeping the place in order.'

'Are you suggesting I'm not coping?'

'Not at all, Daddy. But –'

'I don't need help. I'm happy as I am.'

She shrugged. Lionel's stubbornness was legendary. It would take a lot more than this to shift him, but looking at the state of his kitchen she wondered how much longer she could allow him to continue in this way. She'd have to ring Barbara and see what she could do, though from so far away it seemed unlikely that even she would be able to break down his resistance.

'I'm keeping lists,' Lionel said. 'Maybe you should do the same. Then perhaps you'd remember your commitments, like promising to come to see me at eleven o'clock.'

She felt the blood rise to her face. 'I'm so sorry. It was one of those things. It just slipped my mind.'

'I'm writing everything down, like Dr Caldicott suggested. It seems to help.'

'That's good.'

The kettle had boiled. From somewhere in the depths of a cupboard, he pulled out a small packet of Tetley's tea bags and rummaged about in another for two clean cups. The milk from the fridge had a telltale clot of cream round the rim, as if it were on the turn. He poured a thick slug into each cup. It made her stomach heave. He bent down to open another cupboard and took out a half-eaten packet of digestive biscuits, which he put beside her on the table, pushing the jars of jam to one side.

'I had something I wanted to talk to you about,' he said.

She managed a quick glance at her watch, hoping he wouldn't notice. She'd have to think about leaving in another half hour or so, to be sure of getting to St Pancras in time.

'I've been meaning to talk to you about this for a long time.'

She took a deep breath. This really wasn't the moment; she barely had time to talk to him about the practicalities of the next week or two, let alone listen to his outpourings about the vagaries of his relationship with her, past and present. Whatever he needed to get off his chest would have to wait. But his steely gaze suggested he was determined and she wasn't quite sure how to resist, without signalling abruptly the end of her visit and causing him to take offence. She knew from experience that that was easily done. An artist friend of his had once made a cartoon sketch of him, looking like a porcupine, with sharp spikes spearing out from the back of his body. Everyone had laughed uproariously, except Lionel, who had looked first perplexed and then visibly cross. The friend wasn't seen at their house again.

'Can it wait?' she said finally. 'I've got to be somewhere by two- thirty, I'm afraid. If it's going to take time . . . ?'

'It's about the long term,' he said. 'I'll tell you, then I'll leave you to go away and have a good, long think about it.'

She felt slightly confused. This sounded more like a proposal than a confession, something rather different from what she was expecting.

'I've decided I want to give my body to science,' he said, 'when I die. This annoying stuff with Dr Caldicott has got me thinking. I'm well into my eighties and, like it or not, my time's going to come. The writing's on the wall, as they say. I'd rather do the donation thing than the alternatives – buried in the ground or burnt in a bloody great incinerator in Golders Green. As you know, I have no belief in anything afterwards. Just a dead lump of flesh. I'd like to be of some use to somebody, after I'm gone. But it means there wouldn't be a funeral, as such. You wouldn't get my body after I've gone. You'd have to do something else – a little ceremony, a few people gathered together or something. That doesn't bother me in the slightest. After all, most of the people who might have come are long dead themselves. But would you mind? And Barbara? And how would you feel about me not being put near to

Marje? There wouldn't be a proper place to visit, like there is for her.'

Celia almost laughed out loud. She just managed to stop herself. Whether it was relief, or utter astonishment at her father's way of thinking about himself and his place in the world, she wasn't sure. She sat up straight before replying, placing her hands carefully in front of her on the table.

'Daddy, on something like that, I'll be entirely guided by you. And I imagine Barbara will feel the same. I don't even need to go away and mull it over. I want to do whatever you feel most comfortable with. And besides, I think donating your body is a wonderful thing to do.'

He smiled. 'That's a great relief to me,' he said, patting her hand. 'It's been worrying me for quite some time. Will you talk to your sister? She can be so fierce about these things. Sometimes she won't let me say what I want to, as if I'm being silly in raising it, as if she wants to believe that I'll go on for ever and ever.'

'Of course, Daddy. But I don't think there'll be a problem with Barbara. She'll want to follow your wishes on this. I'm sure of that.'

He nodded. 'Thank you. It's a great big weight off my mind.'

Was now the moment to capitalise on the good will she had generated, his cheerfulness and gratitude to her? Should she leap in now, before the moment passed?

'Daddy, I have something I want to say to you, too.'

He frowned.

'That sounds serious.'

'It is.'

'Well, spit it out then, precious.'

She hesitated for a moment. How could she find the right words?

'You're managing well, as you've always done, ever since Marje . . . Mum died. But, as you yourself say, you're not getting any younger and I really *do* think you could do with a little bit of help. You know Svetlana quite well, she likes you – she always asks after you! I think she'd be very happy to come just once or twice a week, to do a bit of cleaning and washing for you and help lift the burden of all the little jobs around the house. It'd leave you more time to do other, more enjoyable things.'

He made a small sound, like a little grunt.

'You asked me to mull over your idea. All I ask is that you agree to mull over mine.'

He grunted again.

'I think she's looking for a bit of extra work, as well,' she said. 'She sends as much money as she can back to her children in the Ukraine, so she's always after new jobs and they aren't very easy to come by these days.' Not strictly true – she knew that Svetlana was always in demand – but then perhaps Lionel would be more easily persuaded if he thought he were doing Svetlana a favour, rather than the other way round.

'I'll mull it over,' he said.

'Thanks, Daddy, that's all I ask.'

Now she really would need to get going.

'I must dash now but I'll ring tomorrow evening and see how you are.'

'Thank you, my precious.'

That was the second time in ten minutes he'd called her that. She hadn't heard that word in a long while. It was a term he used constantly when she was a child but only in relation to Barbara or Marje. Poor Lionel. How things had changed. Sweet as it was to hear him talk to her like this, she wasn't sure if she really liked it or not, or whether it might be easier, after all, to cope with the months ahead, without any of these new signs of Lionel's affection. After all these years, battling her father might be rather simpler than finding she had to love him.

Chapter 21

She arrived at St Pancras with fifteen minutes to spare and thought she'd surprise Paul by going to meet him at the gate. She scanned the arrivals board. Damn. His train had been delayed for twenty minutes or so. A tannoy announcement mentioned signalling trouble close to Ashford. She needn't have hurried her visit to Lionel. Dismayed by the delay and nervous about what was to come, she wandered around the echoey concourse, drifting aimlessly in and out of the shops – clothes outlets and accessories vendors, gift shops and newsagents, pretending to interest herself in buying a scarf or a hat or a cheap pair of dangly earrings.

In the bookshop, Hatchards, her gaze went straight to the book table right at the front of the store. With her publisher's expert eye, she scanned the stacks of novels to see what they'd chosen to display. Unsurprisingly, Atlas' books didn't figure at all. Dora just didn't have sufficient clout or money to win them these highly desirable marketing spots and though it was nothing new for her, it still rankled. The books looked very similar – bold images and quirky titles, in unusual fonts that mimicked clumsy, childlike handwriting, shouting 'Look at me, I'm new, youthful, a bit zany, the next best thing.' But sitting there quietly, with a simple, understated grey and blue cover, and a restrained, black title, was that novel, *Not Drowning*, that she'd picked out from the slush pile a couple of years previously and tried to persuade Dora and the team to publish. She suddenly felt bereft, looking at it there, its title and author in solid, definite black print. Published by someone else. When she'd picked it up from the pile on her desk, she'd devoured it in a single day. She'd been utterly convinced of its worth, more so than any book she'd ever come across, full of admiration for its intensity, its rich use of language, its unusual and compelling characters. The story came flooding back to her – a first-person narrative set in the west of Scotland about a woman and her failing relationship. It had a double time-frame: the painful, protracted conclusion to the woman's marriage, and her early childhood being abandoned by her mother and brought up alone by her grieving, embittered taciturn father. Needless to say, it had ended in tragedy, but the route to this had been anything but clichéd, a subtle and satisfying build-up to the final, heartbreaking denouement. Dora and the team had been completely unconvinced; they'd refused to budge. She'd argued with them long and hard and privately decided that if she didn't win this one, it really might be the final straw that sent her in search of a new job. But she had finally been forced to concede, and, when it came to it, she hadn't had the guts to hand in her notice. Another book came her way soon after that she rather liked; it was quickly and painlessly accepted by Dora, perhaps by way of compensation for disappointing her over the other one, and she'd settled back down, albeit somewhat grumpily, into her job again.

She took a copy of the book from the stack on the table. It felt thrillingly clean and pure, like all new books, but the cover was particularly elegantly designed and the quality of the paper excellent. A really beautiful object. The back cover had quotes from reviews, praising this new writer for all the qualities Celia had especially admired when she'd first seen the work as a tatty A4 manuscript. The book had clearly attracted big-name reviewers from the broadsheets. She was glad; the writer deserved this. She took the book to the checkout.

Sitting on a bench in the concourse, she flicked through to the end and reread the final paragraph:

Slipping into the water, the bone-cold, icy-clear shallows, edging further in, over moss-covered stones and frail, trailing weeds, till her feet lost touch and her body plunged deeper, her limbs rigid with shock, her breath quick and hard, her heart thundering on, unwilling even now to give up or give in. At last. Drowning, not swimming. Finally.

It brought a lump to Celia's throat. My God, how easy it would be to sink beneath that water. She'd been swimming so hard, trying to keep afloat, dragged up and under by the unrelenting waves. How much longer could she keep on doing this? She needed help, some kind of divine intervention – though of course she didn't believe in that – a lifebelt to pull her out of danger. She hadn't felt quite as bad since those first dreadful days at Anne's in St Albans. She was drowning.

She felt her mobile phone vibrating in her pocket. It was Nick. She decided not to pick up. A few moments later the phone buzzed to alert her to a text message.

'On my way back. Home 5ish. Where are you & when are you back? XXX.'

Should she reply? If so, to say what? Tell him, or deceive him? Postpone. Put off. Decide later. But then, of course, once Paul arrived, it would be infinitely more difficult to find a way to do it. How much harder to speak to Nick, either to tell him she was with Paul, when he was sitting right across a table from her, watching her, or alternatively deceive him and pretend to be somewhere else, with Paul there listening to all her lies. Both would be equally impossible.

She started keying in a message:

'Went into town. Back around . . .'

Around when? Paul had been delayed. He'd come all the way from Paris just to see her. She couldn't just abandon him as soon as he got here. This was crazy, everything about it . . . She wasn't thinking straight. She'd got herself into a horrible mess again. What was happening to her? She wasn't someone who did this kind of thing. By what time could she reasonably get back home? She needed to talk to Nick, to hear what had been said between him and Marina. But she also had to see Paul. What had she been thinking when she agreed to him coming to London in the first place? It had been foolish. Madness. Not swimming. Drowning.

'Back around 6.30 or so. We'll talk then.'

The coward's way out, buying herself time. She pressed Send.

She looked up at the big Dent clock under the domed roof. Just ten minutes or so till the train came in. Below the clock, she couldn't help but notice the striking bronze statue of a couple, locked in a loving, passionate embrace. How apt, she thought, bitterly. She texted Paul to tell him she'd come and meet him at the arrivals area, then wandered down the concourse again, stopping briefly to use the women's toilet, before making her way towards the gate.

As it turned out, the train was a few minutes early, so by the time she got there, passengers were already hurrying through, wheeling suitcases, carrying shopping bags of French goods and Duty Frees, jostling each other in their desire to get out and away quickly, after the frustrations of a very long delay.

Finally, she spotted Paul, strolling along, carrying a large bag over his shoulder. He hadn't seen her yet. He looked relaxed, as always. Maybe he'd had a meal and a glass of good red wine on the train? He'd certainly have chosen a first-class seat – he never showed any reluctance to spend his money on a bit of luxury.

He saw her, smiled and waved.

And now he was with her and giving her a big hug and kissing her on both cheeks and standing back to see how she looked and smiling again. It was good to see him, though she was surprised how much he felt like a stranger to her, despite the fact that it was only a couple of months since the trip to the Alps. There was that sense of having forgotten what someone really looks like when you haven't seen them for a while, the reality turning out to be rather different from the out-of-focus image you had been holding in your head. He looked less attractive, actually, more the middle-aged man he obviously was than the man of her memory, whom she'd admired and flirted with and finally slept with in a posh hotel in the mountains. Though, no sooner had she thought this than she wondered if this perhaps made him *more* rather than less appealing. More vulnerable, rough around the edges, more in need of protection himself.

'Searcys?' he said. 'Or somewhere else?'

'Searcys is fine,' she replied, putting her arm through his as they set off and then, seeing the slightly querying look he gave her, asking herself whether that had been the right thing to do. Perhaps not.

They walked back through the concourse and took the escalator up to the brasserie. He found them a table in a quiet corner, divested her of her duffle coat, himself of his bag and jacket, and sat down opposite her. He called over the waiter and ordered for them – a double espresso for him and a decaf filter coffee for her. As predicted, he'd eaten a good lunch on the train and she assured him that she really wasn't hungry.

'I've booked into a hotel for one night, with the option of staying for a second,' he said, 'just in case you're wondering. On one of those quiet roads in Bloomsbury, close to Russell Square. So if you've only got a short time now and want to meet up again tomorrow, we could do that. Or, of course, I could ring Nick, tell him I'm here and come out and see the two of you together tomorrow. If that would help. It all depends what you want . . .'

She tried to think what she did want. She didn't know. So she said nothing.

'You're looking tired.'

'Exhausted. Absolutely drained. It's been hideous. We had a really good period, soon after I came back from Paris, when things seemed to be back to normal. Both of us were feeling so much happier, on more of an even keel again. And now this!'

'The woman . . . Marina . . . she's definitely pregnant?'

'Definitely.'

'And going ahead with it?'

'Probably. Almost certainly. Nick went off to see her this afternoon. When I get back, he'll tell me the outcome. I really don't want to hear it, though – I can pretty much predict what he'll say but I can't bear to listen to it coming from him.'

'These things happen, you know.'

'Yes. But to other people, not me and Nick.' A tedious and empty refrain. Not to me and Nick, she'd kept saying, kept thinking, when clearly it did; it had.

'Other people find ways of surviving.'

'Do they?'

'I have a good friend – Auguste Leroux – I don't think you know him. Un type très gentil! His mistress had two children. His wife, Delphine, told him each time it happened that she'd accept it, as long as she never had to see either the mistress or the children. He agreed. They live in a neighbouring arrondissement, so he can visit them very often. But Delphine's and the other family's paths never cross – he makes sure of that. They're teenagers now – two boys. He talks about them to me sometimes – very much the proud father. But Delphine pretends they don't exist – she's happier that way.'

'That's Paris, though. The Parisian haute bourgeoisie. The decorous French marriage. Could you honestly see that happening in London, with me and Nick? In Kentish Town? We're extremely indecorous and very English, for all Nick's French roots. English through and through. Do you really imagine I could watch him swanning off for evenings or weekends with Marina and his child in Highgate or Camden Town, or disappearing off to Surrey, if that's where she decides to remain, while I'm left sitting on my own, the ever-patient wife waiting for his return? Penelope to Nick's Ulysses?'

He didn't answer but went straight on. 'In that case, what about embracing the idea of the child? Accept it. Become the good step-parent. People do that, too, you know.'

'I suppose they must. But think about a child on the scene now, at our age! If Pippa or Dan had babies, of course we'd want to help out – that would be a pleasure – but a step-mother to a child of Nick's with another woman – with *that* woman . . . that's quite a different story.'

'And so . . . ?'

'And so! I thought you might tell me to pull myself together, that I'm being stupid and unimaginative and that there's a way out. I thought you might say that my feelings are foolish, that I'll get over it all eventually, that I'll come to love Nick's child, that I should be more pragmatic, less emotional. I hoped you'd be firm with me and tell me to grow up.'

'Your feelings are your feelings. You're entitled to do what makes you most happy.'

'Or least unhappy.'

'Exactly.'

There was a pause, Paul waiting while she collected her thoughts. ' I was able to get over one shock, one thunderbolt – the discovery that Nick had cheated on me – just. Only just. I grieved as if someone close to me had died, as you well know. And then I picked myself up and thought, "This is silly. Why give up on a marriage that's been so successful for so long, if there's even the smallest chance that it can recover?" It's not been easy, but Nick and I have been slowly trying to rebuild our marriage. These last few weeks, I've been . . . not unhappy. But this . . . this new thing, it's like a second lightning strike and I'm grieving all over again. Except this time I'm not sure it's recoverable, because we can never go back to how things were before. Not with a child in the picture. Not with *her* child, a constant reminder of what he's done to me.'

He hesitated before speaking.

'I can see that,' he said finally. 'But what does this mean? A final separation? You'd need to think hard about that. It's a big step. Mon dieu. Starting again.'

'I can't believe that it could have come to this,' she said, dry-eyed for once. 'I can't believe that I could be seriously contemplating it. But I am.'

There was a long silence. She stared into her empty cup, at the rim of coffee-stained milk and the dregs of ground beans at the bottom. She felt conscious of his eyes on her and looked up. He seemed unusually grim. No light-hearted banter, or calm reassurances, no bright, quick responses, not even a pat philosophical phrase, just a serious, concerned expression that she wasn't used to seeing on him. He seemed to be about to speak again. For reasons she couldn't quite explain to herself, she decided she didn't want to hear what he was about to say. Quickly she pushed back her chair, made her excuses and headed off in search of the Ladies.

In the toilet, she stood for a while, looking at herself in the mirror. My God, what a mess! Flushed, hair unkempt, face drawn with worry. It was absurdly stupid of her to keep refusing to face things head-on, irrational and childish – avoiding Lionel's confessions, avoiding Nick's news, avoiding something now with Paul that she couldn't quite grasp but half sensed as dangerous, with that urgent, almost physical awareness of risk. She had run away from it. But soon, when she'd calmed down a bit, she'd go out and ask him, straight out. What had he been about to say?

She opened her bag and rummaged around, looking for her make-up and a comb, to help her look more presentable. She leaned towards the mirror to apply some lipstick. Behind her the door swung open and a young woman breezed in. She didn't look up. Then there was a light tap on her shoulder and a voice that was horribly familiar.

'Celia! Oh my God! What a coincidence!'

Daisy, Annabel's daughter.

'I'm just back from a work trip up to Nottingham and on my way to meet up with Pippa and Jamie for drinks and a meal in Soho! Isn't that weird? Spooky, in fact! What are you doing here?'

Celia hesitated. 'I've been doing some shopping for clothes.'

'Buy anything nice? Let's have a look! I adore your clothes sense. I'm always saying to Pips how she's got the most stylish mum of any of our friends.' Daisy gabbled on, her eyes wandering, looking around for the shopping bags, on the surface by the sinks, on the small table with the paper towels, on the floor by Celia's feet.

There was nothing, not a single carrier bag or shred of evidence of Celia having bought anything. 'Hopeless!' she said, blushing. 'Not a thing that took my fancy. Trailing around the shops for hours and hours and zilch! Here I am, completely empty-handed.'

'Bad luck! That happens to me, too, sometimes,' Daisy said. 'So frustrating, isn't it? All that slog, trying things on for nothing!'

'Lovely to see you, Daisy, but I must dash – Nick's expecting me home soon. Give my love to Pippa and Jamie and your mum, too, if you're speaking to her sometime.'

'I will. Pippa and Jamie will be gobsmacked at my having bumped into you like this!'

'Won't they just?' she said and managed a little laugh.

As soon as Daisy disappeared into a cubicle, Celia hurried out.

Paul was sitting waiting for her.

'This is ghastly. I've just seen the daughter of a really good friend of mine. Pippa's closest friend, Daisy. She can't see us together. I'd better go, right now.'

'Of course. And then –'

'I'll find a way to call you later this evening.'

'Can I see you again tomorrow?' he asked.

'I'll see if I can. I'll try to find a way,' she repeated.

He stood up and helped her into her coat. She moved towards him to kiss him in the usual way, two kisses on each cheek and a rapid departure, but he held her for a moment at arms' length in front of him, looked at her, rather sternly, she thought, then pulled her towards him and kissed her passionately. And she did nothing to resist.

Finally she drew away from him.

'I have to go,' she said, grabbing her bag, then moved towards him and kissed him once more. 'I'll call you this evening.'

Drowning, she thought, as she ran towards the escalator and went down towards the Underground. Going under. And down she went.

Chapter 22

She lay beside him on the bed, the curtains half closed though it was only four o'clock and still light outside. They'd had sex, despite the fact that she hadn't intended for it to happen. She had told herself it wouldn't. Absolutely not. All she had wanted was another conversation, someone to turn to for advice. She must have been a fool not to realise its inevitability, after Searcys and that kiss the previous afternoon. She'd been kidding herself. Somewhere along the line, she must have known that this would follow. From that first text to Paul asking to talk to him, it was almost a certainty, wasn't it?

When she'd returned to the house the previous afternoon, it had all played out much as she had expected – as she had feared. Nick had been distraught. Standing in the hall, still in her coat, with him sitting on the bottom stairs, she had listened as he recounted what had happened. Marina had calmly and coolly explained her plans: she was going ahead and having the baby. She had everything worked out, it seemed. She'd hire a nanny, her mother and father would provide support; she'd moved out to Surrey to be near to them and had found herself a job close to her new flat, in a firm where the hours would be under control and they would put up with a short, unpaid maternity leave. She thought she'd manage; financially it would be a challenge but she'd get by, whether he helped her or not. Of course, she wanted him to play a part. It was, after all, his child. Then, suddenly she'd started to cry. She told him that she still loved him. She wanted them to be a family together, though she knew that couldn't happen. She wanted her child to have a father and she wanted it to be him.

What had he said? What had he done? Stony-faced, tight-lipped, determined, Celia had demanded to know every detail, like an interrogator brutally extracting information from her subject. If she felt any sympathy for him, it was so far beneath the surface as to be utterly invisible to him. His suffering wasn't a pleasure to her, but her pain was everything and there was no room for kindness. His actions had led them here, to this place. And her feelings were all the more bitter for the knowledge that almost certainly, despite everything that he had done, he had not stopped loving her. But he had been careless; he'd thrown their happiness away. His sadness was as tragic as her own, she recognised that. But he'd brought this upon himself, hadn't he?

'What's happened?' he said quietly. 'Something's changed in you. You seem to have stopped caring.'

She'd not replied. That wasn't true. She cared enough to feel utterly empty, as if the juice of life had been squeezed out of her and that the only thing left was a dry, ugly, shrivelled core of bitterness.

'You know what I feel, Celia,' he said. 'You know that, whatever I've done, I would do anything now to save our marriage.'

She had nodded. She did know. But, at this moment, it didn't seem enough.

That night they had slept once again in separate rooms, though he had come to her in the spare room before finally going to sleep, sitting near her on the bed and talking for a while longer, reaching towards her and holding her close as if trying to find a way through to her. She had cried. They had wept together, like lost children unable to comfort one another.

'Go to bed,' she'd said, gently. 'We'll talk again tomorrow.'

On Sunday morning she had woken early to the sound of her mobile phone buzzing. It was Lionel.

'Can you come over to see me today?'

'It's a bit tricky, Lionel. I've got some tentative plans that I need to confirm. Can I ring you back when I know what's happening?'

'I've remembered something I wanted to talk to you about.'

'Can't it wait?'

'Wait too long and I'll be bloody well dead and buried,' he said crossly.

'Now come on, Lionel. That's ridiculous.'

'I need to see you but you're never available. You're always too busy for me. If Barbara were here . . .'

'That isn't fair. It's emotional blackmail. And I'm not going to put up with it! I'll ring you back later, Lionel.' And she brought the call to an abrupt end.

No sooner done than she regretted it and phoned him back straightaway. There was just a dialling tone, ringing and ringing with no reply. Damn. He'd taken umbrage. He'd be in his kitchen, slamming cupboard doors and muttering oaths at her, banging cups onto the table. She knew what he was like when his temper was up. Now she had Lionel to cope with, as if there weren't enough complications in her life already. She'd have to try phoning him again later and find a way to fit him into her day.

Twenty minutes later the mobile was ringing again. Pippa.

'Hi, Mum! Just wondered whether you and Dad fancy coming over today for a late lunch with me and Jamie. Last-minute thing, I know, but we'd like to cook a meal for you for a change. Usually it's us coming to you. Jamie's keen to do a proper Sunday roast, with all the trimmings and everything. We thought we might invite Dan and Lottie as well.'

'How nice!' Celia tried to sound cheerful. 'But I'm so sorry, sweetie – we're both a bit busy. I've got a funny old day.'

'What are you up to?'

'Oh, you know, lots of little commitments. Lionel for one.'

'He could come too!'

'I'm not sure that would work, Pips. He's in one of those moods. He's been on the phone this morning, having a go at me.'

'OK, fair enough. Some other time, maybe.'

She'd sounded disappointed. Celia was sorry. It was a key moment, being invited to Pippa and Jamie's as an adult couple, a symbolic reversal of roles, and she'd had to say no. She almost rang straight back to say she'd changed her mind but then there was Lionel to deal with, working out whether to spend some time with Nick, and somehow or other she was going to have to find a way to meet up with Paul again.

She'd got up, showered and had had her breakfast by the time Nick finally came down, still in his pyjamas, hair on end, looking a bit dazed.

'I took a swig of Night Nurse to help me sleep,' he said. 'Still feeling a bit groggy.'

'Doing that a lot?'

'Just when I really can't sleep,' he said.

She didn't admit to him that she'd been doing the same these past few weeks, a habit caught from him, when desperation for a decent night's sleep overcame her shame at blotting everything out with drugs designed for a bout of the flu. Perhaps Shakespeare was right, she thought. Troubles in love were like a sickness, an ague, like catching the plague. Maybe it was fitting that she and Nick should be treating their suffering in this way.

Her mobile phone flashed. It was sitting on the kitchen table in front of her, next to the bowl of fruit, on top of the *Sunday Times* supplement, an arm's length away. She wondered if Nick would look at it, or reach over to hand it to her. Her heart beat faster. She picked it up quickly, but not too quickly, she hoped. Paul's French mobile phone number. Casually, she put it back down on the table.

'Who is it?'

'Oh, just Annabel. I'll call her back later.'

'I'll go up and shower. Then maybe we should try to do something together today, for a change.'

She said nothing, then as he was going upstairs, called after him, 'Have your shower. Then we can decide.'

She waited till she could hear the bathroom door being closed, the boiler firing up, the water burping its way through the old pipework, then picked up her phone again. Paul's text asked her to call. She rang him straightaway. She needed to be decisive – there weren't going to be many chances to speak to him without discovery – so she made a hurried arrangement to meet him at his hotel at 3 p.m. She'd find a way of working around that, fitting everything in neatly, so as to go undetected. If she told Nick that she was seeing Lionel at three, for a serious talk and a clear-up of his decidedly unhygienic kitchen, she could probably be away till around 7.30 p.m. or so without arousing suspicion. A couple of hours with Paul would leave her time to pass by Lionel's on the way home.

She tried her father again and this time he answered. Her apology for putting the phone down was accepted with moderate grace, as was her promise to come over and see him sometime after 5 p.m. A temporary truce, perhaps made more permanent by a visit. That left the rest of the morning at home. Should she suggest a walk on the Heath with Nick, and lunch at the café at Kenwood? Normal life, or at least the appearance of it, a façade as appealing as the beautiful white exterior of Kenwood House, which both of them had always loved so much. She'd suggest it and see. Better that than both of them moping around on their own at home, avoiding each other, suffering in silence. Perhaps walking along those familiar paths, past the ponds and the chilly ducks and swans, through the wooded enclosure, up onto the frosty summit to look out over London, and then on to the café, might restore something known and knowable to them, if only temporarily.

Nick had leapt at the idea, pitifully grateful for the chance to do something simple and familiar together. Walking, she'd always found, was good for restoring calm, good for thinking, conducive to talking. It proved so now. They'd avoided the obvious topic of conversation right till the end, preferring to stick to safer territory – the erosion of the paths, the renovation of the old dairy, the bad behaviour of dogs and their owners, the much-contested plans for constructing dams. On Pippa and Jamie they were agreed – the wedding was something to look forward to with pleasure and Jamie's growing maturity a good sign for their daughter's future happiness. In terms of Dan, they were also in concert, worrying a bit about what he was giving up with his job and fearful for the stability of his relationship with Lottie, who really was so very good for him. They had always had so much in common, she and Nick: so much to talk about, so many shared attitudes, so little argument or dispute, such strong support for each other. To lose all of this! She felt that fate had dealt her a cruel hand; unjust and undeserved.

They wandered over towards the Kitchen Garden, a favourite place of Nick's. They could never walk on the Heath without finally ending up there. Strolling round the central bed of shrubs and flowers, he stopped abruptly and turned to her.

'You know I've always loved you. Through all of this, I've loved you. I wish . . . I desperately wish we could just go back to where we were.'

Going back . . . no Marina . . . no baby . . . no Paul. She thought of Paul wandering around the streets of London right now and felt sick with the knowledge of it.

And now Nick came close to her and clung to her, holding on for dear life, as if buffeted by fierce winds, though it was a perfectly still day. They stood there for a long time. It was only when she became aware of other people looking at them, smiling at two middle-aged people seemingly locked in a warm embrace, that she finally pulled away from him.

After lunch out on the large patio, wrapped up warm in their coats and scarves, with young couples eating late English breakfasts on nearby tables, and dirty, wet dogs snuffling around them and licking up water from tin bowls, with children drinking hot chocolate from paper cups, and elderly women with sticks edging slowly towards chairs, with thrushes flitting about and pigeons swooping down towards a discarded slice of bread or piece of muffin, they talked again about their troubles.

'I can't refuse to have anything at all to do with it, this baby,' Nick said. 'But I can't bear to lose you, either.'

'Either way, it's a disaster. Whatever you do, either way.'

'Don't let's do anything rash. Give me some time to think. There must be a solution.'

'If there's a solution, I can't think what it might be.' She felt almost cruel in her refusal to provide comfort. But then, what comfort was there?

They walked down to the ponds, past the tennis courts and headed towards home, so that Celia could get herself ready to go to Lionel's, both silent, not sure what more there was to say.

In the hall, as they took off their muddy shoes and peeled off their layers of coats and scarves, Nick said, 'Sure you don't want me to drop you at your father's and then come and pick you up later? I could come in and say hello to him.'

She couldn't bring herself to look at him when she spoke.

'No. He's in an absolutely foul mood. It'd be better to just leave him to me.'

Nick didn't seem to have observed the edginess in her voice; he appeared to be unaware of her intense agitation. Perhaps he put it down to the general ghastliness of the situation. What would make him think that it could be anything else? He had no idea Paul was even in London, let alone that she was planning to see him.

She changed her clothes, put on some make-up, got into the small car and drove not to Lionel's but to a backstreet just round the corner from Kentish Town station, not two minutes away. She caught a Tube to Russell Square and went straight to Paul's hotel where she had arranged to meet him.

She said to herself it was just to see him before he went back to Paris, to show her thanks to him for coming, to talk to him about Nick's and her troubles, to maintain a friendship that might be important to her in the coming months. She would have a drink with him, tell him what was happening with Nick and Marina, share the grief she was feeling and perhaps arrange to talk to him on the phone in Paris, to let him know how things were going. Then she would make her excuses and go. Despite this, she felt a heavy weight on her, a sense of dread, a guilty awareness that really, when it came down to it, even such an innocent meeting as this might not be such a good idea.

Both lay on their backs looking up at the ceiling, neither of them speaking, intimate, yet strangely separate, each lost in their own thoughts, neither wanting to say too much, or the wrong thing. This time she could barely look at him, lying naked on the bed. Even embarrassment at the silence was displaced by other feelings. In among the panic and the guilt – What was she doing here? How on earth had she allowed herself to get into this situation? – she felt some tenderness towards him but struggled to define it more clearly. Tenderness, affection, lust, love, gratitude, guilt, revenge – she really needed to try to explain it to herself, to clarify these things, to understand what she felt. Without clarity, how could she know what to do next?

It did not seem to be lust, pure and simple. More desperation for something she'd lost. Gratitude, certainly. Paul's behaviour towards her had been faultless. He'd done everything she had asked and asked for nothing in return. He'd put her first and if, as it now seemed, he wanted more, was that not only fair? She'd been the one to call him in Paris, she'd agreed to him coming to London, agreed to meet him at St Pancras, to return his kiss, to lie to Nick in order to make another arrangement to see him again. He would be justified in beginning to expect something more. She felt grateful to him for wanting her once and not just once but again, immensely grateful to him for his kindness towards her. It would have been ungrateful, wouldn't it, on her part, to just tell him to go?

Revenge? No, absolutely not. Not that. Once again, Nick had been in her thoughts throughout, intruding on the sex, reminding her of what she most missed. There was no pleasure in imagining what he would feel if he knew where she was right now. She was no Medea, wanting to punish him. What he was going through was punishment enough. Leaving him would, perhaps, be too much for both of them.

Love for Paul? For now, it seemed depressingly unlikely. How easy it would be if she could only transfer her affections, simply and cleanly, to another man, to be able to tell Nick that she'd moved on, to make a new life in Paris with a charming, loving, delightful man who was genuinely fond of her. Perhaps that might come in time. But not now, definitely not yet, possibly – probably – not ever.

As if answering her thoughts, Paul turned to face her.

'If you're trying to decide what next,' he said, 'don't. I think you'll tell me that this was all a big mistake and I really don't want to hear that. You'll tell me you're feeling guilty as hell, that the sex wasn't quite what it could be – which is true and I apologise for that. A man of my age, you know . . . and you being so preoccupied, confused, upset . . . it's not like we're teenagers leaping into bed. The sex isn't the only thing, is it? You'll tell me I'm too much of a ladies' man for you. Not serious enough. Too quick to have affairs. But I've been fond of you for a long time, Celia. Perhaps you didn't know that? Maybe it will come as a surprise? Long before all of this. For many years I've envied Nick what he had with you. I may seem like a shameless old roué to you, but truthfully, deep down, I'm a romantic at heart. I'd say I've had bad luck – I've not found the right woman. And now I don't want this to be the end, just like that. I think, if you want my opinion, that it's better for me to go back to Paris and for you to go home now. Don't make any decisions. Wait and see. That's the best thing, for you. And perhaps also for me.'

She could hardly speak. She didn't know what to say. This was becoming so complicated, so confusing. She dressed quickly, kissed him goodbye rather awkwardly, promising to call him in Paris, and then she hurried to the Tube station to go back to North London and her next stop – her visit to Lionel.

Chapter 23

'I wrote it down,' he said, 'so I wouldn't forget.'

He produced a piece of lined paper, with small yellow sticky notes plastered all over it, covered in his familiar messy scrawl. There were scratchings out and words in capital letters, exclamation marks and double, or even triple, question marks. Typical Lionel, but, even more so, Lionel writ large. The sheet reminded her of her childhood and his case notes which he used to bring home every evening in armfuls of brown cardboard files. Evenings and weekends, he often buried himself in his study. She would go to ask him a question about her homework, or with a message from her mother to say that dinner was ready, and find him furiously scribbling away, adding ideas for a defence, or questions to ask a client, jotting down thoughts and strategies that were decipherable only to him.

Glancing at the sheet of paper, her eye happened on one phrase, larger than the others, occupying its own sticky note, taking up all the space and therefore easily legible upside down: 'BE CAREFUL!!!'

What did he need to be careful about? Careful not to drop something? Careful with his financial affairs? Careful not to give too much away? Or careful of her feelings, careful of his own? It was both intriguing and troubling.

He'd avoided taking her into the kitchen, suggesting that they sit in the living room. It was none too clean either – full of dusty knick-knacks, old magazines, piles of books, and mugs that hadn't been taken through to be washed up – but it was definitely less of a health hazard than the kitchen. He'd made them both a cup of tea, with milk that seemed reasonably fresh, and brought out an unopened packet of biscuits, good ones, chocolate-covered, expensively packaged, as if for a special occasion.

'I thought you might like these,' he'd said. 'Best biscuits. Not cheap ones.'

'Thanks, Lionel. That's nice of you.'

'I've made a few notes for myself, so I get it right. So I say the important things properly.'

'So I see. Punctilious as ever.'

He didn't rise to the bait.

'My memory, you know. Short-term less good than long-term but still, even with the long-term, I can sometimes get in a muddle. So worth getting it all sorted in my head first, don't you think?'

She was taken aback, not only by his quiet reflectiveness, after the spat over the phone that morning, but also by his quiet determination.

'That sounds like a good idea,' she said. 'It's what Dr Caldicott recommended. But Lionel, I'm confused. I can't think what this is about.'

'It's about you and me. It's about how badly we've always got on.'

There was something horribly blunt about this admission. It was painfully direct. She felt impelled to soften it, make less of it, for her sake if not for his.

'We've rubbed along OK,' she found herself saying, though she knew it to be not strictly true. 'Recently things have improved quite a bit. With the odd exception, like this morning, we've been getting on better than before.'

'That's part of it. Since Barbara's been away, I've got to know you better. I've come to appreciate you more. I know I don't see all that much of you – you lead a busy life and really, that's how it should be. I'm pleased for you that you've made a go of your work, now that the children are grown-up. You've had a second wind. For my generation it was different, but you, you've managed things very well, devoting yourself to Pippa and Dan when they were young, then forging ahead with your career later. It's . . . it's admirable, Celia. I admire you. And that husband of yours . . . Nick . . . I think I've been unfair to him. It's just that . . . well, you know how I felt when he broke up with Barbara. But over the years, he's proved himself, hasn't he? He's been a good husband to you.'

She said nothing.

This was Lionel being 'careful', was it? An initial very flattering, conciliatory and totally unexpected preamble before kerpow – the big revelation, the shocker? Her childhood fantasies came hurrying in, yapping at her heels, growling at her, jumping up and threatening to bite.

'As I've already told you, I need to explain some things to you before it's too late. I don't want to go without you knowing.'

'This sounds ominous, Daddy! Portentous! Like some dreadful family secret that I need to be let in on, some skeleton in the closet.'

'Not quite,' he said. 'But nevertheless –'

'I've had my doubts,' Celia told him, before he could say more. She gritted her teeth. Now was the moment for her to come out with her own revelation. There might never be a better time. But could she bring herself to do it?

'I've wondered sometimes myself whether things aren't quite what I thought.' She could hardly carry on. 'I've sometimes imagined – silly though I know it is –

that perhaps I wasn't your child. That I was adopted or something. Or even that Marje had an affair and conceived me with another man.'

He laughed out loud.

'Ridiculous,' he said. 'Whatever made you think that? Adopted? Nonsense! An affair? Absurd!'

And then she cried. She howled. She felt the weight of years of doubt fall away. Unsteadily he got to his feet and shuffled over towards her. He patted her back. He kissed the top of her head. He stroked her face. He sat down on the coffee table so that he could be closer to her.

'How could you have thought that, Celia? A crazy idea! Of course you were ours – mine. Look at yourself! In so many ways you're just like me – your temperament, for instance, a bit too emotional, sometimes rather fierce with people, easily irritated. And those feet of yours – they're just like mine! A perfect match!'

She laughed and then burst into tears again. 'I need a tissue,' she sobbed, like a child with him now, needing to wipe away the snot and tears, asking for help. He got up and went out, coming back with a handful that he passed over to her. He sat back down, perched on the coffee table, close to her.

'And so, my precious,' he said, 'do you want to know what I want to tell you, my daughter? Do you want to hear my story?'

Her face still covered in tissues, her eyes puffy, her nose still running, her face flushed with emotion, her hands trembling, she nodded.

And so he told her. How he and Marje had led a charmed life, schoolboy and schoolgirl together, first loves each for the other, marrying young and setting up home together, like birds gathering twigs and moss to make their nest. And then how they'd been blessed with a baby, a little girl, Barbara, a perfect, adorable little girl. And how they'd loved being parents and decided that they wanted a bigger family – a whole brood – to occupy their nest and fill their lives with joy. And how after a time they'd tried for another child and how happy, how wonderfully happy they had been when Marje found that she was pregnant again, how they'd looked out all the baby clothes and dusted down the cot, how they'd told Barbara about the baby who was coming to be her little brother or sister. And how she was born, a beautiful, bouncing baby, on a Tuesday, full of grace, and how he had come to see her in the hospital and kissed the nurse for joy, for sheer joy, when she told him that he had another fine, healthy girl.

But Marje wasn't well after the birth. She came home with the baby for a few days but didn't want to name the new child, or feed her, or care for her, or care for herself, or for anyone else. She disappeared into a distant fog where he couldn't reach her. With his permission she was admitted to another hospital. The situation was desperate – what else could he do? It was absolutely necessary, so the doctors said. At first he was told that she would stay just for a few weeks and then it turned out to be longer, and longer still, until it seemed she might not ever return. The new little baby required a nurse to care for it and Barbara needed looking after. He had his work obligations, so both children were sent away to his parents in Manchester. The lovely home he and Marje had made for themselves was empty and barren and full of despair. At last, Marje came home and Barbara and the baby were fetched back from his parents', Barbara pale and a little lost, hesitant and shy. And the baby – whom he had named Celia, because, despite everything, she had had to have a name – returned with a nurse to look after her until Marje was fully well again. Which she was, in time. Bit by bit, slowly but surely, Marje became well.

'Your mother came to adore you, you know. That was never in doubt. You've always known that, haven't you? She loved you more than anything, perhaps even more so because she felt that she'd lost you for a while. She wanted to make it up to you. Nowadays they have a name for it – post-natal depression. But then, it was called other things – mental breakdown, insanity, derangement – frightening names. We had to pretend to the outside world that she was physically ill. We told people that she was weak after the birth. It was too much of a stigma to admit that she'd been taken to the local mental hospital. It was a Victorian place of terror in those days, like a prison, with locked wards and iron bars on the windows. Now it's luxury flats. That shows you how much things have changed.

'I blamed myself for it, of course . . . I must have done something wrong. I had been too wrapped up in my work, my cases, my clients. I hadn't given your mother enough support. I hadn't seen the signs. I hadn't been a good enough husband. I had let her down.

'And I blamed you, too. You'd taken away from me my belief in the world, my youth, my optimism, my adored wife. And I didn't really want to get to know you again, when you came back to us. It was Marje and Barbara I chose to dedicate myself to.

'Nowadays, they'd have probably given us counselling, to get us back together as a family. They'd have given me help. There'd have been talk about bonding and suchlike. Psychobabble, maybe, but perhaps not so far off the mark. I read all about this stuff in the papers now and it makes sense to me. I don't think I did really ever *bond* with you. When you came back home, you were a stranger to me.'

Celia listened quietly, her hands clasped tightly in her lap.

'And of course, you yourself were such a nervous little thing. You'd had a difficult start in life, you'd spent your first weeks and months being looked after elsewhere and, when you came back, you must have picked up on the mood in the house. You weren't affectionate or giving. Probably you sensed how I felt.' He paused. 'For that, I've always felt very sad . . . and, I can now admit it to myself and to you, very ashamed.'

'I always thought there was something wrong,' she said softly, her hand still half covering her face with a tissue, 'but I didn't know what it was. I thought it was me. I thought Barbara was better than me, more successful and admirable in all kinds of ways – clever and good and no trouble to you. She was clearly following in your footsteps – she had the same interests, she ended up studying law and has had a brilliant career. I thought you liked her more than me. I was right. But now I know why.'

'I've had to think . . . about my life. Some people keep the cupboard locked right to the bitter end. They go . . . without ever opening it up. Maybe that's what I should have done? But when I began to think . . . when I began to understand . . . I thought I should tell you . . . so you could understand, too . . . I felt it was only fair to you. Specially now, with what Dr Caldicott has told us. The time will come when it won't be possible any more.'

'Thank you,' she said, simply. 'It explains a lot. It's important to me. I feel very, very glad to know.'

He reached out and touched her hand.

'Despite all this, I have loved you,' he said. 'All along, I have loved you. I just didn't know how to show it. I didn't know how to change things. You were distant, you didn't trust me, you seemed to dislike me. I couldn't change that – I didn't know how.'

They sat quietly for a while, him still sitting on the coffee table, leaning in towards her, holding her hand.

'I'm so glad that things worked out for you with Nick,' he said. 'You deserve that happiness. I behaved badly with him and I was wrong about that, too. He was the right man for you.'

BE CAREFUL!!! Lionel's words, there on that sticky note. Difficult subjects that he'd dealt with extraordinarily well, in a way that was so unlike their usual exchanges. He'd chosen his words with the utmost care. Now she needed to do the same.

'It's not always been a bed of roses, Daddy, but we've had a long marriage.'

'And lovely children,' he interrupted, 'and good jobs and a beautiful house, and you're still together after all these years. Marje would have been proud to see the two of you and what you've made of your lives, honestly she would.'

'Yes, Daddy,' she replied. And she said no more.

It was getting late. She asked him if he wanted her to make something for him to eat before she left.

'No,' he said, 'I don't want you going into that kitchen of mine! It'll only get you going again, pestering me about bringing in that Liliana woman of yours.'

'Svetlana, Daddy, Svetlana!'

'Svetlana, Liliana, Luba, whatever! It's all the same to me! I've still got enough marbles to know that I don't want some cleaner of yours coming in and taking over my life, tidying everything away so I can't find a damn thing.'

She laughed. 'OK, you win.'

Though she really ought to go, it was hard to tear herself away. They sat for a while longer in silence, him still holding her hand. Then, at last, she got up to leave.

'Thank you, Daddy,' she said. And then she kissed him and hurried to the door, fearing that a fresh bout of tears would stall her departure. She needed now, above all, to get herself home.

Chapter 24

A week or so later and she was having a drink with Annabel at the Bull and Last on Highgate Road. She hadn't seen Annabel for weeks. Things had been drifting with Nick, nothing had been resolved, both of them paralysed, unable to do anything to drag themselves out of the stasis of indecision, fearful of taking a step in any direction that might take them past the point of no return. There had been no lessening of the suffering, no sign of an end to it all. She hadn't spoken to Paul again; she hadn't told Nick about his time in London, about St Pancras, or the hotel near Russell Square. She had also held off telling him about her father's revelations. The reasons for this particular withholding of information were unclear to her. Perhaps another subtle punishment for him – why should he share in her new knowledge, when they seemed to be pulling apart? Or maybe she feared that telling him might tighten the bond between them more firmly, making it all the harder for her to make the separation that was beginning to look increasingly likely. How much more painful to tear herself away from him, after sharing the details of Lionel's extraordinary revelations.

She'd hoped to postpone seeing Annabel till there was greater certainty but it was difficult to keep avoiding her. She didn't want to tell her about Marina and the baby, or discuss anything more about Nick's and her situation, or, for that matter, say anything else about Paul. She would need to hide from her his visit to London but that wouldn't be easy; Annabel was, after all, her oldest friend and she picked up on things quickly, knowing her too well to be easily fobbed off. But what she said to Annabel could be passed on to Charlie and perhaps even to Daisy and then, who knows what might happen? Daisy was Pippa's best friend. She couldn't risk any of this getting out and making a fraught situation with Nick even worse, perhaps tipping the balance even further towards separation. As far as Pippa and Dan were concerned, everything with their parents was firmly back on track and she wanted it kept that way. The children were making big life decisions. It was an important time in their lives; she didn't want anything being distorted for them by their parents' problems. Pippa must continue, come what may, with her wedding plans and Dan must set off, unencumbered by worries, on his world travels.

But this past week Annabel had kept phoning her. She was worried, she said. She couldn't understand why Celia was being so distant and detached from her. It was quite unlike her. Was she just busy, or had something else happened? There were only so many times that Celia could keep making excuses. Work was demanding and Dora a slave driver – that was a given – but she couldn't keep using Atlas as a pretext for avoiding her. She'd always managed to make time for Annabel in the past, even when there were challenging deadlines and Dora was cracking the whip; now Annabel was clearly beginning to realise that something was up.

The pub was relatively quiet for a Monday evening. Behind the bar, a pretty young woman sporting a ponytail was polishing wine glasses with a plain tea towel. A young man, who looked no more than sixteen or seventeen but surely must have been older, was working to connect up a new supply of beer. She was joshing him, telling him he'd got the wrong technique and that he should leave it to her instead, a form of flirtation that both of them seemed to laughingly recognise for what it was. They were very good at it. A serious-looking man in his late twenties or early thirties, in a sharp suit, sitting on a stool on his own, with a pint of beer in front of him, watched them closely, wishing, perhaps, that he might join in the fun. Two young men, stylishly but casually dressed, clearly gay, were standing near the bar drinking cocktails, laughing, brushing up against each other, occasionally kissing, occasionally holding hands. At a table nearby, a well-dressed couple in work gear were making cheerful inroads into large platefuls of the pub's signature fish in beery batter, with chips and tartare sauce and mushy peas. A large girl with vivid, purple hair, wearing a baggy dress and knee-high black boots, sat alone at a table in the corner, sipping at a half pint of lager. Every now and then she looked at her watch. Whoever she was waiting for was late. She looked uncomfortable, perhaps fearing that her date had forgotten their arrangement, or annoyed at his or her poor timekeeping. Either way, her eyes kept flicking from her drink to her watch, to the door and back again, in agitation or irritation or a combination of the two. Three women in tight jeans and skinny tops, with scarcely enough outer clothing to combat the cold, were standing out on the street, close to the door, leaving it partly ajar so that a strong waft of their cigarette smoke blew in with the chilly air, circling back into the pub and hanging like a light fog over the threshold.

Young people, drinking or eating, out after work, spending their salaries, passing time with their friends, having fun, or not having fun, coming to the pub rather than going straight back to their homes; at the start of their adult lives, finding their way, cementing their friendships, establishing their work lives, their love lives, their relationships, their patterns of being, in London, there, then.

Celia and Annabel were far and away the oldest people there, Celia thought, by at least twenty years. Not unusual these days but, nonetheless, noticeable. They were drinking large glasses of Chablis and had ordered some food – nothing too serious, just a shared platter of mixed starters with pitta bread – hummus, olives, aubergine paté, anchovies, sun-dried tomatoes in olive oil. They were waiting for it to come. The wine was working its magic and Celia was beginning to unwind. Dora had been especially difficult that day, work had been full on and in the little gaps in the frenzy she'd been fretting about how best to handle the conversation with Annabel. But now she began to relax. A nice quiet evening with her oldest friend would do her good. She would talk about other things, steer the conversation away from herself towards the children and their exploits and find out what had been happening with some of their other friends – Mary and Evelyn, the Websters, the Glassmans. Perhaps not Bill and Judy but certainly the others. She'd had tunnel vision for so long now, only thinking about herself and her woes, allowing herself to grow distant from everyone else that she was close to, but now she felt eager to hear about them. Mary and Evelyn were thinking of buying a small house in Suffolk, weren't they? Had it gone through? And Martin Webster was on the verge of retiring. Had Sally decided to give up work as well? If so, what would happen to the business they'd set up? Would one of their boys take over, or were they going to sell it on?

She'd push the conversation in these kinds of directions. She might even tell Annabel about Lionel. It would be good to share that with someone and who better than Annabel? Upsetting though it had been to hear about her mother, and to realise that her feelings about her father's detachment from her had been well-founded, it was also an immense relief to understand why. It hadn't been her fault. There had been nothing that she had done wrong. Her only crime had been to be born and she couldn't berate herself for that. Lionel and Marje and their generation clearly knew little about post-natal depression, but for her and her friends it was talked about openly and much better understood. All that she had suffered as a child – and beyond – now made perfect sense. She felt nothing but sympathy for her poor mother and what she must have gone through, and deep gratitude that, in the end, she had shown her so much love and affection that she had never had even the vaguest of inklings that the origins of the problem had lain with Marje rather than with Lionel.

Annabel had known Marje well; she was fond of Lionel; she would be fascinated by the whole, strange narrative and delighted to discover the difference it made to Celia. She'd be glad for her – one bit of fantastic news in among the rest of her problems.

The platter arrived. They oohed and aahed for a while, then helped themselves to small portions and began to eat. It was lovely, sitting eating delicious food, sipping wine, doing normal things for a change, the kind of thing she and Annabel had done so often in the past but rarely in recent months, escaping from their husbands and families for a girls' night out. Soon she'd find a way to mention Lionel and she'd tell her the secret of her childhood. Annabel would be utterly amazed.

'A little birdy tells me she saw you at St Pancras,' Annabel said, through a mouthful of anchovy and pitta.

Shit. Celia suddenly wished she hadn't drunk her Chablis quite so quickly. It had gone to her head and her brain was working too slowly to process this. What now? What had Daisy told her? What had she seen?

'When?' she said.

'Last Sunday.'

'Daisy?'

'Yes. You didn't say! What an amazing coincidence, don't you think?'

'Amazing.'

'Daisy said you'd been shopping for clothes.'

'Yes.' She blanched. She was a lousy liar. Even now, after everything, she couldn't manage it successfully. How much longer before Annabel cottoned on and asked her what on earth was happening?

'Buy anything nice?'

'No. Nothing at all.'

Annabel stared at her. 'Are you OK, Celia? You look peaky. You've gone terribly pale.'

'Yes, fine. Just feeling a bit tired, that's all. Tell me about Mary and Evelyn. I haven't seen them in ages.'

She tried to turn the conversation quickly, seemingly successfully heading Annabel off, but she scarcely listened to the reply. Annabel's voice was there somewhere in the background, a distant soundtrack to her thoughts, with just the occasional word caught and held by her racing mind.

'You really don't look great, Cee,' Annabel said finally. 'You really have gone awfully pale.'

'I think the wine's gone to my head. I drank too much of it on an empty stomach. I'll be fine in a minute. I just need to eat a bit more and I'll be OK.'

'You know what, Celia?'

'What?'

'I could carry on pretending. But I'm not going to.'

'What do you mean?'

'I could carry on telling you about Mary and Evelyn's new house and we could finish off our platter and chat ever so nicely about this and that. We could make small talk till we're blue in the face. We're very good at that, you and me, rabbiting on. But what would be the point?'

'I don't understand.'

'I'm your best friend, for goodness' sake.' She took a deep breath. 'Christ, Celia. Daisy saw you kissing someone at St Pancras.'

'Oh.'

'She saw you with another man.'

'She did?'

'After she bumped into you in the women's loos. She came out and saw you snogging someone. She rang to tell me straightaway. She phoned from St Pancras. She said you were all over each other.'

'She was going on to see Pippa and Jamie after that.' Celia could hardly breathe. 'She didn't tell them, did she?'

'Don't be stupid. Of course not. She's not an idiot. And anyway, I told her under *no* circumstances – under no circumstances – should she think of – even dream of saying a word. I told her I'd kill her if she did.'

'And do you think she listened to you?'

'Absolutely. She herself said it'd be devastating for Pippa if she found out.'

'It would. It'd be a disaster. She's been so happy since Nick and I have been back together again. Oh God, what the fuck have I been doing?'

'What *have* you been doing? Is it Paul? Or someone else?'

'Paul, of course,' she said, in a slightly aggrieved tone. 'Who else could it be? I called him when I was in a complete state. He came to see me. I agreed to it. But there's more to it than that. It's got very complicated. Ridiculously complicated. If you thought it was confusing before, now it's even crazier than you can possibly imagine. Everything's completely out of control.'

'I thought you'd put the Paul thing behind you. I thought you and Nick were OK again.'

Celia groaned. 'How can a perfectly happy woman, in a perfectly happy marriage, end up plunging so quickly into such an awful, bloody mess? How come, having been so good at relationships and family, she suddenly turns out to be a complete idiot, incapable of taking a single sensible decision? And Nick, too. He was a really nice man, wasn't he? He still is, isn't he? Such a lovely, charming, sweet man. How could he have turned out to be such a stupid fool?'

'Still not able to forgive him, then?'

'I *was* able to forgive him. I did. I forgave him. But things have moved on.'

It was a relief to tell Annabel about Marina and the baby – she'd promised herself not to talk about it to anyone but, when it came to it, she couldn't help herself; she just blurted it out. Much less of a relief was her revelation about the confused, unresolved situation with Paul and the lies she'd been telling Nick about it. 'He doesn't know Paul's been in London. I don't want him to. Not till I'm sure about what happens next. But whatever he's done to me, I'm not sure I've behaved very well myself, either. I feel horribly ashamed. This really isn't me at all.'

Annabel poured herself more wine and took a big gulp. 'As you know, I don't blame you one bit. I swear to you,' she said, 'I won't breathe a word of this to anyone. I'll keep quiet for as long as you want me to. And I'll talk to Daisy again to make sure she keeps what she saw to herself. She's a good girl – she'll understand.'

'And the baby? Am I right to feel that it's the end for me, if he accepts paternity and wants to acknowledge it as his? Am I being stupid about that?'

'I'm not sure whether Charlie and I could survive something like that, if it happened to us, but some people do. It'd take a hell of an adjustment but I expect probably, in the end, I'd come round. Honestly, though, that's something only you can decide. Charlie and me, we've managed to accommodate quite a lot in our time, as you well know. We don't have all that many illusions about each other any more. Neither of us has exactly been an angel over the years, not me nor him. We're neither of us babes in the wood. You and Nick, though . . .'

We're different, she thought. We *were* different. But what are we *now*? She wasn't sure she had much sense of who she was any more, let alone who Nick had become. So much had changed.

They could carry on discussing all this but where would it get her? She'd done so much talking, yet none of it seemed to help.

'Let's talk about nicer things,' she said finally. 'I came to have a good evening out, to escape from my problems, to see you and forget about me.'

'OK, so tell me about Pippa and Jamie and the wedding,' Annabel said. 'That's one thing you must be feeling pleased about. Daisy says the plans are going really well.'

Celia didn't like to admit that the wedding in May was, itself, a source of desperate worry. She dreaded the thought that by then everything would have to be out in the open; the baby would be due, Pippa and Dan would have had to be told. By May, who knows where she would be, what Nick would be doing, whether they'd still be together, whether they'd even be talking to each other? Some happy wedding that was going to be!

With Annabel, she stuck to safe ground – the venue in Sussex, the catering and the invitations, the colour scheme and the flowers, the ideas for Daisy's bridesmaid's dress, the dangers of Jamie having chosen his charming but rather flaky school friend Colin as his best man and the risk – the almost certain fact – that he would make one of those ghastly, embarrassing speeches that resulted in everyone feeling far less fond of the bridegroom by the end of the evening than before.

Annabel then switched the conversation to friends. Judy had gone over to the States for a month to see her ailing mother who lived in Atlantic City; old Mrs Bernstein had had a serious fall and broken her hip. That explained why there'd been no calls from Judy for a while, thought Celia. It was a great relief to have her out of the way; her friendly concern was proving to be more of a problem than a support. She knew too much for comfort and what she did with that knowledge wasn't always entirely helpful, though she clearly thought of herself as the most considerate and solicitous of friends.

Did Celia know about the Glassmans, Annabel asked? Howard had been headhunted for a top job at the European Commission. After his time at the Business School, this seemed like too good an opportunity to refuse. Lois was going to carry on working in London for the time being

– she wouldn't think of giving up her job – but they'd alternate between weekends in London and Brussels.

'Talking of work, one thing I really *have* decided,' Celia said, 'in among all the chaos, is that I do need to do something about *my* work. I'm going to arrange to meet up with Michael Dodd in the next couple of weeks, to see whether his offer is still open. Dora's driving me completely crazy, all my favourite writers have been abandoning us, slowly but surely, and Atlas is on its way down rather than up, in my view. Whatever happens with me and Nick, I'm going to explore the option of moving to Dodd & Co, Michael's new company.'

Having said it made it real. She'd been hesitating about it for so long, cautious, reluctant to make waves with Dora, frightened of such a big change at this stage in her life. It was only now, in saying it out loud to Annabel, that she had finally decided the matter. As far as her work went, she needed to move on.

It was getting late. Annabel looked at her watch. Charlie was out for dinner with a client and Buster would be needing at least a short walk out on the Fields before bedtime.

'Don't keep going AWOL,' she said to Celia, as they hugged each other out on the street, the gaggle of young women curiously watching them through their smoky haze. 'I'm here for you whatever. You can fuck whoever you like, or screw up on things with Nick. You're entitled to be a bit crazy after everything that's happened. And I don't care what you do, anyway. You're my best friend.'

'I know,' Celia said and hugged her again. 'Better get back home. Nick'll be waiting for me, wondering where I've got to. Still worries if I'm back late, you know, in spite of everything. Old habits die hard.' She turned to go. 'Remember about talking to Daisy, won't you?'

'Of course,' Annabel said. 'I'll make sure she doesn't say a word.'

Chapter 25

'If you're conducting an affair, you should at least have the good sense to be careful! Snogging someone in a public place, in full view of everyone, isn't a very brilliant idea!'

'I'm not conducting an affair!'

'What is it then? Come off it, Mum! At your age! With Paul Legrand. It's a total cliché, isn't it? Falling into bed with a French lover. Mills and bloody Boon.'

She hadn't realised how cruel Pippa could be. They'd been so close. Now she seemed remorseless; she had no pity.

'How do you know? Did Daisy tell you?'

'Yes, of course Daisy told me. At least Daisy hasn't been lying to me. At least I can trust her.'

'Oh God.'

'Does Dad know about this little episode in the soap opera – has he been following this particular instalment?'

Celia winced; her voice was quiet. 'No, he doesn't know. When did *you* find out about it?'

'Today. A few hours ago. Daisy had lunch with me and told me. We were chatting about the wedding and I was saying how great it was that you and Dad were back together and so much happier than before and she just went completely silent and I knew something was wrong. She's my oldest friend – she couldn't hide it from me.'

Pippa was standing in the hallway, her car keys clutched tightly in one hand, the other gripping the banister, legs stiff, muscles taut, teeth clenched, like a child on the verge of an explosive tantrum. She'd come round to the house unannounced, straight after work, knowing that Nick was usually home later than Celia and expecting to find her on her own. There had been no preliminaries, no tiptoeing round, just straight in with her rage.

'How can you be so stupid? You don't seriously want to leave Dad for Paul, do you? You can't possibly! And you don't really believe he's interested in you, do you, when he's had so many different women in his time? He'll drop you just like that and go off with one of those attractive young French women he seems to like so much from what you've always told me. Get real, Mum! And when Dad finds out he'll be furious and then all the upset will begin again and then maybe this time he'll really decide to leave you and go back to that woman, which one could hardly blame him for doing, given what you've been up to, and then . . .' By now she was sobbing.

'Stop!' Celia shouted. 'Just stop!' Then more quietly, trying to suppress the rising panic in her voice, 'There's another side to this, Pippa. Perhaps Annabel didn't tell Daisy about that? I asked her not to.'

'What other side? You were supposed to be trying to make it all work. You were supposed to be behaving like adults, both of you, instead of having stupid affairs and hurting each other and telling each other a pack of lies. Where's the morality in that? Where's the honesty and care for other people's feelings that you've always banged on about to me and Dan? I can't see much of that in going off with one of Dad's best friends and lying to him about it.'

'You're upset, I understand that. But at least let me try to explain . . .'

'Whatever happened with him and that woman, Marina, he'd learnt his lesson. He's been trying to make amends and sort things out. He told me that. He said all he wanted to do was make it up to you and make things right again. He's been behaving properly. He's ditched her. Why couldn't you just accept that and get back to normal, instead of this! I don't understand, Mum, really I don't!'

Pippa's scorn, her anger, questioning her judgement and her moral sense, accusing her – it was too much to take. She couldn't just let it go.

'Daisy obviously didn't tell you about the baby. She told you all those stories about my dreadful misbehaviour with Paul but she obviously didn't tell you about that.'

The minute she said it, she regretted it. Whatever Nick had done, whatever she'd done, regardless of the recriminations and anger being directed at her by Pippa, she shouldn't have said it. Not yet. Not in this way.

'What baby?' Pippa said, her voice shrunk to a whisper.

Celia said nothing.

'What baby?' Pippa repeated, her voice rising.

'Everyone's been discussing *my* awful, hideous misdemeanours. But there's another side to it all.' She took a deep breath. 'Marina's expecting your father's child.'

There was a moment of silence as Pippa took it in. Then slowly she sank down to the floor, falling in a soft heap at the bottom of the stairs, her legs folding under her, like a floppy doll. She sat there in the hallway, next to the banister, holding on to it to steady herself.

'I'm sorry, Pippa, you shouldn't have found out about it like this. But you'd have had to be told eventually. We've been working out what to do. We would have told you about it, once we were clear about what it meant for us. And as for Paul . . .' Her voice trailed off. As for Paul, what could she say? She couldn't think what on earth could usefully be said. As for Paul, what? She really didn't know.

'You're supposed to be the grown-ups!' Pippa wailed. 'You're middle-aged, for goodness' sake! You're supposed to know how to deal with these things! How on earth did you let it all get so out of control?'

How had they let it all get so out of control? Celia wished she knew. She reached out towards Pippa, tried to touch her, to stroke her hair, but she shrank back.

'How could he . . . ? How could you . . . ?' she shouted.

Celia shook her head. 'I don't know, Pippa, I really don't understand it.'

'It's like a death wish or something, as if the two of you are just willing your marriage to come to an end, behaving so badly towards each other that it's inevitable.'

'No,' she said calmly. 'Not a death wish. Not at all. Your father and I still have strong feelings for each other, odd though that may seem after everything that's been going on.'

'Strange way of showing them!' she said. Then, becoming quieter all of a sudden, she looked up at Celia. 'Oh God, I shouldn't have said those things. I was just so upset, I got carried away. You must feel awful . . . terrible.' She paused. 'Is Dad going to leave you for her and . . . the baby?'

'The baby changes things. But we're still not sure how. We're trying to work that out.'

She came and sat down beside her daughter on the stairs. Pippa looked at her more softly now, her face filled with a desperate plea for reassurance that Celia felt she simply couldn't give. Through her tears she said, 'I don't think I know who you and Dad are any more. Both of you have been doing things that are totally out of character, totally unexpected. I thought I could always rely on the two of you. And now it's all gone so horribly wrong! I want you to tell me that you'll make it better again!'

She'd have liked to have given her a comforting reply, something that would calm her fears. She'd have liked to tell her not to worry, that everything would come right in the end. But she couldn't. Protecting Pippa from difficult realities had always been such a strong urge for her, almost a compulsion – she was her mother, after all – but it didn't seem possible any more.

'You say that you don't know who we are any more,' she said. 'I'm not sure I do, either. I'm not who I was, that's for sure. I've changed. I've been forced to change. Our lives are different. Like you, I feel as if all my certainties have gone.'

Pippa leaned over and hugged her. 'I should have been thinking more about you. I don't really blame you, honestly I don't. I know what you've been going through and I do, kind of, understand. But it's so hard, when everything I'd ever trusted in seems to have disappeared. And now this . . . a baby. My God! What the hell is happening?'

Celia nodded. She knew what it meant for all of them, the whole family, not just her.

They sat quietly for a while, Pippa holding her mother's hand, Celia stroking her daughter's arm from time to time.

'Where do you think all of this is going to end?' Pippa asked finally, breaking the silence.

'I don't know,' she said. 'I really don't.'

There was nothing more to be said.

When Pippa left, Celia stayed in the hall, sitting on the stairs. Soon Nick would come home. If they followed the pattern of the past few weeks, they would either carefully orchestrate their movements around the house, maintaining a distance that allowed nothing to be said, working hard to create spaces of avoidance, or one of them would force a conversation and they would be locked in deep and difficult discussion, torturing each other and themselves with recurring unanswered questions and painful silences. Brief interludes of normality, such as their walk on the Heath, only served as a painful reminder of what had been lost and ended up provoking an even greater sense of grief. She reflected on which of these equally upsetting scenarios would be played out tonight, when Nick came home.

Pippa knew about Paul's visit to London. She knew about the baby. Soon Dan would find out as well. The time for lying and pretence, for vacillating and hesitating, in the hope that something would eventually just work itself out, was surely coming to an end. Nick would have to be told about Paul. He would be angry and upset, perhaps rightly so. Whatever he'd done to betray her trust, she had also betrayed his. He already seemed to have decided what he wanted to do about Marina and the baby. She would force him to admit that to himself and to her. And then she would have to make up her mind about what that meant for her. Could she accept that, or couldn't she?

She remained in the hall, sitting on the stairs, waiting for the key in the lock, preparing herself for his return from work, running through the conversation in her head. She rehearsed the words and phrases that she would use, imagining his responses and her replies. Finally, after all the doubts, she knew what she had to do.

Chapter 26

The wedding ceremony was over. The Humanist celebrant had done a surprisingly good job. Celia had been sceptical at first, when it had been decided to choose her, but really, it had been very touching and the woman had been extremely good; she'd hit just the right note.

The venue was, thought Celia, rather too small for the number of people who'd been invited, but after the vows, the confetti and the photos, once the caterers had rearranged things, removed the canopy, the rows of chairs and the large table, in readiness for the meal, it looked as if it would all work perfectly well. At least it was a nice, warm day, so they could keep the big barn doors open and spill out onto the grassy bank if it became too crowded and stuffy inside. Picnic blankets had been spread for the children to sit on, covered with pots of coloured pencils and drawing paper, little quizzes and boxes of games. And they'd done wonders with the decorations inside – lovely sprays of flowers dotted around the room, lily of the valley, pink and white roses, dianthus and ferns, with old-fashioned cotton bunting woven in and out of the wooden beams of the barn. It looked delightfully festive, like a traditional country fair from times gone by.

Celia was seated next to Dan on one side, Lottie on the other; Alicia had been very thoughtful in the placings. It was a relief to her that Lottie and Dan had managed to weather the storms and were still together. There'd been a very sticky patch towards the end of Dan's time away travelling, when Lottie had come round to see her in floods of tears, saying that their relationship was over. Dan had met a student backpacker in Thailand, with whom he'd had some ridiculous, short-lived fling, and Lottie, in turn, had comforted herself, briefly, with an old friend of his, a young man Celia had never really liked much. How familiar a story was *that*, Celia thought. Young people showing no more sense than their elders. Lottie had come running to Celia to ask what she should do. Interesting that she'd chosen her over Alicia, her own mother, perhaps thinking she knew Dan best of all, or maybe identifying with her in some way for what she herself had been through. She'd declined to advise her, though, suggesting that Dan himself might be the best person to talk to. On his return, there'd been a frosty period when it looked as if they might go their separate ways, but finally they'd patched up their differences and were back together, seemingly happier than ever. In that way, perhaps the young people were more sussed than their parents. They took these things more in their stride and didn't allow them to get out of hand.

'I'm so glad you decided to come,' Lottie said, as the smoked-salmon starter was placed in front of them and the white wine poured. 'My mother would have been devastated not to have had you here.'

Celia smiled. 'I've always been very fond of your mother, and George, too,' she said. 'It would have been a great pity to miss such a lovely event. But you know how difficult things have been. I wasn't sure I was up to it.'

'We debated endlessly what to do,' Lottie said, 'whether to invite you or Nick, or both of you. My mother wanted you both, so badly. She felt that the two of you were responsible for bringing her and George together. That wonderful New Year's Day party a few years back – that was where they first met and fell for each other.'

'I remember it well,' Celia said. 'Your mother was on top form that day!'

'As always!' Lottie laughed. 'George seems to have calmed her down a bit, though, don't you think? Goodness knows how! It must take up his every waking moment, keeping her energy under control!' Then, more seriously, 'You don't mind that we invited Nick and Marina as well, do you?'

Celia looked across the room. She could see them, through the crowd of guests on other tables. They'd been placed tactfully far away, on a table right the other side of the room. Marina was looking rather beautiful, she had to admit, her blond hair pulled up into an elaborate knot, her dress a turquoise shot silk that on anyone else might have looked garish but on her seemed like an inspired choice. She was sitting quietly, though, looking a bit uncomfortable, or perhaps just bored. Maybe she was feeling that there weren't many people here that she knew? Judy and Bill had been left off the list of guests – they weren't particular friends of George or Alicia – and none of the other Buntings people was there, either. And when Nick and Marina had made a late and hurried entrance, just moments before the ceremony was about to start, neither Pippa nor Dan had been in any great rush to go over and say hello.

Celia caught Nick's eye and gave him a little tentative wave, which he returned. He'd obviously been scanning the room to see where she'd been seated. Marina looked up, following the line of his gaze. Immediately, Celia blushed and looked away.

'Where's Pippa?' she asked Lottie. She was worried that this might not be an easy occasion for her daughter and wondered whether she'd sloped off somewhere to escape all the fanfare and the fuss.

'She's sitting over there with Dmitri and Alex,' Lottie said, and then, as if reading her thoughts, 'She seems fine.'

'I wish . . .' Celia started.

'I know,' said Lottie. 'But really, I think she's OK. Weddings are difficult for *lots* of people.' And then it was her turn to blush. 'Sorry, Celia, I wasn't thinking.'

Celia reached over and patted her hand. 'You're a great girl, Lottie,' she said. 'Dan's lucky to have found you. And so am I. I'm very glad you're back together again.'

'We're not going to get married, though, at least not for a while,' Lottie said. 'We've decided not to bother. Maybe when we have kids we'll reconsider. But really and truly, what with everything that's happened to you and Nick, and with Pips and Jamie, and now all this huge mega-fuss and near nervous breakdowns over Mum and George tying the knot, we're honestly in no great hurry. I do hope you don't mind.'

'Not in the least,' Celia said. 'I sometimes wonder why anyone bothers.' But then that sounded so cynical and such an inappropriate thing to say at a wedding that she qualified it instantly. 'Of course, I don't really mean that at all. I'm delighted for Alicia and, truthfully, even more so for George. He was lonely for so many years – Alicia's been wonderful for him. And the honest truth, Lottie, is that when Nick and I married, it was one of the happiest days of our lives. I never regret it for a moment. It was pure joy. Whatever else has happened since, those years of happiness can never be taken away.'

Dan had turned towards them just in time to hear these last words. He gave Celia a hug. All three of them had tears in their eyes.

'OK. Enough of that!' said Celia brightly. 'I promised myself I'd be good. I promised I'd enjoy the day. Pour us all some more wine, Dan, so we can toast the very gorgeous bride and dashing groom.'

Later, when the tables were being cleared to make space for dancing, Celia wandered outside to see if she could find Pippa. She thought she might offer her a lift back to London, if the younger crew were planning on partying till late and she felt, like Celia, inclined to make an early escape. She drifted past the children on the blankets, some half asleep with exhaustion, or tetchily arguing with their siblings, some intently focused on board games, others cramming into their mouths yet another slice of rich gateau, or covering their faces and hands with melting chocolate fingers.

It was almost dusk, a beautiful, still, summer's evening and, not finding Pippa, she decided to take the path out towards the meadow to enjoy a quiet moment on her own and take in the last of the sun. How lovely this is, she thought. An idyllic place. She spotted a tree at one edge of the field, with an old wooden seat built around the trunk, a perfect place from which to sit and watch the sun go down. And it looked as if she would have it to herself.

She made her way over towards it, carefully negotiating the lumps and bumps in the tussocky grass in her high heels, till she thought better of it and simply took them off and walked the rest of the way barefoot. It felt good to be free of her heels, to have her feet firmly planted on the ground, feeling the grass and the soil, still warm from the heat of the day. Sitting on the bench, swinging her legs, she almost felt like a child again. She watched the sun edging its way slowly downward, till the shadows gathered and it began to grow almost dark. Across the meadow, in the barn, the fairy lights were beginning to glow.

And then she noticed him, strolling slowly across the grass, towards the bench, towards her. He was on his own. She felt a moment of sudden panic, a desire to run away. But that was stupid. What had she to fear?

'Hello,' he said simply.

'Where's Marina?' she asked, and then instantly regretted it.

'She has a headache from the champagne. It doesn't agree with her. George found her a bed in one of the cottages the family have rented. She's having a lie-down. Trying to recover a bit before we head off back to Surrey. Avoid it becoming a full-blown migraine. She's prone to these things.'

Neither of them looked at each other; both stared out, towards the barn, the stand of oak and beech trees in the distance, the hill beyond, the setting sun.

'How have you been?' she asked.

'Oh, fine, you know.' There was a pause. 'And you?'

'Yes. Fine.'

'The house?'

'Same as usual. Not much has changed. Though, of course, I had the outside painted in the spring. I thought it needed it. The usual pattern – three years of total neglect, then a proper facelift.'

'Good idea,' he said. 'Stick to the usual pattern.'

They fell silent.

'Christ,' he said. 'This is awful.'

'Is it?'

'Don't you think so?'

'I thought it was all rather nice. Alicia seems so happy and George seems like a new man.'

'Not that. Not the wedding. The wedding is fine. I was talking about everything else.'

She hesitated, weighing her words carefully. She didn't want to say something out of place. She didn't want to say the wrong thing.

'Are you happy, Nick? You and Marina?'

'In a way, yes. I suppose so. Happy enough, all things considered.'

'Has she got over losing the baby?'

'Not really. I'm not sure one ever gets over something like that. It was so late, like a proper birth but with nothing to show for it in the end. Such a terrible shock for her.'

'And for you.'

He didn't reply.

'What about you?' he asked. 'Are you OK?'

She nodded. 'I suppose so. Happy enough, all things considered.'

He laughed.

'And Paul?'

'I haven't seen him in a very long time,' she said. 'I made the break quite a while back. I thought it was for the best. Fairest to him, really.'

She thought about how badly it had ended with Paul, just a few months after her separation from Nick. He'd been angry and resentful, accusing her of being careless with his feelings. It was true that she hadn't been able to commit to him, or promise him anything, nor had their time together been particularly pleasurable or happy; she had been too consumed by grief, too shocked by the change in her life, to be anything other than anxious and confused. In a way, he was right; she had used him. All that talk of not making demands on each other and no regrets hadn't meant much in the end. They'd parted on hostile terms.

'We have no contact any more, Paul and I.'

'I shouldn't be pleased,' he said. 'It's entirely unreasonable for me to feel pleased. But I have to say that I am.'

'I shouldn't feel pleased that you're pleased. It's ridiculous and pointless. But I have to say that I do.'

They looked at each other directly, for the first time.

'How the hell did this happen to us?' he asked.

'You did some bloody stupid things.' She paused. 'But so did I. We weren't experienced enough, or clever enough, to do the things that we did and come out of it unscathed. We were innocents. We should have known better than to pretend otherwise.'

'If you'd known then, what you know now . . . ?'

'Ah, if I'd known then . . .'

They sat in silence for a while. Then Celia noticed a figure coming towards them out of the darkness. She was almost upon them by the time they realised who it was.

'Mum, I think I'd like to go home. Would you drive me back to London?' She ignored her father, even when he stood up and reached out his hand towards her, to draw her to him for a kiss. 'I've had enough of this, all this happiness, all this love,' she said bitterly. 'It's too upsetting.'

Neither of them replied.

'I'm tired. I'll get my coat and meet you at the car,' she said.

'OK, Pips.'

'And maybe I could stay over tonight with you and Lionel, if that's OK? Save you having to drive me over to Stroud Green so late.'

'Of course. Lionel will be pleased to see you in the morning. You can have breakfast with us.'

She picked her way awkwardly over the bumpy grass and they watched her go.

'Lionel?' he asked.

'Oh, didn't I say? He's moved in with me. It's quite a recent thing. He can't really manage on his own any more. You'd have thought it'd be ghastly but actually I don't mind too much. Svetlana helps me and he's turned surprisingly sweet these days.'

'Give him my best,' Nick said.

'Of course. I will.'

They wandered slowly back towards the barn. She wished he would take her in his arms and kiss her, before they got close enough to other people to be seen. In the darkness of the meadow, they could hold each other tight and no one would know. A Mills and Boon ending, that's what she wanted. The kind of ending she hated in the novels she read. The sort of thing she'd scornfully reject, scoring through it with a red pen and the word 'Rubbish' scrawled in big capital letters across the page. She thought perhaps that's what he wanted, too. But she knew it wouldn't happen. It was too late for that now.

At the open door, he turned and kissed her once on the cheek. This was it. The farewell. On impulse she suddenly grasped his hand. He squeezed hers and held on as if he might never let go. At last they moved apart. Nothing more was said. And then he was gone.

When they arrived home in Kentish Town, Pippa went straight up to the spare room. Celia put on her slippers, went quietly into the kitchen and shut the door, fearful of waking Lionel. She put on the kettle and made herself a cup of tea.

Before long, the kitchen door opened and Lionel came in, wearing only his pyjama bottoms and his open dressing gown, his bare chest showing through.

'So you're back at last,' he said.

'Yes, Daddy.'

'Out at the theatre?'

'No, Daddy. I told you, I was at a wedding, Alicia and George's wedding.'

'And where's Nick, that husband of yours? Parking the car?'

'No, Daddy. You remember, don't you? Nick doesn't live here any more. Our divorce came through last year.'

'Divorce?'

'Nick and I aren't married any more.'

'Why, whatever happened? He was such a charming man. You know, Celia, how much I always liked him. You should have stayed with him, you know.'

And as she did every day, she sighed, took a long slow breath, and repeated the story that needed to be told over and over again, a story that for Lionel, at least, could never be satisfactorily concluded.

'He was such a charming man,' he said, as he always did.

'Indeed,' she replied, as always. 'He was.'

Also Available by Barbara Bleiman

Off the Voortrekker Road

Off the Voortrekker Road is a personal family story, a courtroom drama and a political narrative, casting a light on a pivotal moment in South Africa's history. It weaves together two narratives. In Cape Town, in 1958, a young Jewish lawyer, Jack Neuberger, prepares to defend a minister in the Dutch Reformed Church who stands accused of 'immoral or indecent acts' with a 'non-white' woman. The novel also transports us back to Jack's childhood, when he sat 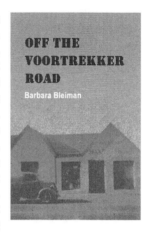 silently on a sack of beans in his father's hardware store, the Handyhouse, bearing witness to the comings and goings of the colourful community of Parow and navigating his way across the wash of his parents' turbulent marriage.

The novel spans the twenty years in which the National Party or 'Nats' came to power and the apartheid movement gathered momentum. For adult Jack, the secret police are watching his every move, key testimonies are proving unreliable and his career and family are threatened. For young Jack, as well as finding a way of coping with the discord within his family, he struggles with his sense of self: how to be a good son, a good Jew, a good person or mensch and, most importantly, how to be loyal to his best childhood friend, Terence Mostert.

Years later, in a courtroom in Cape Town, this loyalty and Jack's personal courage face the ultimate test, in a case which will impact upon those he loves, those he feels responsible for and future generations of South Africans.

Reviews

'I enjoyed and admired this novel very much. It is so well written, a fine example of how close and honest observation of a particular situation can speak volumes about larger issues.'

Diana Athill

'A great historical novel that deals with issues of race, humanity, and coming of age. I highly recommend this novel. It would also be a great book club book as there is much to discuss.'

Laura Gerold, Laura's Reviews Blog

'A South African version of *To Kill a Mockingbird*. Beautifully written with a compelling central idea and engaging characters. *****

Laura Ballantyne, Amazon.co.uk

'This is a simply stunning book, one of the cleverest I have read. It will appeal to anyone interested in the Jewish diaspora; apartheid in South Africa; justice and the law; in fact anyone who likes a good story.' *****

H. M. Sykes, Amazon.co.uk

Off the Voortrekker Road is available on Amazon, in two formats, in paperback and as an ebook for Kindle.

A NOTE ON THE AUTHOR

Barbara Bleiman lives and works in London. She has an MA in Creative Writing from Birkbeck, University of London.  Her first novel, *Off The Voortrekker Road* was published as an eBook in 2013 and in paperback format in 2014, and is available on Amazon. Her short stories have featured in *The Mechanics Institute Review*.

12723660R00154

Printed in Poland
by Amazon Fulfillment
Poland Sp. z o.o., Wrocław